Intellectual Property

Also by the author in reading order:

Destiny: Union Station
Date Night on Union Station
Alien Night on Union Station
High Priest on Union Station
Spy Night on Union Station
Carnival on Union Station
Wanderers on Union Station
Vacation on Union Station
Guest Night on Union Station
Word Night on Union Station
Party Night on Union Station
Review Night on Union Station
Family Night on Union Station
Book Night on Union Station
LARP Night on Union Station
Career Night on Union Station
Last Night on Union Station
Independent Living
Soup Night on Union Station
Assisted Living
Freelance on the Galactic Tunnel Network
Con Living
Empire Night on Union Station
Space Living
Traders on the Galactic Tunnel Network
Orphans on the Galactic Tunnel Network
Swap Night on Union Station
Slow Living
Artists on the Galactic Tunnel Network
History Night on Union Station
Bits of Anarchy
Double Living
Bits of Flower
Synergy on the Galactic Tunnel Network
Substitutes on Union Station
Bits of Catalyst
Elder Living
Royals on the Galactic Tunnel Network
Deal Night on Union Station

Intellectual Property

Book One of EarthCent Families

Foner Books

978-1-948691-95-6

Hardwick, Massachusetts.

One

The Director of EarthCent Intelligence struggled to his feet, one hand pressed to the small of his back. "New rule," he said to his sparring partner with a groan. "No flipping the boss."

"Did I do it wrong?" Thomas asked, a look of genuine concern on his handsome android face. "I take notes whenever I test these personality upgrades for QuickU. Two more evaluations and I'll reach a hundred."

"You must be their all-time beta tester," Clive said, jogging a little in place to try to loosen up. "Which one of the martial arts are you testing today?"

"Cage fighter," the artificial person replied. "I heard that you spent a year on the professional circuit after getting out of the mercenaries and I was curious what it would be like to channel a cage fighter myself."

"I thought the only one outside my wife and the Stryx who knew about my missing year was M793qK, and doctors are supposed to keep patient information confidential."

"Are they?" Thomas asked. "I think the practice is limited to a subset of humanity. The advanced species all believe it's important for medical information to be shared as widely as possible."

"You're talking about statistical information," Clive said, trying a little shadowboxing to see if his back would spasm. "That's not the same as—no?"

"Wouldn't you want to know if somebody living on your corridor was carrying a plague or was subject to seizures and reliant on passersby for help?"

"You're telling me that the aliens share that kind of information?"

"Yes. Perhaps it's part of how a species builds longevity," Thomas mused as he resumed a fighter's stance. "Are you up to another round?"

"Wait a minute," Clive said, raising his hands. "I'm curious how my year fighting as *The Masked Mercenary* came up in conversation with the Farling doctor."

"We were discussing sports betting, and M793qK said he'd made a tidy sum wagering on you during your brief career. I used to restrict myself to gambling on poker, but since Live Action Role Playing took off with the Professional LARPing League, I've developed a system for—"

"Stop right there," Clive said, walking off the mat and grabbing his towel from the back of a chair. "Unless your system involves paying players to fix matches, it's no better than throwing darts at a board. One of the things we need to discuss today is a proposal from the league that we join the Inter-Species Police Operating Agency's gaming security group to help police human competitors. That means all our personnel involved with the ISPOA contract will have to agree to forego gambling on LARPing and other covered sports."

"But my system is almost perfected," Thomas protested. "It would be a crime to waste it."

"So don't waste it. Publish a booklet on how to choose winners in the Professional LARPing League. I guarantee you'll earn more from royalties than you would from placing the bets. Blythe can help you get set up."

The artificial person, who hadn't bothered pretending to sweat, retrieved his tailored business suit from the back of another chair and began to change. "Maybe that's not a terrible idea," he said. "But your wife publishes alien romances in translation and my gambling system is nonfiction."

Clive snorted. "I'm not an expert on disclaimers, so talk to Wrylenth, and don't be surprised if he tells you to include something about your system being for entertainment purposes only. If you're really that excited about the idea, drop by the Galactic Free Press and ask my sister-in-law for an introduction to whoever is printing the *For Humans* series these days."

Thomas considered the suggestion. "I wouldn't be able to sell it on Earth and that's half the market."

"I don't follow."

"Earth's copyright laws specifically exclude works created by artificial intelligence. Any publisher could copy my book verbatim and I couldn't do anything to stop them."

"That's insane," Clive said. "Have you ever asked our embassy to check into it? You're a sentient being, recognized by the Stryx, and under tunnel network law, you have the same legal rights as the species that created you."

Thomas shook his head. "Copyright is one of those funny things that get separately negotiated in treaties. When the Stryx first opened Earth, none of the advanced species paid attention to our laws protecting intellectual property, not that there was much they were interested in stealing. Signing reciprocal deals with the other tunnel network species was one of the first things President Beyer did when he took the helm at EarthCent. Our negotiators based the local deal for Earth on the last international copyright treaty from before the Stryx opened the planet."

"Before we had developed sentient artificial intelligence." Clive thought for a moment. "It's the first I've heard about this. Why did Earth want to prohibit artificial intelligences from copyrighting their work?"

"People were concerned that what passed as artificial intelligence at the time was creating new works purely through imitation, with no genuine thought or intent. After the Stryx came and governments began collapsing under their debt loads as the population emptied out to the stars, updating copyright law for sentient artificial intelligence just wasn't that high on the priority list."

"Let me grab a shower and then we can walk and talk," Clive said, employing their code phrase for taking a short ride in a random rental ship to avoid electronic surveillance. "I'll meet you there."

Thomas nodded, completed a perfect Windsor knot in his necktie, and headed for Mac's Bones. Rather than visiting the training camp that he'd run for over a decade for EarthCent Intelligence recruits, the artificial person strode up to the Tunnel Trips kiosk and greeted the Horten girl who was breaking in a new employee.

"Any returns due in?" he asked by way of a greeting.

"A two-man trader just came out of the tunnel," Marilla replied. She pointed out the blinking ship's identification number in the holographic projection above the kiosk that registered rentals owned by Tunnel Trips in local space and made sure that the young man she was training could duplicate her gestures in the control field.

"Can I grab it for a half-hour?" Thomas asked.

Marilla waved the holograph out of existence and brought up a schedule on the display surface of the kiosk, again demonstrating the steps to the new hire as she went. "It's not going out again until this evening, so we'll have plenty of time to clean it after you bring it back."

"But you just told me that the number one rule is to always clean returns before letting somebody else take them out," the young man protested. "If it turns out the ship was damaged, we won't know who is responsible if we don't do a thorough inspection between uses."

"Gary, meet Thomas," Marilla said instead of directly answering the objection. "Thomas is with EarthCent Intelligence, and he ran the training camp on the other side of Mac's Bones for longer than I've been with Tunnel Trips. We have an arrangement with EarthCent Intelligence to let their senior personnel borrow returns for a quick jaunt outside the station, providing we have something available."

"Are you chasing somebody?" Gary asked Thomas, plainly excited by the idea. "I started watching that new immersive series about a spy who goes undercover as an independent trader, and there's a chase scene in every episode."

"I'm not chasing anybody, and Stryx Gryph controls all ships in the vicinity of Union Station, so any chase wouldn't be very exciting," Thomas told him. "I hadn't heard of a new espionage series. What's it called?"

"*Bad Trade*. It's supposedly based on reality."

"I've been in the business for over twenty-five years and I've yet to have occasion to go on a space chase. Unless the two ships were identical, it would be over pretty fast."

"You have to dodge into an asteroid belt," Gary explained. "Or dive into an atmosphere or a minefield. There are a lot of ways to escape."

"A minefield?" Thomas asked, turning to Marilla. "Have you ever heard of minefields in space?"

"Not on the tunnel network," the Horten girl replied. "And asteroid belts are nowhere near as dense as they look in immersives," she told Gary. "You could plot a course straight through one as if it wasn't there and the chance of hitting anything would be a trillion to one."

"How about entering a star's corona?" he asked hopefully.

Marilla deferred to the artificial person who said, "It would depend on the type of ship you were in and what was chasing you. Any of the military vessels that the advanced species build would follow you right in. A two-man-trader, like the ones Tunnel Trips rents, wouldn't survive the heat or be able to pull away from the star's gravity."

"There's Director Oxford coming now," Marilla said, pointing out Clive to the new employee. "Any time he or Thomas asks for a return, give them the master key."

Clive glanced up as the massive bay doors in the ceiling of Mac's Bones opened onto Union Station's core. A two-man trader, manufactured on Flower under license from the Sharf, entered the bay and set down next to a row of Dollnick space taxis, which made up the bulk of the Tunnel Trips fleet.

"Is that ours?" Clive asked.

"Yes," Marilla said. "I was just about to give Thomas the master key."

The salesman returning the ship was traveling with the complete setup for a tradeshow booth. Clive and Thomas pitched in to help remove the cargo netting and roll all the travel cases down the ramp, which took upwards of ten minutes. Then the two EarthCent Intelligence employees climbed the ladder to the bridge and the ship retraced its path through the atmosphere retention field and out into Union Station's core.

"Are you going to accept the LARPing league's proposal?" Thomas asked after the ship cleared the station.

Clive stretched, causing something in his back to pop. "We need to start thinking about the day you replace me as director, so you should take part in all of these decisions."

"You're only fifty-six years old. Even by human standards, you're just entering your prime for managing an intelligence agency."

"I think it's obvious to everybody by now that the Stryx are pushing the Human Empire to get through the accelerated startup phase and take over from EarthCent. My intention is to hand over the reins when that happens, though maybe I'll stay on in some sort of emeritus role."

"But EarthCent Intelligence is the most successful government agency that humanity has," Thomas pointed out. "I've talked to Samuel and Vivian, and the Human Empire is counting on us to provide continuity during the transition."

"Have you forgotten that Vivian is my daughter? It's just a bad look for a government and a spy agency to be too closely related."

Thomas shrugged, obviously unimpressed by the argument. "What's so important that you're hoping to prevent eavesdropping?"

"The Human Empire," Clive said with a sigh. "Vivian is a little more paranoid than Samuel, thanks to the time she spent working for Drazen Intelligence. How well do you know Dewey?"

"Flower's Dewey?"

"That's the problem. He's become a vital link between us, the Human Empire, and the community on the Miklat, but after talking with Vivian, I'm not sure who owns his first loyalty."

"Flower," Thomas said. "After her, the expatriate Bits community, but he's close with the Farling doctor as well."

"And you don't think we should be worried?" Clive asked.

"Dewey is a bit of a special case. Most human-derived artificial people were created for a purpose, often as academic or showcase projects, like Chance and I. Dewey came about by accident when the hackers on Bits were trying to create a non-sentient librarian and underestimated the power and neural network-like architecture of the alien hardware they were running to simulate Earth's old Internet."

"Is that a traumatic experience for artificial intelligence?"

Thomas shrugged again. "It's nice to be wanted, and Dewey was the last thing the Bitters were hoping for. They had to abandon the project as soon as they recognized that he was sentient. Mouser, who is now the Miklat's mayor, helped Dewey build his first body. As soon as Dewey was mobile, he left Bits and joined Flower to work in the library there. I know that he still takes part in a role-playing game with Mouser's group when he has the chance, but he also carries messages between the alien intelligence agents on Flower and the freelance spies on the Miklat."

"How smart would you say he is?" Clive asked. "Average human but with a photographic memory, or something more?"

"A lot smarter than he was when I first met him," Thomas said. "When Dewey transferred out of the librarian robot that Mouser helped him build, he bought a human-style android body off the shelf from one of the advanced species. I'll bet that Flower has been helping him upgrade its processing capabilities."

"Vivian said pretty much the same. She likes Dewey, but she assumes that anything she involves him in will be reported to Flower, and probably end up reaching the ears of the intelligence agents on board as well."

"I thought the real reason we invited the advanced species to place intelligence agents on Flower in return for helping subsidize her costs was to prove to them we have nothing to hide."

"From the standpoint of our Intelligence Steering Committee, that was the main reason for offering the deal," Clive said. "Being open with the aliens has worked well for us so far, but I'm beginning to think that when EarthCent is replaced by the Human Empire, it would be wise to have a few clandestine assets that they can build on."

"You mean, real secret agents?" Thomas asked. "You know that Chance and I are always game."

"You're the deputy director. You've represented us at every major interspecies intelligence conference for the last two decades. I'll bet half the counter-intelligence agents on the tunnel network know you by sight."

The artificial person smiled and tapped his chest. "It's just a body, Clive, and I finished paying off the mortgage a long time ago."

Clive stared for a moment. "I forgot you could swap to a new one," he admitted. "But it would show up on every security scanner in the galaxy."

Thomas smiled again, reached into his pocket, and brought out the pinky ring that he'd removed before their training session. "You never asked why I went to see M793qK in the first place," he said. "This is a Farling medical transponder. It can spoof any active scanner on the tunnel network, and I've improved my internal shielding enough to prevent passive radio-frequency leaks."

"You went to M793qK to get tech that will let you pass as human on a scan?"

"I've already tested it a few times."

"But if it's that advanced, we have no way of knowing what else it might be doing, like letting the Farling doctor track your location or listen in on your conversations."

"He'd need a local relay station for real-time electronic surveillance, and he's done surgery on you," Thomas pointed out. "Don't you think he could have planted an undetectable bug in your body if that's what he wanted to do?"

Clive grimaced. "I never thought of it until now. All right, maybe running some agents that none of the other species know about is a pipe dream, but I think we owe it to ourselves to try. All our employees who went through the training camp are blown, we knew that from day one, but the opportunity has come up to hire a covert operative. I want you to meet him."

"A human agent?"

"Yes. He's a referral from John who had an encounter with him on Earth. John convinced him to talk with us and arranged for a meeting in Manhattan next week."

Thomas nodded. "I can take Chance on vacation to go clubbing for cover," he said. "But John hasn't been back to Union Station recently. How did he get word to you?"

"Handwritten note carried by an independent trader and passed to Joe at Mac's Bones," Clive said. "It's a risk, but I have an excuse to meet with Joe any time thanks to our kids being married. The potential agent gave John the number of one of those disposable phones they use on Earth, so you can contact him when you get there to set the meet."

"Did you get any background information on him at all?"

"Nothing, and John was smart not to put any more in writing than necessary. He only said that the man has skills, and we can guess what that means."

"Good," Thomas said. "Are you going to continue negotiations with LARPing league security while I'm away?"

"There may be some benefit to letting them cool their heels for a couple of weeks, so we don't come off looking needy," Clive said. "Which we aren't, if you were wondering. The main attraction is that whoever we put on it will end up working with agents from all the other tunnel network species, and the same is true for any other ISPOA gaming security investigations we're pulled into. I'd pay to get our agents that kind of experience, not to mention the opportunity to make personal connections inside some of the intelligence services that we normally only hear from if they're complaining about something."

Two

"Mom is at a *Cookbook* thing and she won't be home for dinner," Bethany told her father. "I'm making spaghetti."

"Great," Walter said. "I love your spaghetti. What's the sauce?"

"Flower's Own," the young teen said and checked the label on the jar as she returned it to the fridge. "Garlic."

"Do I like that one?"

"You did last time we had it. I still think that Drazen Foods makes the best spaghetti sauce, but they only bottle it in season using sun-ripened tomatoes, and the stores have been out of stock for months."

Walter filled a glass of water for himself from the chilled tap and watched his daughter's preparations. "Did you make a whole box for just the two of us?"

"Pava feels like pasta," Bethany said, turning her head a bit sideways to look under the kitchen table where the giant Cayl hound was napping. "She doesn't like garlic, though, so I let the leftover chili warm up to room temperature and I'll put it on hers."

"Just as well. That chili was a bit too strong for me and Pava has an iron stomach. How was school today?"

"Weird. Libby is still trying to get me to learn trigonometry even though I keep telling her I'm only interested in writing. I'm going to be a newspaper editor like you."

Walter put a fond hand on his daughter's shoulder as she stirred the sauce and couldn't help marveling that she was already taller than her mother. "I do math at work all of the time, and not just business math," he said. "As managing editor, I have the final responsibility for all of the stories we publish, and a basic knowledge of trigonometry has come in handy more than once."

"Did Libby put you up to saying that?" Bethany asked without turning around.

"I haven't talked to her about your schooling since the last Parents Day."

"Can you give me an example of how you use trig at work?"

"Sure," Walter said and sat down at the kitchen table to make sure he was out of the way. "One of our technology reporters wrote a story about the Miklat and compared it to a modern colony ship. He confused the formulas for the volume and surface area of a cylinder and none of the proofreaders caught it. If I didn't remember the basics of trig, we would have gone to press with the error, and you know what would happen next."

"The Grenouthians would do a satirical segment on their news reporting a story about colony ships and intentionally getting all of the math wrong," Bethany said immediately. "Okay. I can see how being able to do some math in your head would come in handy editing news stories."

"Do you know the difference between a billion and a trillion?" her father asked. "I don't just mean counting zeroes. When you hear the numbers, do they give you a sense of proportion?"

"Sure," Bethany said, turning off the induction heating element below the spaghetti and carefully pouring the contents of the pot into a colander in the sink. "There are around a billion humans in the Conference of Sovereign Human Communities, which makes them citizens of the Human Empire, and someday when we all join, there will be almost ten billion of us. But there are more than a trillion Vergallians spread across their empire and the Fleet worlds, which means that the Human Empire will have less than one percent of the Vergallian population."

"Did you just do that in your head?"

"I'm not sure. It might have come up in school."

"Well, numbers are one of the big bugaboos at the Galactic Free Press since Libby raised her price for proofing in order to get us to stop relying on her services," Walter said. "I have reporters who don't know the difference between a million and a billion, and it's gotten to the point that I had to draft a team of editors who aren't afraid of math to do a final review of every story that includes numbers higher than a hundred."

"You're making it up to get me to like math," Bethany said as she dumped half of the drained spaghetti into a large serving bowl and poured the heated tomato sauce over the top. The rest of the spaghetti went into a large bowl labeled, 'Pava', and with the help of a spoon, she added the leftover chili and mixed it all up. She barely finished lowering the bowl to the floor before the Cayl hound began eating.

"It's all true," Walter insisted. "I have perfectly intelligent writers whose minds go on tilt when it comes to big numbers. Somebody wrote a piece about InstaSitter and said that the business employed thousands and was valued in the millions of creds."

"Are you kidding? They employ hundreds of thousands of part-timers on Stryx stations, and the business must be worth billions of creds."

"You're hired."

"You *should* hire me," Bethany said before placing the serving bowl on the table next to the salad and sitting down across from Walter. "Mom was already working with her father and sister at Kitchen Kitsch when she was my age. I've been reporting over the teacherbot network for the Children's News Network from Union Station for two years, but there are so many other kids that they ration assignments. I've been thinking about asking Grandpa to hire me to work at Kitchen Kitsch, but the last time he said I don't have the right personality."

"No," Walter said. "I can't see you shouting, 'Egg slicers, onion dicers,' at the top of your lungs in competition with all the other barkers in the Shuk, and I was serious about hiring you. How many hours do you want to work?"

"Libby?" Bethany asked without even glancing up. "How many hours can I work?"

"If you continue to study four hours in the morning, you'll be ready to start at the Open University in two years," the station librarian replied. "The rest of your time is your own."

"And your mother's," Walter reminded his daughter. "Weren't you going to help her with the *All Species Cookbook*?"

"That was before you offered me a paying job at the Galactic Free Press," Bethany said happily. "Mom doesn't need me to work for her. She and Aunt Shaina have plenty of help, plus the part-time alien university students Cousin Mike hired for them."

Walter used the plastic tongs from Kitchen Kitsch to build a heaping serving of spaghetti on his plate, but he paused, fork in hand, before he began to eat. "Were you serious about Pava telling you that she wanted pasta?"

"Do you think I'd make up something like that? She'd fill my school backpack with sand and make me run laps on the park deck."

"I know that you and Pava are on the same wavelength most of the time. What I meant was, do you hear the words in your head, or does an image of a Cayl hound eating spaghetti suddenly appear in your vision? You've never explained how it works."

Bethany held up a finger, and for a moment, her father thought she was pointing at her ear to indicate she was hearing instructions over the translation implant she'd received that year. Then he realized she was signaling that she needed a minute to finish chewing and swallowing.

"I can't explain it any better than I have," she said. "I just know what Pava is thinking sometimes. Grace is the same with Queenie, but Mike isn't, so maybe you have to live with a Cayl hound from birth."

"Or it only works with the females on both sides," Walter said. "Queenie's three littermates were male, and I'm sure we would have heard something from the ambassador's family if any of the children around Beowulf or Alexander could hear them."

"I don't know," Bethany said. "Cayl hounds are pretty good at getting their point across without words, so maybe the males are just lazy about it. Or maybe me and Cousin Grace are the only ones on the Union Station with the right mix of genes or—" she cut herself off and looked over at Pava who had already finished off her bowl of spaghetti and chili. "Who?"

"What is it?" Walter asked.

"Pava says she can talk to that woman who started training as Baa's apprentice at SBJ Fashions before Mom and Aunt Shaina sold their shares back to Jeeves and left to run the *All Species Cookbook*."

"Jyndal," Walter put a name to the young mage's apprentice and took another forkful of spaghetti. Then the door of their apartment slid open and a petite woman carrying a large cake box entered.

"Mom," Bethany cried, jumping up from her chair. "I thought you weren't coming home until late, so I made dinner."

Brinda set the cake box on the table and crouched to give Pava a quick scratch behind the ears. "There's something wrong with people born on Earth," she said with a sigh. "Somebody told the delegation that the cheapest way to travel is as supercargo on independent traders, so that's what they did."

"And they all got Zero-G sickness and couldn't make the meeting," Walter surmised, neglecting to remind his wife that he had been born and educated on Earth.

"Worse," Brinda said, getting herself a plate and taking a seat at the table. "There was a communications breakdown, and they ended up at Reunion Station."

"I never heard of Reunion Station," Bethany said. "Did the Stryx just build it?"

"It's not a Stryx Station. It's a Frunge manufacturing orbital in one of their oldest star systems which is so far from here that it's a three-day trip in the tunnels." Brinda took a small serving of spaghetti, hardly enough for a child, and began winding it onto her fork.

"I made plenty, Mom. You can take more."

"Do you think I would bring home an empty cake box? I bought it from the new bakery to impress the delegation since they're all in the dessert business."

"The Healthy Baker?" Walter asked. "Our local food writer just did a story about them that will be in the weekend edition. The owner claims that their cakes are so healthy that she's been living on nothing else for the last three years."

Pava got up and nosed the box.

"I don't think you'll like it," Brinda told the Cayl hound. "It's a nut-based flour with lots of fruit and no added sugar or salt."

"If we're having cake, I'll make coffee," Walter said. He pointed at his ear and then continued eating.

"Sending a command over your implant doesn't count as making coffee," Bethany said. "Mom's the one who adds the roasted beans to the machine and changes the filters."

"Your father is an intellectual," Brinda reminded her daughter. "The last time he tried servicing the coffee maker himself we ended up with filters in the grinding section and I had to ask my dad to come fix it."

"Grandpa can fix anything."

"Anything in a kitchen. He's a specialist."

Pava delegated herself to guard the cake box until her family finished their spaghetti and salad, and then she watched closely as Brinda undid the flaps and dropped the sides. The Cayl hound shook her head in dismay that anybody would go to the trouble of making a cake out of such healthy ingredients and took herself off to the living room for a nap on the couch.

"It's not terrible," Walter said after chasing the first bite down with coffee. "A bit heavy, maybe."

"Not the worst," Bethany agreed. "It reminds me of some of those fancy breads parents bring to Libby's school for bake sales."

"When they're trying hard to impress everybody how health-conscious they are," Brinda said. "It's edible, but it's no Harry's Fruitcake."

"Not terrible, not the worst, and edible," Walter recounted their judgments. "I'm beginning to wonder if our food writer took a page out of your visiting delegation's book and went to the wrong bakery."

"To be fair, I asked the owner for the healthiest cake they had, and she was a bit hesitant about selling it to me. It was in the back of the case."

"Dad hired me to work at the Galactic Free Press afternoons," Bethany announced.

"Did you check with Libby?" her mother asked. "One of the conditions for attending her school is that you have to follow the program she creates."

"Libby says I'll be ready for the Open University when I'm sixteen as long as I continue studying mornings, and you said that you didn't want me going to college younger than that."

"How about I give tentative approval, pending a discussion with the managing editor after you go to bed?"

"Don't you think I'm mature enough to even listen to a discussion about *my* future?" Bethany asked as she began clearing the plates. "I've tried all the afternoon clubs and craft circles that you suggested, but now I'm ready for a real job. The older kids managing the Children's News Network on the station divide the assignments evenly between everybody who signs up so I can't increase my hours there."

"It's not the idea of your working afternoons that concerns me," Brinda admitted. "It's the newsroom."

"All the news our readers can use," her daughter quoted the paper's motto. "What's wrong with that?"

"You explain it to her, Walter."

The managing editor of the Galactic Free Press took a moment to gather his thoughts. "What concerns your mother is the news that doesn't make it into the paper," he finally said. "Parents try to strike a balance between preparing their children for the world they'll face as adults and protecting them from all of the bad things there are out there."

"Libby won't let anything *really* bad happen on Union Station," Bethany asserted. "And I learned how to read from the Galactic Free Press."

"You know that newspaper editing isn't limited to making sure that our stories are clear and concise," Walter said. "Chastity and I meet every day to decide which stories we want to pursue and which stories, despite being factual, don't deserve a place in a paper with our motto."

"Especially violent crime," Brinda said, getting to the point that her husband was dancing around. "There's a reason I've never let you watch shows from Earth before sitting through them myself, Beth. You know that there are bad people who do terrible things. There's nothing to be gained from watching actors portraying the perpetrators and victims of terrible crimes. It's a kind of voyeurism."

"But you can't just ignore the bad things in the universe," Bethany objected.

"There's a difference between recognizing that some people live in a sewer and choosing to wallow in it yourself. And none of your academic twaddle," she continued, turning on her husband before he could muddy the waters with what he had been taught in graduate school on Earth. "You know I'm right."

"I'm not contradicting you," Walter said mildly. "But I wouldn't want Bethany to start judging people by their circumstances without knowing anything about how they ended up in your allegorical sewer. Some people dive in, others fall in, and there are even those who are pushed."

"That sounds about right," Bethany said. "You only publish stories about those who are pushed?"

"We don't publish stories about any of them unless they've done something that we think our readers will benefit from knowing. There are news organizations on Earth that cover crime and victims in excruciating detail as long as the stories are salacious enough for them."

"And my concern about you working for the Galactic Free Press is that you'll be exposed to all of those stories because reporters are the galaxy's worst gossips," Brinda said. "The last time I went to a party with your father, I heard things that made my hair stand on end."

"What if I work on the Union Station desk?" Bethany asked. "You like Bob, and he's the senior reporter. I won't have to hear about all sorts of terrible crimes because there aren't any on Union Station."

"Unless The Healthy Baker continues falsely representing five pounds of compacted granola as a cake," Walter said. "Our daughter has a point, Brinda, and Bob has been running himself a bit ragged lately trying to cover the tunnel network commissions that have moved to Union Station, in addition to his regular beat."

"Do you think, and don't take this the wrong way, Beth, that our daughter is ready to report on a commission meeting?"

Walter laughed and used his napkin to cover the remains of the slice of cake he'd given up on. "Bob doesn't just cover diplomatic activity. Since he took over the Union Station desk, he's responsible for all our local news as well, though he leans on part-timers for that. Bethany could start out reporting on schools and sports. We don't expect any of our trainees to write stories that will earn us a profit. The training is an investment in our future."

"What about the book division?" Brinda asked in a resigned voice. "I thought you always needed help with the *For Humans* series."

"After four hundred-plus books, we're running out of subjects to cover," Walter said. "The only manuscript in the works right now is a book tentatively titled *Humans for Aliens*."

Bethany sensed an opportunity for a compromise. "I could start with that and then move to reporting when it's done. Does the new book have a human author, or is Jeeves writing it under a pseudonym?"

"It will be a team of authors when it's finished. The idea came about when Ambassador McAllister suggested we might want to publish a guide written by Λabina, her special assistant, and Affie, the Alt's contract queen."

"They couldn't finish it or something?"

"The guide was written for Vergallian princesses on their way to volunteer as government administrators on Earth, which is a minuscule audience. In addition, the draft she showed me was written way above the level we target with the *For Humans* books."

"Like, eighteen and over?" Bethany asked.

"Our books are targeted for readers who have the equivalent of an eighth-grade teacherbot education,"

Walter explained. "Vergallian princesses spend around fifty years in royal training."

"Ugh. As much as I like Libby's school, I wouldn't want to go for fifty years. Will you hire another author to dumb down what Affie and Aabina wrote?"

"You're forgetting about the lack of an audience. But after the ambassador brought it up, I talked to some alien acquaintances, and they all thought that a concise guide to humans for the advanced species would be useful. There probably isn't enough demand to do one for each species, so I thought of including all of them in a single book."

"Do you think that the Dollnicks will be interested in reading a Frunge author's take on human foibles?" Brinda asked.

"For the audience on Stryx stations, yes," Walter said. "The manager of the Empire Convention Center came in to renew their sponsorship of the weekend travel section, so I bounced the idea off him. Granted, he deals with aliens all day long, but he said that learning what the Frunge or the Drazens thought about humans would be just as valuable to him as finding out what another Dollnick thought. Then he drew a sort of pie chart and began explaining the Theory of Perspectives, but fortunately, there was an emergency on the Freelance Desk."

"Aren't emergencies usually bad?"

"Yes, but it got me out of admitting that I didn't understand what he was talking about."

Three

As Thomas and his partner walked off the dance floor to the thunderous applause from the crowd in the retro discotheque, Chance issued a silent command, and the heels of her SBJ Fashions dancing shoes began to thicken and collapse. By the time they reached their table, her eyes had dropped from the level of her partner's ears to his mouth.

A waitress, who ignored several patrons trying to attract her attention along the way, reached their table just as they sat. "The manager sent me over to tell you that your drinks are on the house," the waitress said. "And that goes for any time you want to come back and dance." She lowered her voice as much as she could and still hope to be heard over the pounding music before adding. "If you ask me, he'd pay you guys to dance. Everybody who was here pinged their friends to come and the place hasn't been this packed since New Year's. You guys are the best dancers I've ever seen."

"Thank you," Chance said, displaying her dimples with a smile. "I'll have a double vodka, or you could just have the bartender fill a water glass if there isn't a law against it."

"Same for me," Thomas said. "The cheap stuff is fine as long as it's a hundred proof."

The waitress laughed, clearly not taking them seriously about the water glasses or quality. "I'll be back in a flash with two double vodkas."

"That was fun," Chance said, opening her fashionable purse, a five-feather model from Baa's Bags which she'd left on the table. "Oops, looks like somebody got their fingers burned."

"I thought that the protective enchantment Baa put on the purse to keep anybody other than the owner from picking it up did so by making them believe that somebody was watching," Thomas said.

"That works against the light-fingered crowd in most places, but not on Earth. I asked Baa to add a little electric shock, and now she's thinking about making it an option on all the four and five feather bags."

"And you can tell somebody touched the bag by looking inside?"

"There's a counter." She opened the mouth of the purse again and displayed it to Thomas. "Baa thought it would make a fun addition, and now that I've seen it in action, I agree."

Thomas turned his chair a little to keep an eye on the door. After he and Chance finished their virtuoso performance, the patrons crowded back onto the dance floor, improving the lines of sight in the rest of the club. "I wonder if anybody has ever told him that early is on time."

"Too early is rude, and you shouldn't judge potential agents on their manners," Chance said.

The waitress returned with their drinks, and the two artificial people drained them before she could turn away.

"Again," Thomas said, returning his empty glass to the tray. "Chance?"

"You know I can't stand seeing you drink alone," Chance said with a wink, setting her glass next to his. "You don't have to rush back with them," she told the waitress and added a five-cred piece to the tray. "And there's no reason for you to lose out because your manager is feeling generous."

Thomas waited for the waitress to leave before asking, "Have you forgotten that the exchange rate here is running over five eBucks a cred? I wish somebody would give me an hour's pay for carrying a couple of little glasses of vodka to a table."

"That's for the whole evening. I might forget later." She looked deep into her husband's eyes and asked, "What efficiency are you at?"

"Ninety-six-point-two percent on that last drink," Thomas replied. "I should probably change the filters on my backup microturbine. You?"

Chance broke into a wide grin and did a little victory dance in her chair. "Ninety-eight percent," she boasted. "Who would have dreamed when we first met that I'd keep my body in better shape than you."

A wiry man in his late twenties wearing an oversized bomber jacket and a knit hat stepped up to their table and addressed Thomas. "Want to buy me a drink, buddy?" he asked.

"Only if you want lemonade," the artificial person completed the code phrase. "Grab a chair."

"When the message said I'd recognize you because you'd be the best dancers in the room, I thought it was a test," the man said, pulling out a chair and sitting down. "You could have told me that you'd be the best-looking people in the place and it would have been equally true."

"What happened to your face?" Chance asked him. "Is that some sort of combat injury?"

"Chicken pox, and I scratched. I was living on my own by then and I didn't trust the public health clinics."

"What should we call you?" Thomas asked. "John didn't include a name."

"If I had any friends, they would call me Henry. I'm not going to—" he stopped talking and leaned back as the waitress returned and placed another two double vodkas on the table.

"And what can I get you?" the waitress asked Henry.

"How about a screwdriver without the vodka," he said.

"You mean an orange juice?"

"I thought this was one of those places that only sells alcoholic beverages. If orange juice is cheaper than a screwdriver without vodka, that's what I'll take."

"Or you could give me his vodka," Chance said. "I'm running ninety-eight percent tonight."

The waitress left, and nobody spoke during the sudden lull as the DJ missed a track change. Then the loud music started up again.

"This is your idea of a secure meeting place?" Henry asked.

"We avoid using active shielding technology on Earth because it stands out like a sore thumb," Thomas said. "Every alien agent in the city would be on their way within seconds of their detectors picking it up. We took the subway to get here, including jumping off a train and running across the tracks to the opposite platform. If anybody tried tailing us from the Elevator Transit Authority spaceport, we lost them."

"That's reasonably aggressive," Henry said in an admiring tone. "I cut through Central Park and then climbed up the fire escape next door and jumped to the roof of this building, but I've been on the move since breakfast." He took out a smartphone and swiped it to life on a screen that was showing live feeds of street scenes from eight different cameras. "I've got a tap into the city-state surveillance cameras and didn't see anybody following me."

Thomas and Chance exchanged a grin. "Work smarter, not harder," Chance said. "I like it. Where did you meet John?"

Henry checked to see if the waitress had returned before replying. "He didn't say anything about it?"

"We haven't caught up with him yet. He sent headquarters a short message requesting that somebody come to meet you, but he'd already left Earth by the time we got here yesterday."

"John showed me his spaceship. If I sign up, will I get a ship?"

"That depends on where we send you, and at best, it would be a Sharf two-man trader," Thomas said. "John bought that four-deck Grenouthian job with the prize money he picked up while working with an alien agent, but I can't go into the details."

"You mean if we seize enemy assets, we get to keep them?" Henry asked, his eyes lighting up.

"Not exactly, but if you work with aliens, they have different rules." Thomas leaned back again as the waitress returned with an orange juice, placed it in front of Henry, and made a show of checking that Thomas and Chance hadn't finished their drinks.

"How much do I owe you?" Henry asked.

"The table is comped," the waitress said. "Are you a dancer too?"

"If you're asking me to dance, I can fake it."

"I can teach you," Chance said after the waitress moved on. "Thomas and I have trained hundreds of agents to dance."

"Is it really that important?" Henry asked.

"Depends on where you're assigned." Chance waited for Henry to swallow a sip from his orange juice before prompting, "So back to how you met John."

"He caught me breaking into the EarthCent president's office. Not my finest hour."

"Picking locks without setting off an alarm is tricky," Thomas said sympathetically. "And I'm sure they have surveillance cameras in the elevator lobby."

"I was going in through the window," Henry said with a sigh.

"The window? But the EarthCent president's office is on the twenty-second floor."

"Don't remind me. It took me half the night to climb that high. Somebody must have finked on me. It's one of those old buildings where the windows open, though I had to cut a hole to get at the locking mechanism. Just when I was about to swing in, the lights all turned on, and there was John standing in one of those black mercenary uniforms with his arms crossed."

"What did you do?" Thomas asked.

"I was so surprised that I lost my balance and fell," Henry said. "I wasn't tied off to anything, and half of my life flashed before my eyes. Then an alien cross between an eagle and a lion grabbed me by the shoulders, flew back up to the window, and tossed me through."

"Semmi, a Tyrellian gryphon. She travels with John, but she's not on our payroll."

"I've been in some tough spots without spilling the beans, but that little trip down memory lane made me question a few things. Including why I took a job from a mystery alien to break into QuickU to steal a prototype personality upgrade for artificial people."

"Wait," Chance said. "If you were hired for industrial espionage, why did you break into the EarthCent president's office?"

"QuickU leases the whole floor, and the president's office sublets from them," Thomas reminded her. "Henry probably assumed, and rightly so, that QuickU's security would be better than EarthCent's."

Henry nodded. "All I saw in the president's office were some locally made motion detectors and a Drazen anti-surveillance system that on a good day might prevent the Hortens from eavesdropping. QuickU is kitted out with Dollnick security, but the alien who hired me gave me something from the Verlocks that would have gotten around it."

"That's the second time you've referred to your alien employer without identifying who it was," Chance said. "You have to let go of your old life before we can hire you."

"It's not loyalty," Henry said. "You know what the contractor game is like. My employer might have been the one who ratted me out. Maybe he hired multiple contractors for the same gig, already got what he needed, and didn't want to pay the rest of what he would have owed me."

"You never met in person?"

"I met somebody, but he was so covered with tattoos and body armor that I couldn't tell if he was a human or a Horten. But I can guess from his attitude that he was a contractor just like me."

"Meaning that anybody could have hired him to hire you," Thomas said and began thinking out loud. "QuickU started out creating personality upgrades for human-derived artificial people, who turn out to be a sort of lowest common denominator for artificial intelligence on the tunnel network, the same as most human food can be digested to some extent by all the advanced species. How much were you paid?"

"Ten thousand creds, plus I got to keep the alien tech," Henry said. "Two thousand up front, the rest on delivery."

"We're in the wrong business," Chance groused. "I only made twenty thousand for all of last year."

"Do you get benefits?"

"Best benefits you'll get from a human employer," Thomas told him. "The EarthCent Intelligence package is modeled on what the aliens give to contract workers. I asked what your mystery employer was paying because you could buy any personality upgrade in QuickU's catalog for a couple of thousand creds and have enough left over for a vacation to try it out."

"I was given a map of the QuickU offices and the location of the workstation where I was supposed to plant a data bug," Henry said. "I'm not sure whose technology it was, but I gave the bug to John, along with the Verlock tech."

"Do you still have the map?" Thomas asked.

"The tattooed guy showed it to me on his tab and I memorized it. I have perfect recall for diagrams, though it fades after a couple of weeks."

Chance reached into her small purse and produced a notebook that shouldn't have fit inside. She pulled the pencil out of the spiral binding, checked the point, and then put both on the table in front of Henry. He stared at her purse, started to say something, and then took up the pencil instead. Turning to a random blank page, he began to sketch and talk at the same time.

"Open workspace, so there aren't any cubicle walls confusing things," Henry said as he drew a rough rectangle and began rapidly filling it with smaller rectangles that represented desks. "I hate breaking into places with cubicles, makes me feel like a rat in a maze."

"Interesting," Thomas said. "Perhaps we should be promoting cubicles as a passive deterrent to crime."

"Not to mention discouraging communications with your co-workers. Four desks from the door, two desks over, I was supposed to place the bug on the back of the shallow drawer that all those desks have."

"That's Jasmine's desk," Thomas said and appeared to be staring off into space for a moment. "She's one of the lead developers, and the last time I was there, she told me they were trying to capture the fundamental essence of being a chef."

"For artificial people?" Henry asked in surprise. "What's the point? They don't even eat."

"We eat when we socialize," Chance said, adding a dazzling smile.

Henry's mouth dropped open as if he'd just been given a dozen shots of Novocain. "You mean…"

"We're both artificial people," Thomas told him. "Coincidentally, I'm the top beta tester for QuickU, which is why I'm familiar with the employees and what projects they're working on."

"But I have a detector ring for artificial people," Henry protested. He tapped the large blue stone in the class ring on his left hand and then angrily twisted it off his finger. "Serves me right buying alien tech from somebody I didn't know."

"We're both very good at shielding—it comes with the territory."

"Yeah, but it's supposed to detect poison and electronic eavesdropping as well. It probably doesn't work for any of them."

Chance picked up the ring and stared at it for a moment. "It's just a chunk of blue glass in a brass setting," she said. "If you sign up with us, you'll get a Drazen poison detector ring, though you probably shouldn't wear it."

"Why not?" Henry asked.

"Because every intelligence agent on the tunnel network knows what they look like."

"Why did you think you would need a way to detect artificial people?" Thomas asked.

"I heard you all worked for the Stryx," Henry said.

"That's a common misconception, though many of us take out mortgages with the Stryx to purchase a body from one of the advanced species. If we did work for the Stryx, we wouldn't have any interest in you."

"Aren't they the galaxy's policemen of last resort?"

"Only for artificial intelligence," Chance told him. She tossed off the rest of her vodka, caught the eye of the waitress, and signaled for another round. "But to be honest, you won't get any top-of-the-line tech working for us because the aliens don't share their best stuff. We have pretty good access to Gem nanobot gear, and the Drazens help us as much as they can, but nobody is going to give anything away that could be used effectively against them if it fell into the wrong hands.

"You don't have to recruit me," Henry said. "I told John that I was willing to work for EarthCent Intelligence as soon as he brought it up. I've always wanted to see the galaxy, but everything I've heard about places run by aliens is that they don't tolerate people like me."

"They certainly wouldn't tolerate you climbing up skyscrapers for the purpose of industrial espionage."

"Here's the thing," Thomas said. "Since our founding, EarthCent Intelligence has always operated in the open. We can't compete with any of the aliens on tech, so we focus on human resources and gathering business data that we can sell to subscribers to encourage humanity's economic growth and fund our efforts to support EarthCent's diplomatic service."

"If you're looking for somebody to stare at a hologram of business data all day, it's not me," Henry said. "I want to work in the field, like John."

"That and your prior experience with breaking and entering at a high level is why he wants us to hire you. As I was saying, we've always worked in the open, to the extent that the alien intelligence services monitor our training camp and identify all our employees before they even start working. We also host alien intelligence agents on Flower, the colony ship that—"

"I took the shuttle up and visited when Flower stopped at Earth. I would have stayed on board, but every time I looked at a reflective surface, I saw a four-armed bot floating behind me."

Chance laughed. "Flower is a sharp one. She probably runs a background check on everybody who takes her shuttles and keeps an eye on them if something looks off."

Henry took a long swallow from his orange juice and a wistful look passed over his features. "Flower has great produce. I took a tour of the ag deck, and I was ready to sign up as an apprentice in the orchards."

"You'd make a living, but it would be quite a pay cut from what you're used to." Chance thought for a moment, and then asked Thomas, "But why would anybody hire him to steal a personality upgrade in development for artificial people to experience being chefs?"

"Chefs make good money, especially if they can work around the clock," Thomas said and turned back to Henry. "I brought up Flower as an example of how EarthCent Intelligence has been operating in the open, not because we want you to live on board. Director Oxford and I agree that we need to start establishing a more clandestine branch of the service to give the Human Empire a head start when they take over from EarthCent. John thought you were an ideal prospect."

"Because I'm deniable?" Henry asked.

"You're human, you've never been away from Earth so you aren't on the radar of any of the alien intelligence agencies, and you climbed up the side of a skyscraper the old-fashioned way when you could have bought a floater belt and done it in thirty seconds."

"I did a few exploratory runs and the building's security system sent an automated drone to investigate whenever floater technology was detected within the immediate airspace."

"Is that ours?" Chance asked Thomas.

"Probably something one of the alien tenants set up," Thomas replied. "This is the first I'm hearing about it. I'll have to check the building registry and work out who it is. Maybe they're the same ones who tipped off EarthCent that somebody was climbing the building."

"Look," Henry said. "I fell into the industrial espionage business when I was a kid on the streets and I got hired to do all sorts of weird jobs, like collecting turtles in the park and harvesting seeds from private orchards. Eventually, they had me breaking into laboratories to steal genetic samples, and some of those labs were in skyscrapers. I only found out after the Alts bought Earth Two that I'd been working for a Dollnick subcontractor gathering samples for terraforming. I trust John because he could have told that gryphon to drop me in the street, and he said I can trust you. But I work by myself, and I use my own judgment on how to get the job done. I'm not training camp material."

"That's exactly what John told us," Thomas said and slid a programmable cred across the table. "I'll be blunt. I'm the deputy director of EarthCent Intelligence and I was the first agent they hired. There aren't many Stryxnet registers where you're going, but there are a few, and if you need a recharge, the funds will show as coming from a Thark bookmaking outfit."

"That's smart," Henry said, nodding his understanding.

"Your contacts for now will be John, Chance, and myself. If anybody else approaches you saying that they're from EarthCent Intelligence, your cover has been blown. We're sending you to Farling Four, the only open world in the Farling Empire. They just got a tunnel connected thanks to building a sovereign community of twenty million humans. Your mission is to go there undercover and get a job that gives you time to investigate a list of exporters that we'll provide."

"Industrial espionage."

"Yes, but the exporters we want you to look into aren't tunnel network members," Thomas explained. "We don't even have an exact count of the alien civilizations participating in the Farling Empire, but early reports suggest they specialize in different commercial areas, much like the advanced species on the tunnel network."

Henry finished his orange juice and began rolling the programable cred across his knuckles. "You'll be adding the information I send you to your business database?" he asked.

"We hope to barter it with the advanced species. This is the first intelligence-gathering opportunity that's come up where we aren't at a disadvantage on the ground. In fact, the Farlings need to stay on good terms with humanity to keep the tunnel open, and since we're there in much larger numbers than the other tunnel network species, you'll have an easier time blending in."

"What happens if I get caught?" Henry asked. "I've heard that the Farlings have drugs that could make a man talk."

"The Farlings have drugs that can make a man do anything," Chance said. "We aren't going to give you a suicide tooth. There won't be any repercussions for us if you get caught and the other species might even think better of us for trying. But you can't expect a rescue either, so my advice is not to get caught."

Four

Clive felt his eyes glazing over as he attempted to read the junior analyst's report about the interstellar trade in fine wool from sheep being raised on Earth Two and several open worlds with large Old Way colonies. It wasn't that he didn't appreciate a good pair of woolen socks, but after a morning of reading reports by recent hires who hadn't yet learned how to write executive summaries, he was ready for something that provided any hint of excitement.

"Kroap, from the Professional LARPing League to see you," the receptionist's voice chirped through his display desk's audio system. "No appointment, but he claims it's urgent."

"Show him in," Clive said. He hesitated for a moment, considering whether to pretend to be immersed in his reading when the alien entered, but the report was so mind-numbingly dull that he put it aside and rose to his feet.

"Director Oxford," the Horten said as soon as he was through the door. "I just came from a meeting where we were finalizing the new arrangements for league security and my assistant told me that you never signed the contract."

"Kroap," Clive said, offering the alien a slight nod, but not a handshake, since the Horten was excited enough to have forgotten his gloves. "Our legal people are still looking it over, and I have a meeting scheduled this afternoon with my deputy director to—"

"Nonsense," Kroap interrupted, and his skin color began tinting red. "It's the standard contract for intelligence agencies policing gaming activities, and all the other species belonging to ISPOA have already signed. My colleagues on the board of directors suggested that your tardy response would make an excellent excuse to disqualify human players from the upcoming season, but I staked my reputation that the only possible reason for your delayed response was incompetence on the part of your underlings."

"Are you serious about the other intelligence agencies signing on? Nobody has said anything to me."

"Then you need to get out more." The Horten produced a secure holo memory and tossed it to Clive. "Slot that in your display desk."

Clive caught the crystal, tapped the icon on his desk that was supposed to force the reader to access holo memories in display mode to prevent any spyware from transferring, and slotted it in. Nine documents in different languages and scripts appeared in the hologram, all of them easily identified as signature pages from a contract.

"Translate text and dates," Clive instructed the display desk. Then he scanned the signature lines and determined that all the contracts had been signed within a twenty-four-hour period two weeks earlier. He frowned and made the appropriate gestures to change the display to the cover sheet of each contract, which in translation, looked identical to the one he'd been offered. "You won't be offended if I confirm these."

The Horten's lips drew back, and his skin was rapidly approaching the shade of a boiled lobster, but he managed to say, "Confirm all you want."

"Access the Thark registry of bonded signatures and confirm these documents," he instructed the display desk.

This time an artificial voice replied, "The Thark registry charges ten creds for each signature check for bonded documents. Confirm payment?"

"Confirm," Clive said, and then subvoced, "Libby? Is Thomas back on the station?"

"He arrived twenty minutes ago and is catching up with Joe in Mac's Bones."

"Can you put me through to him?"

"Thomas here," the artificial person responded a second later.

"Sorry to interrupt, but my contact from the LARPing League is here claiming that all the other species signed the security contract as soon as it was offered," Clive said. "Can you come immediately?"

"On my way."

"I can see your lips moving," the Horten said with a hint of a sneer. "Are you satisfied with the confirmation?"

Clive refocused on the hologram and saw that five of the nine documents were now framed in green. A sixth was confirmed even as he looked.

"I invited Deputy Director Thomas to join us. He'll be here momentarily."

"The artificial person," Kroap said, and the translation Clive heard over his implant gave the Horten's words a tone of heightened interest. "His position in your agency is the most interesting thing about your species."

"You don't think Horten Intelligence employs artificial intelligences?"

"I imagine there are a few crunching data, but leadership roles in government agencies are taken by biologicals."

"Why?" Clive asked. "Are you worried about their loyalty?"

The Horten's skin color shifted from red to brown in a matter of seconds and his face showed genuine amusement. "Loyalty? What does that have to do with it? If any of our artificial intelligences want a job leading flesh-and-blood Hortens, they're welcome to apply. What fascinates me about your deputy director is that he would accept the job in the first place."

"Could I ask if the same was true when you first developed artificial intelligence?"

"A surprisingly astute question, and the answer is, I don't know. That would be over a half-million years ago, before we perfected interstellar drive."

"Do you have any artificial intelligences that have been alive, well, conscious since that time?" Clive asked.

"Is asking me questions your idea of spying?" Kroap countered, unable to hide his amusement as his skin turned an even deeper brown. "I'll be eating out on this story for the next century."

"I didn't realize it was a sensitive topic."

"Where do you buy your clothes?"

"Uh, my wife usually shops for me," Clive admitted. "I think this suit might be from SBJ Fashions or a Vergallian boutique."

"It just gets better and better," Kroap said, pulling out the Horten version of a tab and sketching some quick notes with his fingertip. "You won't mind if I do an impersonation at the next retirement dinner, all in good fun," he continued, looking up at Clive. "I'll need a wig and a fake scar, but as long as I do my Human accent, the right audience should get it. Proceeds go to charity."

"Deputy Director Thomas is here," the receptionist's voice issued from the display desk. "Should I send him in?"

"Yes," Clive said with relief.

Thomas entered the office a moment later, walked up to the Horten, and offered a handshake. "I heat sterilized my hands on the way here," he told Kroap.

"Still warm," the Horten said after returning the handshake. "Shaking hands is a Human tradition that must have evolved to spread germs as rapidly as possible to achieve herd immunity. Such a strange species."

"I also checked with legal while I was in the lift tube," Thomas told Clive. "It turns out that the contract we were offered was standardized back before the Hortens and Drazens joined the tunnel network. It seems that gamblers trying to fix competitive interspecies events is the oldest profession and the sport or game in question doesn't even appear in the contract language."

"Other than as the party of the first part, which in this case, is the Professional LARPing League," Kroap said, putting away his tab. "And the reimbursement rate is set the same for all of the police or intelligence agencies involved."

"I don't remember seeing anything in Stryx creds," Clive said.

"We share the one percent enforcement fee on the official betting," Thomas said. "The Tharks probably carry more action, but they have their own investigative teams keeping an eye on insiders rigging the results."

"Those aren't investigators, they're handicappers," the Horten said. "The Tharks don't care if somebody is trying to rig the outcome as long as they know about it ahead of time and can work it into the odds."

"You have a bonded Thark tab with you?" Clive asked.

Kroap's fast draw of a device not much larger than a smartphone out of a special pouch on his belt would have put a gunfighter from the Wild West to shame. "The camera is enabled," he said, handing it over.

Clive skimmed through the contract again on the way to the signature page, then set down the tab and signed with the stylus. The screen changed to a display box that was showing live video of the ceiling. He picked up the bonded tab, changed the camera orientation so his face filled the box, and said, "Clive Oxford signing for Earth-Cent Intelligence." As he spoke, a flat line below the box ballooned into a waveform, and a green check appeared.

"Excellent," the Horten said, practically snatching the tab out of Clive's hand. "There's an orientation meeting for all the security contractors a week before the season starts. Be prepared to share a list of your key personnel with the other contractors so you can coordinate."

"Aren't you going to sign?" Clive asked.

"It's my contract. Why should I sign it?"

"Don't we get a copy?"

"Haven't we already been through that?" Kroap asked in exasperation. "It's the standard contract. Get it out of a history book, or if you have creds to waste, order a copy from the Tharks. If a ten-cred hologram isn't good enough, you can get calligraphy on parchment, and I believe the Tharks have a deal with Frunge to inscribe contracts on stone tablets if you're old-fashioned." He hesitated for a moment and then offered Thomas another handshake. "It was a pleasure. My strong preference for any future contacts would be to meet with you alone so I don't have to go through decontamination when I return to our deck."

Thomas glanced at Clive before replying. "Director Oxford has requested that I head up the LARPing security team, so I believe we can accommodate your request, provided that I'm on the station."

"Thank you." The Horten made a curt head bob in Clive's direction, then exited the office.

"I didn't want to say anything while he was here, but doesn't the new season for the Professional LARPing League start in ten days?'

"Meaning we have just three days to put together a team for the orientation with the other contractors," Clive said grimly. "Serves me right for playing hard-to-get."

"You made the right play based on the knowledge we had," Thomas said. "I'd never heard of standard contracts myself. I thought everything was always negotiable."

"We'll have to ask legal to find out if there are any other fields where tunnel network members have settled on standard contracts, though now that I think of it, the labor contracts offered to workers from Earth were all built on the same template."

"The minimum terms and conditions for members to hire contract laborers from another species are set in the tunnel network treaty, so it's not the same thing. Especially since the Stryx reserve the right to change the treaty language at their discretion."

"It will be your team, so you choose the members," Clive said. He indicated the chair across from his desk for Thomas to sit, even though the artificial person would have been equally comfortable balancing on one leg. "Do you expect any difficulties?"

"I stopped by QuickU while Chance and I were vacationing on Earth and picked up the personality enhancement for sports gambling so I could gain some insight into the problems we'll face," Thomas said, at the same time flicking his chin with his thumb, a set signal to tell Clive that the subject would require further discussion in a location with better security than the office. "I used the time on our trip back through the tunnel to watch some LARPing reruns from the last season and it's going to be a real challenge."

Clive nodded. "By the end of my brief career cage fighting, I could have earned more money by throwing fights than winning them. I never ate out in the days before a match for fear that the food would be drugged, and I only drank bottled water and juice that I bought from random markets."

"It will be educational to see how the security contractors from the other species operate."

Clive swiped at his display desk and did a reverse hand roll, bringing up the hologram with the bonded Thark contracts again, and now all of them were framed in green. He scanned the signature pages and then used both hands in the control area to turn the hologram so it faced the artificial person.

"I didn't notice the first time, but the Empire of a Hundred Worlds and the Fleet Vergallians signed separate contracts, so their intelligence services are still independent," Clive said. "And the Sharf signed on. They're in ISPOA even though they aren't tunnel network members."

"Based on the reruns from last season, around a tenth of the players in the Professional LARPing League are Sharf," Thomas said. "You'll get your wish for our agents to experience working with alien intelligence services."

"I can't imagine the other agencies need the income so they must be doing it for practice."

"A large part of the work is going to be monitoring the finances of the players and their families for unexplained asset growth or lifestyle changes. What does that sound like?"

"Counterintelligence," Clive said. "If we were worried about EarthCent diplomats selling out humanity, those are exactly the same indicators we'd be watching."

"Do we even have access to that sort of information?" Thomas asked.

"I checked into that while you were away since I couldn't see the point of signing the contract if we didn't have the ability to fulfill the basics. Thanks to all the city-states and legacy nations on Earth signing the treaty to get access to ISPOA databases, we can make reciprocal data requests."

"It's a bit ironic, isn't it? We're humanity's intelligence agency and have the authority to police any populations of humans without formal governments, yet we have to go through the Inter-Species Police Operating Agency to get financial data about our own people."

"Which means you'll need analysts familiar with the process on your security team," Clive said. "I think we should go with our full-time field agents to do any leg-work, both to get them the practice, and because it wouldn't be appropriate to activate sleepers or casual assets for the sake of trying to protect gamblers."

"Agreed," Thomas said. "While watching those reruns, I realized that we're going to need people with experience in LARPing to watch every match and look for suspicious mistakes or missed actions on the part of human players.

The ideal would be if we had somebody with the right credibility to mix with the players."

"Send out an agency-wide notification to all our agents and analysts asking for volunteers. The security contract isn't secret, and if getting people talking discourages a player from thinking about getting rich quick, all the better."

"How about Jonah?"

Clive shook his head. "For one thing, he doesn't work for us. For another, when he's not busy with *Stone Soup* or his family, he still puts in a little time at InstaSitter—"

"Running their amateur LARPing league for current InstaSitters and alumni," Thomas interrupted his boss. "Jonah probably has more experience in LARPing studios than anybody working for us, and now that I think about it, he might know former InstaSitters from multiple species who have gone on to play professionally."

"Blythe will kill me if I add to his workload. And I don't want Jonah feeling that he's required to spend whatever free time he has remaining watching Professional LARPing League contests to help out his father."

"Maybe he's already watching them," the artificial person said. "I've got three days to put together a team. Let me ask him, and if he's not interested, maybe he can point me to somebody with similar knowledge looking for a part-time gig."

The director of EarthCent Intelligence began to formulate a rejection and then changed his mind. "I'll talk to him, and I'll tell him that it's your baby so he doesn't feel like he's making life harder for me if he declines."

"Fair enough," Thomas said rising to his feet. "He can ping me any time, day or night. I'm going to take care of sending everybody an announcement about the new contract and see how many of our analysts and agents respond before I have to start volunteering them."

That evening, Clive was sitting on the living room couch with a Cayl hound's head on his lap when Jonah entered the apartment carrying a large recyclable foil pan. "Where's Mom?" he asked.

"Working late," Clive said. He tried to move the giant hound's head so he could get up and help Jonah, but Bodie chose to play dead, complete with rigor mortis.

"We had the Fillinduck ambassador on today and he cooked some weird meat, but I think it will be safe for Cayl hounds," Jonah said. "But it looks like Bodie died, so I'll bring it by Mac's Bones and see if Beowulf and Alexander want it."

Bodie yawned as if just waking up and deigned to lift his head.

"Bring it over here and let him have a sniff," Clive said. "He's skeptical."

Jonah placed the pan on the coffee table next to the couch and carefully peeled back part of the foil covering. The Cayl hound kept one foreleg across Clive's thighs to inform him that he wasn't yet dismissed from pillow duty, put his other foreleg on the floor for balance, and brought his nose near the tray. Then he nodded, got all four paws on the floor, and headed into the kitchen.

"Sephia taught him that," Jonah said over his shoulder as he followed the hound with the pan of leftovers. "Her family has this weird thing about only eating in the kitchen."

"Maybe they grew up with white rugs," Clive said. He attempted to stand and discovered that both of his legs were half asleep. "Do you have a minute to talk?"

"I assumed that's why you invited me by. The leftovers are just a coincidence."

"That and you think that your mother and I starve Bodie when he stays with us, but I haven't noticed him losing any weight."

A deep growl came from the kitchen, followed by loud slurping noises that could only be made by a giant tongue.

"You know that his metabolism adjusts to the available food supply," Jonah said, as he came out of the kitchen to meet his father, who had only managed to limp the length of the couch. "Sephia says she'd be fine with having Bodie all the time, and with you and Mom working so much, it would probably be better for him. Sephia hates to leave Adam with InstaSitters unless Bodie is there."

"Do you find yourself using sitters a lot?"

"Sephia gives me grief about it, but I think that calling InstaSitter for Adam as often as possible shows that we're still involved. Mom and Chastity meet with Tinka once a week, but I'm the only one left in the family who spends any time in the offices. I still teach the cooking course for our continuing education program once a week."

Clive stood crabwise to massage the back of his legs, and looked up as he said, "So you don't deal with the internal LARPing league anymore."

"I'm never going to drop that," Jonah said. "I stopped talking about it because I know that you and Mom think that dressing up like medieval warriors and bashing away at each other with noodle weapons and magic spells is silly. I don't have time to coach the Union Station InstaSitter team anymore, but our internal league has gotten so competitive that the players pool their money and hire a real coach to scout the other teams and work on strategy. We would have won last year, but Echo Station has a mage with a crazy repertoire of cantrips that our team wasn't prepared for."

"Cantrips?"

"Think of them as ready-to-go spells and incantations that don't take any time to cast. I tried getting Baa to rent us Jyndal but she wanted too much money."

"You were going to pay Jyndal to be a ringer on your InstaSitter team?" Clive asked.

"I was going to pay Baa to let Jyndal go through our training and work a few hours as an InstaSitter," Jonah said, trying to look offended. "A ringer is somebody who doesn't technically qualify to be a member of the team."

"Then I'll keep this brief. EarthCent Intelligence just signed a contract with the Professional LARPing League as outside security to prevent match rigging. All the other alien intelligence services work through ISPOA to prevent match-fixing in sporting events, and this is our first invitation to participate."

"Because there are so many humans in the Professional LARPing League," Jonah said, nodding. "We don't have anybody on the leaderboard, but most teams have at least a token human."

"Why did I think that teams were made up of members from the same species?" Clive asked.

"That's a separate tournament that the league runs, sort of an all-stars thing that doesn't have any significance, other than bragging rights and gambling. Do you need me to come in and give your analysts a briefing?"

"Thomas is in charge of our security team, and he wants to talk to you about working with him a few hours a week. He thinks it's critical that we invest the majority of our available resources for the job looking in the right places."

Jonah grinned. "You mean, EarthCent Intelligence will pay me to watch Professional LARPing League matches and tell them if I think a player is underperforming his or her potential?"

"I guess we'll have to pay you, and I think he'll want you to make use of your contacts and celebrity to attend some player events and see what you can pick up," Clive said. "He said you can ping him day or night to talk about it."

Five

"Cop—e—right," Wrylenth said, enunciating the syllables so slowly that his audience wondered if he had reverted to speaking at the normal speed for Verlocks. "Breaking the word down, we find its roots. 'Cop' is a Humanese slang term for police, derived from a time when officers of the law wore copper badges, and 'e' refers to ebooks and other electronic media, such as streaming video. The last root word in the construct, expressing the core concept of proper or correct conduct, is 'right', which —"

"What are you talking about?" Roland interrupted impatiently. "Copyright existed long before electronic media, and the important part of the word is 'copy', as copyright law offers economic protection to authors and other creators of original works from indiscriminate commercial copying. On top of that, it's a 'y', not an 'e', and policemen didn't wear copper badges, they copped criminals. It's a verb."

The owner and publisher of the Galactic Free Press began to laugh and poked her Freelance Desk editor in the arm. "I can't believe you fell for that," Chastity said to Roland. "Wrylenth always starts briefings with a joke."

"I thought it was rather good," the Verlock said. "I've been practicing my timing."

Roland groaned and rubbed his temples. "Got me, but in my defense, I'm running on caffeine this morning. The press syndicate Ellen helped set up on Earth has been too productive, and last night I had to winnow through almost a hundred potential stories that she passed along."

"Do you need a bigger budget for acquiring content from Earth?" Chastity asked.

"Yes, but more than that, I need another body to help sort through it all. The number of freelancers we have working in sovereign human communities scattered around the tunnel network has been doubling every year, and if we don't figure something out soon, we'll be publishing a million words a day."

"It's an electronic paper," Wrylenth said, obviously puzzled by Roland's concern. "Why count words?"

"We have almost two hundred editors at various levels working on Union Station," Roland said. "To handle a million words a day, call it a thousand articles averaging a thousand words, we'd need another two hundred."

"Are four hundred editors too many?"

"You'd be surprised how difficult it is to train new editors," Chastity told the Verlock. "We get a hundred applications for every editor we hire, and half of those don't last a year. The profession attracts too many people who already know all the answers and want to shape every story to fit their favored narrative. We aren't in that business."

"You could hire more non-Humans," Wrylenth said. "I know a Verlock statistical journalism professor at the Open University who stays in contact with his former students."

"We're humanity's flagship news organization so I'm trying to avoid relying too much on aliens. But if you can suggest any analysts who—"

"No," the Verlock cut her off. "Director Oxford was very upset with me the last time I gave you a list of our intelligence analysts who had expressed an interest in exploring other job options."

"Twenty-three out of the twenty-six I hired away are still working for us," Chastity said with a wolfish grin. "My sister wouldn't talk to me for a week."

The door on the Galactic Free Press side of the shared conference room slid open and Walter entered with a recyclable cup carrier in one hand holding four large coffees and a Dollnick tab in the other.

"I found what I was looking for and grabbed a coffee while I was out," Walter said. "Did you start without me?"

"You missed the joke," Chastity informed him.

"I could tell it again," Wrylenth said.

Roland shook his head. "It won't work now that he's expecting it. And when are we going to get the coffee machine fixed?"

"It's their turn," Chastity said, pointing at Wrylenth as the representative of EarthCent Intelligence. "The machine that failed was the spare from one of our breakrooms, and I bought the one before that which somebody destroyed trying to make invisible ink. Spies drink at least as much coffee as we do. They're just freeloading."

"Is anybody else coming?" Wrylenth asked.

"Bob Steelforth will be here as soon as the meeting he's covering wraps up," Walter told him. "I asked Roland because he's our main editorial contact for journalists working on Earth and it's their copyright system that's messed up. The four artificial people we have working for us are all away on assignment."

Wrylenth stood and began a prepared speech. "As you know, over a dozen artificial people are working for

EarthCent Intelligence. That almost certainly makes us the largest employer of human-derived artificial intelligences, thanks to the recruitment efforts of Thomas, our deputy director. He recently brought to the director's attention an egregious case of discrimination against artificial intelligences in Earth's copyright laws. Since the other tunnel network species have agreed to honor our intellectual property laws through bilateral agreements, that means that original works created by human-derived artificial intelligences aren't protected."

"That's crazy," Roland said. "How did such a rule ever get included in Earth's copyright laws?"

"I've been doing some research on the subject, and it's clear that the real intent wasn't to deny protection to works created by sentient artificial intelligence, but to protect the jobs of Human writers and artists from competition by early machine learning systems that were capable of almost instantly creating new works based on simple prompts."

"Original works, or copies?"

"That's where it got tricky," Wrylenth said. "You could ask one of these large language models to write a story about Easter in the style of Dickens Christmas Carol and it would create a story that didn't violate the copyright laws of the time. But there was a debate over whether that work could be classified as original, and of course, opportunists immediately began training these chatbots to flood the market with look-alike titles that were intended to tap into the audiences of famous authors."

"But were they original?" Chastity repeated the words of her Freelance Desk editor.

"Based on the century-old examples I looked at, I would have to say that they meet the Humanese definition of original."

"But not the Verlock definition?"

"No. Our copyright laws place great weight on the intent of the creator, and a non-sentient chatbot cannot have intent by definition," Wrylenth said. "My specialty, to the extent which I can claim to have one so early in my career, is in tunnel network law. If I had trained in intellectual property law, I might be able to tell you more about the origins of our current copyright law, but I wouldn't be surprised if those records have been lost over the millions of years."

Walter frowned. "Stryx Jeeves has ghostwritten quite a few *For Humans* books and we publish them with copyright notification. Are you telling me that if a publisher on Earth wanted to copy them word-for-word, we'd have no legal recourse?"

"That's exactly the case, and a competing publisher with deep pockets might even attempt to sue the Galactic Free Press through a city-state court system claiming economic damage caused by a false copyright notification."

"Is that just a theoretical, or could such a thing happen?" Chastity asked.

"I'll repeat that I'm not an expert in intellectual property law, but under the systems with which I'm familiar, copyright protection is implicit, with no filing or notification required. Filing for copyright and supplying deposit copies to the registration authority, in Earth's case, gives the claimant the ability to collect statutory damages and legal costs. Perhaps a particularly litigious adversary could sue for false advertising, but it would be difficult to prove lost profits for books that they never published, and I doubt the courts will be sympathetic. Keep in mind that I'm comparing apples to oranges here since the intellectual property laws of all the advanced species protect works created by artificial intelligence."

"Then I don't understand," Roland said. "If we all honor each other's copyright laws, why couldn't Jeeves or Thomas claim protection under Verlock copyright law?"

"They could do so everywhere other than Earth," Wrylenth said. "Given the depth and complexity of intellectual property law, treaty agreements always include a 'home rule' clause that gives priority to the legal code of the signatory species on their designated homeworld. Away from the homeworld, we follow a simple majority."

"Hold on," Walter said. "Are you telling me that rather than sitting down and working out a uniform set of intellectual property laws for the tunnel network, all of the species agreed to honor each other's laws without knowing what's in them?"

"Experts know what's in them, though to put it in context, if you started reading through Verlock lawbooks related to intellectual property, you'd be hundreds of years old before you got halfway through. Negotiation is ultimately about compromise. Rather than investing millions of legal hours into settling every little difference between our intellectual property laws to come up with a uniform version for the tunnel network, our ancestors left it to the judges and attorneys to hash out in court."

"But isn't it terribly inefficient to leave the law so unsettled that the same questions get litigated over and over again?"

Wrylenth now assumed the pose of a Verlock lecturer, which informed his listeners that he had something to say that he believed was fundamentally important to the issue at hand. "First," he said, "the judges, attorneys, plaintiffs, and defendants all have access to precedent to guide their actions. More importantly, intellectual property law is not a physical law, like gravity. When Earth signed onto the copyright treaty, it meant that the law changed for all of us. I'm aware of at least one case in the field of anime where your version of copyright law which granted protection to characters based on the pointiness of their chins and the size of their eyes tipped the balance in favor of a claim that a Grenouthian producer had been pushing in recent centuries."

"Centuries?" Walter asked in astonishment. "How long does copyright protection for anime characters last?"

"In Grenouthian law, copyright protection for anime characters lasts as long as the original creator or his legal heirs keeps producing new content based on those characters," the Verlock said, resuming his seat. "Reruns are fair game."

"It's a bit surprising that Jeeves never brought it up given that it could affect the royalties on the *For Humans* titles he ghosted," Chastity said, and turned to Roland. "Do any of Ellen's freelancers report about intellectual property law on Earth? Maybe we could put out some quiet feelers to find out what would be required to get it updated."

"I've already looked into that," Wrylenth said. "The history of copyright law is a patchwork because there were always nations that either didn't honor the commitments of prior governments or never signed onto the international treaty in the first place. I think our best chance of getting anything done in the near future would be to push the inter-species aspect and claim that EarthCent has the right to negotiate for all of humanity. Even if that stand is challenged by the city-states or remaining nations, it wouldn't cost that much to tie it up in court for years while working on the other approach."

"Negotiating with all of Earth's governments separately? Never mind. If a problem comes up with the *For Humans* books, Jeeves can take care of himself."

The door on the Galactic Free Press side of the conference room slid open again and a serious-looking man in his forties entered with two oversized takeout cups of coffee, each of which had the capacity of two mugs.

"I thought you might be running low by now," Bob said. "They're both black without sugar, so you'll have to add packets."

Chastity pointed at her ear to let the others know she was communicating over her implant. Walter and Roland took advantage of the break to top off their coffees from one of the cups Bob brought, and Wrylenth stood up again and began gathering his things.

"It's done," Chastity said when she lowered her hand. "I ordered one of those expensive Dollnick universal brewing machines with a lifetime warranty. They'll install it this afternoon, and if my sister won't pay half for EarthCent Intelligence, I'm going to hire away more of their analysts."

The three men grinned at each other like schoolboys, and even the Verlock couldn't hide his pleasure at the announcement.

"Is your daughter starting this afternoon?" Bob asked Walter. "Stephanie Hertz agreed to let Bethany use her desk in the afternoons since she doesn't come in before evening."

"Beth will be here after she finishes school for the day, around noon," Walter said.

"Why didn't you give her to me?" Roland asked. "Bethany is a smart kid, and I need help more than Bob does."

"Because you need help sorting through news stories from Earth, and that's exactly what my wife doesn't want our daughter doing at fourteen years of age."

"Brinda has a point," Chastity said. "Do you think Bethany would be interested in working with Lena? I've been thinking about asking her to open an office for us to coordinate with the Children's News Network. There are kids in all of the sovereign human communities submitting stories through their teacherbots and Lena has an eye for which ones warrant following up and a byline."

"Walter's daughter hasn't even started working for me yet and you're taking her away?" Bob protested "Give the kid a chance."

"It was just a thought. The Children's News Network sets a standard word rate that we pay when we rerun any of their content, but Lena learned her journalism chops working for them before she aged out, and she thinks it would be a good idea to invite those kids to Union Station for a journalism boot camp."

"You mean, Lena thinks it would be a cheap way to recruit the next generation to work for the Galactic Free Press."

"It did come up in our conversation," Chastity said with a grin. "Lena won't commit to anything at the moment because she's traveling with her boyfriend, but I suspect she'll be ready to settle soon enough."

"I hate to disappoint the three of you, but Bethany will be working as a junior editorial assistant on the new *For Humans* book for the next three months," Walter told them. "My wife agreed to Bethany shadowing Bob on days where there isn't anything for her to do on the book, which is why he arranged for her to share a desk near his."

"I thought you were sunsetting the *For Humans* brand," Roland said and turned to the publisher. "Didn't you end up canceling the last book just before the release?"

Chastity grimaced. "*Sanitation for Humans*. The Grenouthian network got ahold of a draft and used it as fodder for the comedy part of their late news broadcast for a week. We probably shouldn't have included all the helpful hints about washing hands and wiping."

"Why did you want to publish the book in the first place?"

"We received thousands of requests, and with a little editing, we'll release it as *Sanitary Engineering for Humans*. That's what ninety percent of the book was about, but the acquisitions editor liked the shorter title. Then she decided it would be useful to start with a basic guide to hygiene and didn't think it was worth bothering the editorial board about the changes."

"Is she still with us?" Bob asked.

"I didn't have her eliminated, if that's what you mean," Chastity said, then displayed a cat-that-ate-the-canary smile. "I arranged a job interview for her at my sister's publishing company and provided an excellent reference."

"Who's the editor of the new book?" Roland asked Walter.

"Finalia. She edits the alien cultures section for the weekend edition."

"Good choice," Bob said approvingly. "I run into her at more alien events than any other human journalist on Union Station. She's a sponge for alien cultures, so she should understand the context of their take on us."

"We must have too many editors working for us because I'm having trouble putting a face with the name," Chastity said. "How long has she been working here?"

"I noticed her showing up at events when the ambassador was away filling in for the president, so, two years?" Bob concluded uncertainly.

"That sounds right," Walter said. "She worked the culture beat back on Earth for almost twenty years before coming to us."

"Oh, the woman from Rome," Chastity said. "I remember her now. I wonder why her name didn't stick with me. She married into one of the top families in the Roman city-state and came here to get away from a messy divorce."

"Bit of a workaholic, which is to say, our kind of people," Bob said with a grin.

"I'll have to start reading our alien culture section. How is she doing at lining up aliens to write chapters about humans from their perspective?"

Walter drooped. "It's turned into a bit of a diplomatic kerfuffle. Ambassador McAllister mentioned her idea for the book in one of her committee meetings with the alien ambassadors, and—"

"Don't tell me," Chastity interrupted. "They all have a favorite author in mind?"

"Worse. They all believe themselves to be uniquely qualified to write the chapter for their species."

"What's so bad about letting them each write a chapter?" Bob asked. "It's all going to get whittled down into the *For Humans* template, with short sentences, limited vocabulary, and half of the page being taken up by colored boxes with pulled quotes and helpful hints."

"Would you want to be the one editing the Verlock ambassador's mathematical proof of why we act the way we do?" Walter asked. "And how much experience with humans do any of them have outside of diplomacy?"

"But Finalia has a secret weapon," Chastity said slowly. "All she has to do is explain to the ambassadors that the series is written for the eighth-grade level. And unlike Ambassador McAllister, I suspect that the aliens won't have any trouble following the guidelines for length and content."

"Hey," Roland said. "Wouldn't Bethany be in eighth grade if she was going to one of those old-fashioned schools on Earth that separate classes by age? Attending Libby's school, she's more advanced academically, but she could still give the ambassadors instant feedback on what they're writing."

Walter looked intrigued for a moment but then frowned. "I already told Kelly that it was a bad idea and asked her to let the ambassadors know that we were looking in a different direction."

"When was that?" Chastity asked, pointing at her ear.

"This morning when she went into the embassy, maybe a half hour before this meeting."

The publisher of the Galactic Free Press was silent for almost a minute, then she smiled and lowered her hand. "Kelly hasn't talked to any of them yet. She said she thought about your objections and she was still planning on trying to convince us to use the ambassadors. Aabina was helping her make up a list of reasons when I pinged."

Walter began to raise his coffee cup and realized from the weight that it was empty. "Then I guess we can try it," he said. "I suppose Brinda can't complain about our daughter being exposed to what the advanced species think about humanity."

"Don't you want to know what Kelly's reasons were?" Chastity asked.

"She read you the list?"

"The ones they had written down. At the top was that the alien ambassadors have staffs and access to their intelligence services. She thinks that rather than their personal opinions, we could end up getting concise summaries of the problems the advanced species have dealing with us, and at an eighth-grade level so we can all understand."

Six

Henry squeezed the neck of the new sick-up bag closed even though there hadn't been anything left in his stomach to fill it. "How much longer?" he groaned.

"Another hour and we'll arrive at Void Station," the trader said sympathetically. "You might want to spend a few days recovering there before the next leg of your trip. Where did you say you were going again?"

"Timbal," Henry lied. "I always wanted to be in the immersive business and a cousin there can get me in as an extra so I can make some money while I'm auditioning for better parts."

"Then you're in luck because there's good liner service to Timbal. The way they spin those ships up, you'll think that you're walking on the surface of a planet. Or you can go for the cheaper stasis option and sleep the whole trip."

"Stasis is cheaper than staying awake? If I had known that I would have asked you to freeze me."

The trader laughed. "I can guess how you feel, but I barely have enough room on the bridge for one passenger and the exercise equipment. I've never heard of somebody carrying a stasis pod on a Sharf two-man trader, though if it can be done, I'm sure Flower Shipyards will be announcing it as an option one of these days. Why didn't you grab a car up the elevator stalk and take a liner in the first place? You only would have been weightless for a couple of hours instead of a couple of days."

"I've never been off the planet before," Henry lied again, rather than revealing that he'd made the deal to fly supercargo on a trader to avoid any official records of his leaving Earth from being generated. "It's like anything else, right? The next time I'm weightless it won't be as bad?"

"Some people get used to it. Others never do. I wish I stocked Zero-G sickness meds, but I never needed them myself, and I don't carry passengers often. I bet you would have paid anything for a pill."

"You bet correct. I haven't kept anything down in two days."

"I noticed," the trader said, striving to maintain a sympathetic expression even while he pondered adding a few embellishments to the story of the trip and entering the Tall Tales contest at the next Rendezvous. "At least you were able to sleep."

Henry winced. "I hadn't had nightmares about falling since I was a kid. I hope I wasn't yelling and disturbing you."

"Not a peep," the trader said, even though he would have loved to ask whether his passenger's mumbling about breaking into a government agricultural vault to steal rare heritage seeds was true.

After they came out of the tunnel, the trader handed over control of the ship to the Stryx owner of Void Station, who used manipulator fields to bring it into the station's busy core and land it at the far end of the travel concourse reserved for independent traders. Henry began feeling better as soon as his weight returned to something like the eighty percent of Earth-normal that the station's spin imparted to everything on the innermost deck, and after thanking the trader and shouldering his backpack, he set out to look for something to eat.

"Hey, not in there," a passing woman hissed in Henry's ear as he started to enter a restaurant with holograms of entrees that made his mouth water. "That's a Drazen joint. The food will kill you."

Henry turned to ask the woman for details, but she was walking rapidly toward a queue of people and aliens waiting to board some sort of shuttle, and he didn't want to make her late. He gave the holograms a final wistful glance, this time noting that he didn't quite recognize any of the entrees, and decided to keep looking for a place with a menu in English. He walked another ten minutes with his stomach growling so loud that several aliens glanced in his direction, including a tall fellow with four arms who pressed a coin in his hand.

"Hey, I'm not a charity case," Henry called after the alien, but the last thing he wanted was to draw attention, so he gave up and examined the coin. "Ten creds!" he couldn't help blurting out. "You could beg on a street corner in Manhattan all day and not make this much."

"Are you looking for a guide, sir?" a child's voice inquired. Henry looked up, and then down again, to see a ten-year-old boy with a buzz cut wearing some sort of uniform with a handkerchief tied around the neck. "I'm Scout Earnest, and I can help you find whatever you need."

"How much do you charge?" Henry asked, having plenty of experience with street kids in the city and their offers to help.

"Station Scouts don't charge for help, sir, and we don't accept tips. I'm working on a new badge."

"Sorry, I thought your name was Scout. I'm Henry, and if you thought I looked lost, you're a hundred percent right. But I just spent two days in Zero-G getting sick and my priority is to find something to eat. Is there anything for humans around here? I haven't seen a menu in a language I recognize."

"There are three human restaurants further up the travel concourse, where the liners dock," Earnest reported. "It's about a fifteen-minute walk for me but your legs are longer. There's a Vergallian vegan restaurant back the way you came, which is closer, but," he lowered his voice, "it's not a good one."

Henry's stomach offered a loud objection to the scout's options. "The closest food is fifteen minutes away?"

"If you aren't transferring to a liner right afterward, it would be quicker to take a lift tube to the Human Deck and get off at Chinatown. It's not all Chinese food, it's just what everybody calls the restaurant section."

"How long would that take?"

The scout glanced in the direction of the nearest bank of lift tubes to see if there was a crowd. "It looks clear now, sir, so less than five minutes."

"Thank you," Henry said, starting in the direction the boy was pointing. "What do the lift tubes cost?"

"Nothing, sir." The boy hesitated a moment, and then called after the man, "Have you ever been in a lift tube, sir?"

"My first time in space," Henry lied reflexively without even being sure why.

"I can guide you to Chinatown if you want. It's on the way back to school and recess is almost over."

"I'd appreciate the help. Is there something I can sign for you to earn your badge?"

"It's on the honor system, sir," Earnest said as he accompanied Henry to the lift tubes. "Chinatown," he declared out loud when they entered.

"Voice controls?" Henry asked, even though he already knew that was how it worked from his visit to Flower. "That must be a trick with all of the languages spoken by the different species."

"I think the station librarian runs the lift tubes, sir. He knows all the languages."

"Even alien travelers who show up from random worlds? We must have hundreds of languages just on Earth. I can't imagine how many languages the aliens on the tunnel network speak."

"One per species, sir. They all standardized long before humans began speaking, or that's what my third-grade teacher said." The boy rubbed at the side of his buzz cut and asked, "Do you have an implant?"

"No. Do you?"

Earnest shook his head sadly. "My parents say I'm too young and my head is still growing."

"I'm planning on doing some traveling and I've been told that an implant would be a good investment," Henry said. "I didn't want to buy one on Earth because I've heard horror stories. Do they sell them on the Human Deck?"

"Yes, sir. There's a shop that has a robot surgeon to do the installation in Chinatown."

"Then it sounds like we're going to the right place. You wouldn't know what they cost?"

"No, sir," the boy said as the capsule doors slid open on a busy marketplace with smells that made Henry's stomach growl even louder. "But I've heard that you can get cheap ones or expensive ones." He turned his head slowly, like he was searching for something, and then pointed off to the left. "There, sir. The shops selling technology are past the water fountain."

"Thank you again, Earnest. I think I can find my way from here. And good luck with your badge."

As the scout hurried off to school, Henry couldn't help thinking that the boy was a bit young to be engaging with strange adults on the travel concourse, but then again, he'd heard that there were surveillance cameras everywhere on Stryx stations and violent crime was unheard of. He resisted grabbing the first empty seat he saw at a sushi bar because they were a long way from any oceans and ended up in a self-service cafeteria-style place with hot food in a steam table. He went for a plate of macaroni and cheese, a piece of pie, and a bottle of lemonade. The cashier gave him seven creds change for the ten-cred piece the alien had pressed on him, plus a few smaller coins that he dropped in the tip jar.

"Good stuff cheap," he said to the cashier. "This would cost at least twenty eBucks on Earth."

"Sounds like a rip-off," she replied. "I've never been there myself."

Henry took his tray to one of the tables in the shared courtyard area and found that despite all the noise his stomach was making, he felt full before finishing the pie. "Probably shrank in Zero-G," he muttered to himself. "Now to see about an implant."

The scout's description proved accurate, and just beyond the parabolic fountain he found booths selling everything from tabs to holographic projectors for home immersive systems. The shop selling implants was exceptional in that it had four glass walls and a door that swung open on a pivot point rather than sliding.

"Can I help you?" a dark-skinned woman wearing a white medical jacket asked as soon as he entered. "We have a special on the new trader implants this week. Just five hundred creds with the installation."

"That's over twenty-five hundred eBucks," Henry said. "Not cheap. What are the other options?"

"The most basic implant that only handles tunnel network languages spoken by oxygen breathers and doesn't come with any visual enhancement or a heads-up display is one hundred creds, installed. But more than fifty percent of people who buy it decide to upgrade after a few years, and there's no market for used electronic devices that have been inside somebody's head."

"No, I don't imagine there would be. What other options are there?"

"The regular business implant comes with a translation pendant so you can speak to alien customers in their language, and that's just three hundred and fifty creds," the woman told him.

"Less than the trader model," Henry said. "What am I losing?"

"You don't get the visual enhancements with the business model. That means you won't be able to capture images of signs or documents in alien languages and have a translation appear on your heads-up display."

"Okay, I can see where that would be valuable for traders. Are the implants manufactured by the Stryx?"

The woman opened the glass case she was standing behind and brought out a retail box with a picture of a Sharf two-man trader on the cover. "No," she said. "All of the implants we sell are made by the Dollnicks under license to the Grenouthians. I think that the Verlocks manufacture diplomatic implants, though those would be licensed by the Stryx."

"Warranty?"

"Lifetime plus a hundred years, but it's not transferable."

"Very funny," he said, though the corner of his mouth quirked up in appreciation of the joke. "I'm in transit and the trader's implant sounds good, but could you sharpen your pencil a little?"

The woman appeared puzzled. "I don't think I've ever owned a pencil, though I've heard of them."

"I'm asking if you have any room for negotiating on the price," Henry said. "Five hundred is a bit of a stretch."

"I'm afraid I don't have any flexibility on pricing. We're just a franchise."

"Payment plan?"

She made a face rather than replying.

"All right," Henry said, getting out the programmable cred that Thomas had given him. "Charge it to this."

"Charge?"

"Sorry, I meant, take it out. I keep confusing these things with credit cards."

The woman flipped over the programmable cred, looked at the balance, and then back to Henry. "There. I almost felt bad about not being able to give you a discount. Your balance is ten times mine."

"Everybody on Earth dickers over prices these days," Henry told her. "I thought we picked it up from alien tourists or people retiring to Earth after working a few labor contracts."

"Barter is better, but we aren't set up for it here," she said, slotting the coin into her mini-register. "Five hundred cred purchase of a trader's implant, installed." Then she looked at Henry like she expected him to do something.

"I approve," he said hastily, giving himself a mental kick for having forgotten that transactions for more than a handful of creds required voice confirmation.

"Good. We can do the surgery right now as long as you haven't eaten anything in the last twelve hours."

"It's going in my head, right? What difference does it make if I've eaten."

"The surgery is done under general anesthesia, which can lead to your food," she made a lifting gesture, "and choking you."

"I hadn't thought of that part," Henry said. "Is there a workaround? How about a local anesthetic and doing the surgery while I'm sitting up?"

"Hold on. I think we have a hold-harmless agreement for that if you want to risk it." She brought a bonded legal tab out from under the register, flipped through a few screens, and said, "Here. If you sign that and give voice confirmation, we can proceed."

Henry skimmed the document in which he accepted all responsibility for the implantation surgery and agreed to hold harmless a laundry list of vendors. He felt a little less sure of himself, and asked, "Does this come up often?"

"I've only been working here a few weeks, but I was told it's not uncommon for people who buy an implant while passing through the station on their way elsewhere," she said.

"And the surgeon has done this before?"

"The surgeon has probably done more surgeries than there are people. That," she pointed at a stainless-steel hand attached to a robotic arm in a glassed-in booth, "is just there to hold the tools. The real surgeon is the station librarian who subcontracts to do the work."

"You mean a Stryx does the surgery?" Henry asked.

"That's how the franchises were set up. I'm not sure why the aliens don't take advantage of all the services the Stryx offer on stations."

"Then let's do it." He used the proffered stylus to sign the tab, gave his voice confirmation, and entered the small booth.

"The glass is going to get dark now," she warned him. You wouldn't want passersby seeing the inside of your head."

Henry sat in the chair, which included a yoke-like device to hold his head steady, and then he felt several lightning-fast pricks on the scalp just behind his ears. "Local anesthetic," an artificial voice announced. "Tell me if you feel anything, but avoid speaking otherwise." A few minutes passed while the robotic arm did some prep work, and then the yoke released. "All done."

"Is this a joke?" Henry demanded. "You didn't do anything."

"It's a simple procedure. I installed the implant and the shunts, but the delicate surgery is done by nanobots over the next several hours and days. They'll make the necessary connections to your nervous system and brain that allow the implant to block you from hearing the dialogue in the original language that's being simultaneously translated."

"What about the heads-up display I paid for?"

"That will also become functional once the nanobots make the connections to your visual cortex."

"Then who would ever go under general anesthesia for this surgery?"

"People who want to limit the number of nanobots in their heads," the station librarian explained. "A few million are unavoidable for a surgery that involves making changes inside the brain, but in your case, the nanobots will also form themselves into wires to make the necessary connections. Under general anesthesia, I install a complete wiring harness which lowers the resistance of the connections and is less likely to fail within the warranty period."

"Thank you," Henry said as he got out of the chair, but then he stopped. "How will I know that it's working?"

"Will you be remaining on Void Station? I can inform you when the connections are complete and provide the initial training."

"I was planning to leave as soon as I can make a connection to the mining colony at Pzerous. A friend told me that tickets are cheaper if you buy them last minute on Stryx stations."

"The next liner stopping at Pzerous leaves in three hours and nine minutes from the Frunge Imperial Lines gate," the station librarian informed him. "A tourist class ticket is three hundred and seventeen creds, or two hundred seventy-five if you travel in stasis. I can process the purchase against the programmable cred you just used."

"Does the ship have gravity?"

"It spins up to provide passengers on the outer decks a weight approximately the same as the travel concourse on this station."

"Then I'll stay awake, though I don't get why it costs more," Henry said.

"You'll be in transit for three days, so the difference covers meals and service. The only reason they don't charge more is to subsidize traffic to the bars and casino."

"Sounds like my kind of ship. Go ahead and sell me a ticket."

"Processed," the station librarian announced. "I'm sending the ticket to your smartphone since you don't have a tab, but you should know that the phone won't be able to connect to any networks other than on Stryx stations and Flower."

"Buying a tab is next on my list. My friend said—"

"You'd get a better deal on a Stryx station than on Earth. Your friend was correct. May I recommend an eBook purchase after you acquire a tab?"

"Are you an author?" Henry asked suspiciously.

"Yes, but in this case the book I'm recommending isn't my own. It's *Implants for Humans*. If you want to get the most out of your trader's implant, you'll either need a tutor or a reference."

"I'll get it. Thank you."

Henry spent almost an hour wandering through the booths selling tabs before settling on a foldable Dollnick model that fit easily in the lower pocket of his cargo shorts. He was so surprised that it cost just ten creds that he paid in cash, and only as he was walking away did he remember that there may not be many Stryx registers where he was headed and that Thomas had suggested paying with the programmable cred whenever possible. When he located the bookstore at the other end of Chinatown, he had less than two hours before the liner departed and was feeling rushed.

"*Implants for Humans*," the clerk repeated his request. "Do you want that on paper?"

"I just bought this tab so I may as well stick with electronic," Henry said, unfolding his recent purchase and laying it on the counter. "I've never done this before, so..."

"Got it," the clerk said and waved a hand over the mini-register. "One copy of *Implants for Humans,* local electronic delivery."

"Four creds and ninety-nine centees to purchase *Implants for Humans,* electronic edition," the mini-register responded, and the amount appeared floating above the register in a hologram.

Henry confirmed the decimal place and said, "Authorized," then watched as the screen of his tab blinked, and then showed the cover of the new book.

"Will there be anything else?" the clerk asked. "Perhaps a novel?"

"My phone is loaded," Henry said, drawing a look of incomprehension. "I'm all set, thank you." He refolded the tab, returned it to his pocket, and found the bank of lift tubes. "Frunge Empire Liners," he told the capsule confidently.

"Frunge Imperial Lines," the familiar artificial voice of the station librarian corrected him. "I would offer to send a map to your implant, but the heads-up display will be one of the last functions to come online."

"Do you mean some functions are?"

"The basic translation of alien languages will be active soon, though you might still hear the source language at the same time. It depends on how much trouble your antibodies are giving the nanobots." When the capsule stopped and the doors slid open again, the station librarian added, "Count two hundred steps to your right, and then head straight for the green arbor with the vines."

"Thank you again," Henry said. "If the service is always this good, I could get used to living on a Stryx station." He followed the instructions, turned on his heel after the two-hundredth step, and spotted the green arbor in the distance. After another three minutes of walking, he found himself marveling over the thickness of the vines and the density of the leaves. The arbor was tall enough to fit over a two-story house.

"May I help you, sir?" asked a cheerful alien female with vines of her own threaded through a trellis on top of her head.

"I have a ticket for Pzerous," Henry said. He thought he saw her expression change, though he didn't know what it meant. "I'm not too late, am I?"

"Too early," she told him. "The liner doesn't leave for another hour and a half. It's only picking up a few hundred passengers here, so boarding won't begin until a half-hour before departure."

"Don't I have to go through anything first? Security?"

"Do you have a ticket?"

"On my phone," he said, bringing up the ticket.

"Then you're all set to go. Just be back here in an hour on your clock."

"You speak English very well," Henry said.

"I don't speak Humanese at all," the Frunge gate attendant told him.

Seven

"Where's Tinka?" Chastity asked her sister. "I know she would never miss the awards."

"Her blind date spilled his drink on her, so she ran home to change," Blythe said. "It was red wine."

"I don't understand how Tinka's blind dates all turn out so badly," Marcus said as he carefully filled Chastity's wine glass. "She's attractive, successful, has a wonderful sense of humor, and most important of all, she's a great dancer."

"Tinka isn't ready to get married but she's under a lot of pressure from her family," Blythe explained. "Her solution is to only accept dates with guys that she's sure will go wrong because then her family stays off her back for a few months."

"Tinka has phenomenal instincts for picking bad dates," Clive observed. "She's been getting away with it for a decade."

"Happy Awards Day," Jonah said, pulling out a chair for his wife, Sephia, and then pushing it in as she sat. "I thought we would be the last ones here, but it looks like Tinka must have gotten her date over early."

"You missed the classic jostle and spill trick," Chastity said. "I worry that she's developing a reputation in the Drazen community, and when she's ready to meet somebody, they'll be too frightened."

"Drazen males don't scare easy," Sephia said. "My toughest competition on the racing circuit is Lorn, and he'd rather wreck a floater than give up position."

"She's back already," Blythe said, her eyes on the entrance. "I knew she wouldn't miss the opening monologue."

A graceful Drazen sporting a large blue shawl that didn't match her lighter blue dress smiled when Jonah jumped up to pull out her chair, and she employed her tentacle to keep the shawl clear as she sat. "I didn't have time to go home and change so I ran into a shop and bought this to cover up," she said, lifting the shawl away from her dress to show an ugly red stain that ran down the side, almost like the flame motif on Sephia's racing floater. "Oh well. It's a small price to pay for another two months of freedom."

"Just two?" Chastity asked. "Spilled wine might not rise to the level of accidentally tripping you while dancing, but I would have guessed four months."

"The noose tightens," Tinka said dramatically. "In another year, I'll be old enough for my family to build an official compatibility testing profile without my cooperation."

"I thought there was a battery of questions and tests that took three days to get through."

"Three days if you're fast. That's one of the reasons that close family are allowed to act as proxies for adult children, and that's what I'll be next year."

Chastity put a hand on the forearm of her childhood friend, who had taken over managing InstaSitter for the sisters and was the minority stakeholder. "Maybe you should do it yourself, Tink," she said. "Just because you've completed a compatibility profile doesn't mean that you have to marry whoever matches."

"No, but it gets harder to reject the candidates who are perfectly aligned," Tinka said. "I do want to get married, someday, but I want a little more time."

The banquet hall was rapidly filling up with InstaSitters from all the oxygen-breathing tunnel network species, with the pre-determined winners and their families from more than a dozen Stryx stations taking up whole tables. Waitstaff from as many species began to circulate taking orders, and the professional master of ceremonies who had been doing the awards dinners since the beginning hopped over to the head table and asked, "Who's giving the family statement this year?"

Blythe and Chastity both pointed at Jonah.

The Grenouthian hooked the thumbs of both paws over the opening to his belly pouch like a young tough and growled at Jonah, "From one professional to another, I do the jokes. Got it?"

"I know the drill," Jonah said. "I'm just going to say a couple of words about our history and make a few acknowledgments."

"Stick to that. I'll welcome everybody to the banquet, do a brief introduction, and then we'll get you out of the way. You can have a hundred words, tops. Everything is timed so that the meals will start coming out right after I announce the InstaSitter of the year and she gives her acceptance speech."

"He seems pretty keyed up," Clive observed as the Grenouthian hopped away. "Is his contract up for renewal?"

Blythe laughed. "We're lucky to get him. I think the only reason he still works for us is because we helped give him a start in the business. His daughter was an InstaSitter and he volunteered to do our first awards dinner."

"Are you nervous after all of those instructions?" Sephia teased Jonah.

"He makes my director on *Stone Soup* look like a sweetheart," Jonah said with a grin. "And I can empathize with what he means about not stealing his thunder. Sometimes the guest cooks on my show treat it like their personal platform."

Marcus, whose seat at the round table facing away from the stage gave him a good view of the banquet hall, said, "I think Alinka is here."

"The Vergallian girl who's been winning all of the local junior ballroom competitions?" Chastity asked, leaning a bit to the side for a clear path in the same direction her husband was looking. "Yes, that's her. We ran her picture on the front of the dance supplement in the entertainment section a couple of months ago. Is she here because she has a sibling who won an award?"

"Alinka works for us," Tinka said. "Just a few shifts a month, which is probably all the time she can spare from her studies and dance practice. She's a good sitter, but if I had to guess, she started working for us to join our internal LARPing league."

Jonah took a glance over his shoulder and said, "I'm not as involved as I used to be, but I think I would have remembered if I'd seen her."

"Alinka attends the workshops, but she hasn't participated in a LARP yet. I suspect she's in training to try out for the professional league in a supporting role as an elf dancer."

"Do you know anything about her family? Are they royal refugees from a succession fight?"

"If you go back enough generations, all upper-caste Vergallians are royal refugees, but nothing recent," Tinka said. "Both of her parents dance competitively and work for Astria's Academy of Dance."

"Then there's a good chance they work for Vergallian Intelligence as well," Clive said as the Grenouthian MC passed the table again on his way to the stage. "Looks like he's ready to start."

Most of the crowd noticed the alien bounding onto the stage in a single leap and quickly ended their conversations. Those who hadn't noticed took their cue from the rapid drop in the volume of sound in the banquet hall. The Grenouthian waited until there was complete silence before blowing a puff of air, which was picked up and amplified by the sound system.

"Welcome to the Twenty-Sixth Annual InstaSitter Awards Banquet," the Grenouthian master of ceremonies began. "I welcome one and all, and—" he turned his head as if talking to somebody offstage and asked, "—is it too late to warn them about ordering the dish with the imitation Sheezle bugs?"

A collective groan went up from the Dollnicks in the audience, and the Grenouthian pretended to be surprised that he'd been overheard. "I just want to say that the rumors about the Sheezle bugs being artificial are completely unfounded, and if anybody thinks they taste strange, it proves the power of negative suggestion. This is my twenty-sixth time doing this gig, and it's a pleasure to see the founders of InstaSitter in attendance. For anybody who doesn't know them, will you please stand up, uh—" the MC cocked his head and looked puzzled, then grabbed the sash draped from his left shoulder to his right haunch and turned it inside out at the top to squint at something written on the backside, "—Blip and Chatty. Would the two of you stand up and let everybody see you?"

Blythe and Chastity rose from their chairs and received a thunderous round of applause mixed with laughter from the InstaSitters and their families.

"Before we start with the awards," the Grenouthian continued, "this year's representative of the founding family has a limited number of words to share, and if he exceeds the count, I'll belly-bump him into next year. You all know him as the marginally competent cook hosting *Stone Soup* and the former coach of Union Station's InstaSitter LARPing team, so without further ado, I give you Whale-bait Oxford."

Jonah, who had risen and began edging toward the stairs at the start of his introduction, mounted them rapidly and turned to the audience. "That's the first time I've been called whale bait today," he began, drawing a cautionary scowl from the Grenouthian. "My mother and aunt, Blythe and Chastity," he enunciated the names, "started InstaSitter with the help of their former teacher, station librarian Stryx Libby, and were soon joined by Tinka, who continues to run the business. I want to take a moment to offer our family's congratulations to the InstaSitters who were voted awards by their peers this year, and to add that in our eyes, you're all winners." He waited a few seconds for the applause to die down, and concluded, "I see a big furry guy edging in my direction, and I must be getting close to ninety-nine words, so thank you all, and please enjoy."

"Let's give a big round of applause to Fish Food," the Grenouthian said, hopping forward to barely miss Jonah's retreating back. "You can tell he's a professional from the way he avoided me, and you can tell he's a Human because he lost count of his words and went over. To make up for the lost time, I'm forced to leave three words out of my next introduction. The award for Most Likely goes to Orsilla."

A Horten girl rose from her seat and quickly made her way to the stage amidst the applause. The Grenouthian began rummaging through what looked like an old interstellar liner trunk, throwing bits of this and that randomly over his shoulder into the wings before pulling out a glass plaque with a metal plate.

"Isn't she Marilla's little sister?" Clive asked his wife while the girl was approaching the stage. "I don't see Marilla, but she could be facing away from us at their table."

"Yes, and Orsilla was on *Let's Make Friends* years ago," Blythe said. "She was in the cast rotation with Daniel's son, Mike."

"That reminds me that we need to find a new artist for our internal avatars. The one Mike did for me is much better than my official one."

"When Emanuel got nervous about starting in the *Let's Make Friends* cast, Mike came by our apartment and gave him some pointers," Marcus contributed. "Nice kid, but two left feet."

Orsilla accepted her award from the Grenouthian and read off the plaque, "Most Likely to Fill In. It feels funny to receive an award for something I see as a privilege, being asked to help when something prevents a fellow InstaSitter from arriving on time or completing an assignment. I've been doing homework while babysitting for years and it almost feels like I'm getting paid for advancing my education. I want to thank everyone for being so kind to me, especially our clients."

"Did you notice that her skin color didn't change at all," Jonah asked Sephia over the applause. "Orsilla has tremendous control for a Horten. She could be a professional announcer."

"I met her sister when I went to rent one of the two-man traders from Tunnel Trips," Sephia said. "Flower's special assistant contacted me about potentially doing an advertisement for Flower Shipyards. One of those, 'When I'm not racing floaters, I like to relax flying a Sharf two-man trader,' type things."

"—and that's how Humans came to be," the Grenouthian MC concluded to a roar of laughter from the non-human members of the audience. He pulled a bottle of clear liquid from his pouch and drained half of it while waiting for the room to quiet down. "It's just water. I keep it in a Ghazey bottle because I got a scary ping from a law firm after appearing in public with a Union Station Springs water bottle that I'd refilled from the tap. Which brings us to the award for Best Aquatic InstaSitter, which goes to Squeelch, from Red Station."

"InstaSitter employs Dquariums?" Clive asked in surprise as a sleek alien who might have been mistaken for a walrus on Earth floated up to the stage in a tank of water on a mobility platform. "I knew that they were a tunnel network species, but I've never seen one on Union Station, and they don't have an embassy here."

"It's tough being a mammalian aquatic species in space," Blythe said. "Do you know how many Dquariums we have working, Tinka?"

"Less than a thousand," the Drazen replied immediately. "Red Station is probably their largest population center away from their worlds. The Stryx added a salt-water deck for them because they spend more time in the water than on land."

"Do our implants understand their language?" Marcus asked.

The walrus-like sitter opened her mouth to speak, and whatever sound came out was canceled by the high-quality implants of the humans at the head table, who instead heard, "This is the first award I've ever been given. I want to thank all of my fellow InstaSitters who voted for me, and I can't say enough about our employers who paid for this mobility platform so I could attend the ceremony. Thank you."

The Grenouthian retook his place as the Dquarium floated off to a round of applause. He stared up at the ceiling for a moment as if he was trying to remember something, and then flipped the top of his sash inside out again. "Chatty, whale, goody two shoes, tusks," he muttered. "Uh, oh. Here comes trouble." He backed up a few steps as if he wanted to make sure he had a head start in case the next InstaSitter to come up attacked him. "Best Dragon Variant Sitter," he said, and then leaped off the back of the stage and pretended to be cowering in a tight ball.

A pink Huktra lumbered up, her wings neatly folded and tucked to avoid hitting anybody. Her eyes were fixed on the Grenouthian, and there was a brief moment when everyone in the audience really thought she might attack him. Then she reached the stage and thanked each of her clutch mates for coming out to support her, all twelve of them. The Grenouthian stopped faking and presented her award, and so it went until the InstaSitter of the Year was named and dinner was served.

"Did we give out more awards this year?" Chastity asked Tinka. "I thought the ceremony was finished in just over an hour last year."

"Have you already forgotten about the MC's gag with the helium?" Tinka asked in response.

"That's right," Jonah said. "He kept pretending to take hits of helium gas off a tank that looked like he borrowed it from a welder and then he'd talk really fast. He even got some of the award winners to pretend they were doing it too."

"I think I put it out of my mind on purpose," Chastity said. "We got some complaints from parents about that one."

"Have any of the syndicated reporters on Earth followed up about the copyright laws related to artificial intelligence?" Blythe asked her sister. "Abs House retains an intellectual property lawyer on Earth, and after Clive told me about the problem, I sent along a few questions and got back a bill that could have paid for a family vacation."

"It probably did pay for a family vacation," Clive said. "Just the wrong family."

"One of the syndicated journalists is looking into it, and she already confirmed the gist of what Thomas and Wrylenth told us," Chastity said.

"Is there a problem with Earth's laws?" Sephia asked. "I thought that tunnel network law always took precedence."

"On open worlds it does, but not on Earth," Blythe explained. "And according to the lawyer, some of the translated romances that Abs House has published are at risk of piracy there because I paid Libby to help with the translations."

"But you have editors rewriting those books so that they make sense for a human audience," Chastity said. "According to the outline a syndicated journalist submitted to get approval for an in-depth investigation, the problem only comes in with works created by artificial intelligence."

"Our expensive lawyer says that the governments on Earth never agreed to a single definition for what constitutes creation, and when it comes to translated books, the amounts of money involved are usually too low to gamble on taking infringers to court in every jurisdiction. He advised we avoid employing artificial intelligence at every stage of the publishing process so as not to leave the door open a crack."

Eight

"—and here's where the magic happens," Walter concluded, leading his daughter into a large cubicle whose walls consisted of shelves that looked like they'd been designed to display old-fashioned magazines in a library, except the spaces were all taken by *For Humans* books. "The acquisitions editor for each book pulls together a temporary team of experts from the regular staff of the Galactic Free Press to offer suggestions, but the authors are expected to submit a manuscript that doesn't require much more than formatting and illustrations."

"Jeeves doesn't do his own illustrations?" Bethany asked.

"Stryx Jeeves is an exception, and it's not widely known that he ghostwrites *For Humans* books on the side, so please don't spread it around." Walter checked his implant and frowned. "It's not like Finalia to be late."

"That's okay, Dad. You don't have to wait with me." She took a book off a shelf and showed it to her father. "*Starting a New Career for Humans*. I've never read this one."

"All right. But if she doesn't show up in the next fifteen minutes, ping me."

Bethany settled into one of the padded chairs at the table and began to read, but she soon started flipping the pages. "I don't need a chapter on dressing appropriately and not showing up for my first day at work after spending a night in a bar," she muttered as she ran her finger down the helpful tips in the margins that summarized the text. "Don't forget to bathe?"

"Sounds like good advice to me," a woman said as she entered the conference-room-sized cubicle carrying a large plastic box. "I'm Finalia, and I apologize for being late. I didn't realize that I'd be responsible for your employee orientation, and I hadn't left sufficient time in my schedule to pick up the package for a new employee."

"I just got here two minutes ago," Bethany said. "I already know where everything is from coming to visit my dad at work, if that's what the orientation is about."

"Good, we can skip that part, but first," Finalia produced two take-out cups of coffee from the box and followed up with a bag from the bakery. "It's traditional to welcome all new employees with stimulants, and I went with cupcakes because not everybody is a donut fan. Do you drink your coffee with cream or without?"

"With," Bethany said, though her coffee drinking to date had been limited to trying her mother's and making faces. "And I love cupcakes."

"Well, these are interesting. The bakery is run by a couple who moved here after working two contracts on a Drazen world and their cupcakes can have quite a kick to them. The ones with the white frosting aren't supposed to be that hot."

Bethany pulled down enough of the cupcake wrapper that she wouldn't be eating paper and took a tentative bite. "It's good," she said, and then her eyes went wide and began to water. "It's hot."

"Don't feel you have to finish it," Finalia said. "Here," she continued, taking the lid off the coffee with cream and handing it to the girl. "I got the coffee before stopping at sentient resources, and if anything, it may need reheating."

"Thank you." Bethany took a small sip, having learned her lesson about the relative nature of heat from the cupcake, and while the coffee was fairly hot, it didn't burn her mouth and she was able to swallow. Then she took another careful bite from the cupcake, avoiding the frosting. It still reminded her of the special peppers that her mother and Pava liked, but it didn't make her turn bright red and start to sweat.

Finalia ate half of a cupcake with red frosting in a single bite and her olive skin grew a shade darker. "So," she continued. "Have you ever been to an orientation before?"

Bethany nodded. "A lot of the activities I sign up for have them. They're usually about what not to do in an emergency."

"What not to do rather than what to do?"

"Don't panic, don't throw water in burning oil, don't crowd the exit. It's not like anything can go really wrong on a Stryx station."

"You grew up here," Finalia surmised. "Sometimes I wonder if children raised on Stryx stations are ill-prepared to live anywhere else, but I haven't heard of problems yet."

"What do you mean?" Bethany asked.

"You know that the Stryx don't babysit the rest of the galaxy, right? They may be manipulating everything behind the scenes to move biologicals toward some best possible outcome, but they won't protect you from getting mugged or dying from smoke inhalation anywhere other than on their stations."

"Every year in Libby's school we have an Earth Week where we act out the safety plays that the kids who learn from teacherbots do. It's not the same as living in a big city on Earth, but I know enough not to get in a floater with a stranger. And I've helped at my grandfather's shop during school vacations."

"Good," Finalia said. "Retail is an excellent way for a young woman to learn about human nature. Did you ever catch somebody stealing?"

"I'm not sure," Bethany said. "She said it was a mistake and she just forgot to pay."

Finalia laughed. "From now on, you can answer that question in the affirmative." She took a sip from her coffee and another cupcake with red frosting, then pulled a tab out of the plastic box. "This is a standard reporter's tab, which I'm sure you've seen a million times growing up with our managing editor. I have to watch while you go through the setup."

Bethany swept the tab to life, looked straight into the lens, and said, "Bethany Dunkirk."

"Identity confirmed," an artificial voice responded. "This tab is granted standard cub reporter access."

"Editorial override," Finalia said in irritation. "Add *For Humans* imprint access."

"Facial recognition required."

Bethany passed the tab to her boss, who turned it so the camera could see her face and then passed it back without even waiting for the confirmation.

"Override recognized."

"And give her biographical access to the embassy files," Finalia added.

"Access granted," the tab responded.

"What are the embassy files?" Bethany asked. She handled her reporter's tab with new respect like it was a loaded weapon.

"A combination of our obit files and the information on Union Station diplomatic personnel we get through our EarthCent Intelligence subscription," the editor explained.

"Obits are obituaries. Why would I need those?"

"Obituaries for those who are still with us. It's probably a waste of time when it comes to the alien diplomats since they all live so much longer than we do, but standard newsroom practice is to maintain running obituaries for diplomats, celebrities, and wealthy entrepreneurs," Finalia said. "If there should be a sudden death, we can just add a few details and publish a story while the interest is still peaking."

"So more like biographies," Bethany said. "Doesn't it feel weird to read about somebody's life knowing that it's actually a story about their death that's been written ahead of time?"

"You'll get used to it. Famous people have a way of getting into the news on a regular basis, or maybe they're famous *because* they get into the news, but everybody uses the obit files for research." Finalia paused and stared off into space for a moment, either checking her implant or simply trying to call something up from memory. "Walter said that you worked for the Children's News Network."

"Writing, mainly. I was never much of an on-camera person."

"CNN is the best match for kids who like reading their stories on camera. I came up through the teacherbot student newspapers and they don't put any emphasis on performance. Which brings us to what you're going to perform today."

"Which is?" Bethany asked when the editor didn't say anything.

"I'm thinking," Finalia said. "How many *For Humans* books would you say you've read? An estimate is fine."

"A hundred maybe? Dad brings home the paperbacks and there are always a few in the basket in the bath—" She broke off the word halfway through.

"—room. Don't be embarrassed, they're designed to be picked up and put down. I'm not going to have you sit around and read more of them since you must know the format and style by heart at this point. There's not anything else to do on the book while we're waiting for the ambassadors to submit their drafts. Didn't your father say something about having you shadow Bob Steelforth?"

"To learn about fieldwork and covering live events," Bethany said. "I don't think he'd want me sitting beside him and looking over his elbow while he's typing."

"Bob types?" Finalia asked in surprise. "I'm strictly a speech-to-text person myself. And before you ask, we like to avoid the word 'dictator' in the newsroom when referring to journalists."

"Dad types, and I use a keyboard at home because he taught me. I don't know how Uncle Bob writes his stories. I was just guessing."

"Are you related, or is this one of those friend-of-the-family things that drives me nuts?"

"Sorry," Bethany said, unsure of exactly why she was apologizing. "Bob used to come to dinner a lot before he and Judith got married. I guess Dad sort of dragged him to make sure he ate something healthy at least once a week. I think Bob used to live on coffee and donuts."

"Better than alcohol and peanuts like some journalists I know." She pointed at her ear to indicate she was communicating over her implant and Bethany thought she heard the editor muttering Bob's name under her breath.

Then Finalia mumbled some more, a sign she'd received her implant later in life and never mastered subvocalizing, followed by, "I'll send her over," at regular volume.

"Did he say what he'll be doing for the rest of the afternoon?" Bethany asked.

"He's going to Mac's Bones for a Tunnel Trips press conference. Everybody knows that they're launching a passenger service, but I guess they felt the need to make it official since it's tied in with a Human Empire benchmark."

"I'll ask him if I have time to stop home and bring our Cayl hound. She'll be mad if I go to Mac's Bones without her."

It turned out that the press conference wasn't for another twenty minutes, and Union Station's senior reporter didn't want to get in trouble with Pava any more than did Bethany. They stopped to pick up the hound, who promptly dumped them as soon as they reached Mac's Bones.

"She might have pretended to be interested in why we're here," Bob said in amusement.

"Cayl hounds have an incredible sense of smell, and if she doesn't outrun her own scent, she won't be able to—" Bethany broke off as a loud yelp was heard, followed by furious baying and howling coming from at least two throats. "I think she caught Alexander sleeping on duty."

They continued toward the Tunnel Trips rental lot which was strung with bunting that looked like it was left over from one of the McAllister parties. A dozen carbon fiber chairs capable of bearing the weights of alien species up to Verlocks were set out in a semi-circle around the kiosk that served as a rental counter.

"The reddish Horten wearing the mask is the bureau chief for the Horten Gaming Gazette, the Drazen works for their Shipping News, and the Grenouthians are with their network, though I'm sure you figured that out from their cameras," Bob told her as they approached the aliens. "I was expecting a bigger turnout, but the other reporters have probably written their stories already and are just waiting for confirmation before they file."

"How can they have written stories about something that hasn't happened yet?" Bethany asked.

"It's an open secret that the Stryx made sure an obsolete Horten liner abandoned in long-term parking found its way into the lot that Paul McAllister's wife bought for him at auction a decade back. Tunnel Trips had to invest some money in refurbishing the drive and piles and it took some back-room deals to get the parts. The real challenge was arranging for gates at the elevator hubs where the Rainbow will be stopping, but everything eventually fell into place. I can zap you my series of articles about it if you're interested."

"Yes, thank you." Bethany waved to Marilla, who she knew from making frequent visits to bring Pava to Mac's Bones. The Horten girl was the minority owner in Tunnel Trips after Paul and Joe McAllister, and she managed all the scheduling and rentals. Marilla waved back, her skin a rich brown tone indicating happiness blended with a sense of accomplishment. Then she whispered something to Paul, who stepped up to the old-fashioned microphone somebody had placed on the kiosk as a prop for the speakers.

"Welcome to Tunnel Trips for the launch of our passenger service," Paul began. "The Rainbow is too large to be brought into Mac's Bones, but it's here in Union Station's core—" he pointed over his left shoulder, "—attached to one of the radial docking arms that accommodates smaller liners."

"So why didn't you schedule the presser there?" the Horten correspondent asked when Paul paused to catch his breath.

"The Stryx don't allow press conferences anywhere on the docking deck to avoid inconveniencing the paying travelers. While we're on the subject, I'd like to take a moment and thank all the ambassadors who helped us navigate the labyrinthine process of obtaining docking gates at space elevators in their empires, and a special thanks to Ambassador Ortha, without whom we would still be waiting for parts to rebuild the jump drive."

"How could you rebuild a jump drive when you don't know how they work?"

"You don't need to understand the theory of operation to assemble parts. Stryx certification for tunnel network passage requires that the jump drive be maintained and operated by sentients who do understand how it works, and we've arranged with the Zarents to supply the Rainbow with a rotating crew of engineers and apprentices."

"How much of the Rainbow's capacity is reserved for the maiden voyage?" the Drazen reporter asked.

Paul stepped back to let Marilla handle the question.

"We intentionally limited the number of tickets available to the public to give the Rainbow's staff time to adapt, since most of them are Humans who haven't served on a passenger liner," the Horten replied. "I don't see the point in talking about capacity utilization before we make it all available."

"Good evasion," Bob muttered to Bethany, and then politely raised a hand.

"Yes, Journalist Steelforth," Marilla said.

"Bob Steelforth, Galactic Free Press. Our readers who aren't comfortable in Zero-G will want to know how long they will experience weightlessness at each stop."

"Excellent question. All the Rainbow's scheduled stops are at elevator hubs, orbitals, or Stryx stations, so the ship will never need to spin down. On Stryx stations and orbitals, the Rainbow will attach to a radial docking arm with a moving seal at the center of the core. At elevator hubs, the Rainbow will also dock to a radial seal and remain spun up. Passengers will only experience Zero-G when they enter or leave the ship through the transfer point at the axis, and of course, while they remain on a space elevator hub."

"Is it true that the Humans only made you a minority owner in Tunnel Trips to make the technology transfer possible?" the Horten reporter asked.

"Why is he so angry?" Bethany asked Bob while the Horten girl's skin color became blotchy and she struggled to regain her composure. He shook his head, either to indicate he didn't know or that it wasn't the right time to ask.

Marilla drew a deep breath and stated, "The McAllisters insisted on giving me shares when I started working here and they began vesting over three years ago, long before anybody knew about the Rainbow. If you publish otherwise, I'll be forced to seek legal advice."

"I must have received bad information," the Horten reporter said hastily. "You don't have to get worked up about it."

Paul stepped back up to the kiosk and said, "If there aren't any further questions, we'll be conducting a tour of the Rainbow after a short refreshment break. It's self-service," he added, pointing at the folding table where a couple of trays of sliced fresh fruit and a few bottles of wine had been set out.

Bob waited until the other journalists mobbed the table, then said to Bethany, "Some elements in the Horten Empire aren't happy about Tunnel Trips ending up with one of their old liners, and I guess that reporter works for one of them."

"But why?" Bethany asked.

"Internal politics?" Bob shrugged. "There must be twenty times as many Hortens as there are humans, if not more. It would be surprising if some of them didn't have a bone to pick with us. It's just a shame that Marilla had to bear the brunt of it."

"Are you going to write about it?"

"No. You're going to see a lot of unpleasantness if you keep attending press conferences. There's always somebody unhappy about something or trying to make a name for themselves. Your father and our publisher deserve a lot of credit for setting the tone at the Galactic Free Press. If you want a story to reflect the reality of a situation, sometimes leaving out the noise from a few malcontents creates a more accurate picture than putting it in."

"You're saying that we shouldn't give people a platform just because they're angry or loud," Bethany said.

"I try to focus on what an event means to our readers," Bob said. "I happen to know that Marilla is telling the truth, and I already reported about how her minority ownership helped ease the way for Tunnel Trips to get parts." He tapped and swiped at his tab. "There, I just sent you the articles. And you'll notice that I left out the part about her engagement to the Horten ambassador's son."

"Because it's not material?"

Bob shook his head again. "One of our publisher's policies. We don't bring in private relationships unless it's critical to understanding a story that needs to be told. In this instance, Marilla's relation to Mornich is a small factor. If she hadn't asked him to approach his father for help getting the parts, the Horten ambassador would have offered himself. It was good business for everyone involved."

Nine

"Bank," the inhumanly beautiful Vergallian woman across the gaming table declared. The other players deferred, and she retrieved the cards from the automatic shuffler. Henry rose from the table and left a red chip for the croupier who he couldn't help thinking of as the dealer, even though the Frunge never touched the cards. Nobody paid the slightest attention to his abandoning the game, which made sense, since he'd only placed minimum bets and had broken even.

After cashing out his chips at the window, Henry stepped behind a row of what might have been slot machines to get out of the way of traffic and commenced staring at nothing. The heads-up display appeared in his vision, and he painstakingly navigated with eye movements to the information channel. The ship had entered a parking orbit around Pzerous and shuttles to the surface were leaving several times an hour, but he had no interest in seeing the mining colony and began searching the list of connections. There, the Miklat was scheduled to arrive in twenty-three minutes, just enough time for him to return to his cabin, grab his bag, and find a space taxi to take him to the other ship. He flinched at the thought of spending any more time in Zero-G, but comforted himself that it would be a short trip.

"Here," the middle-aged woman piloting the space taxi said a half hour later as she held out a fresh Zero-G sickness bag. "I've never seen somebody fill one up so quickly. I'm sorry I can't accelerate all the way to give you some weight, but fuel packs are expensive."

"The waitresses in the casino kept bringing trays of complementary food to players at the tables and I thought that having a full stomach might help," Henry said in a thick voice while tying off the first bag. "I think I got it all out."

"Better safe than sorry," she said, insisting that he take the bag. "I don't charge for them, but I do charge for cleaning."

"Sold." Henry contemplated the new bag for a moment, considered making a deposit, and then found he no longer felt sick. "Hey, I feel better."

"Maybe you're getting your space legs. It will take us another fifteen minutes or so to get close enough to the Miklat for their A.I. to take over navigation and bring us in to the docking deck."

"I can manage fifteen minutes. Have you ever been on the Miklat?"

"This is their first stop at Pzerous and I'm looking forward to seeing the ship. I may even join."

"What about your business?" Henry asked.

"How do you know I'm not an employee?"

Henry pointed at her license that was taped to the viewscreen alongside printed pictures of a boy at different stages of development, or maybe two boys who shared a strong family resemblance. "Owner-operator," he said.

"I forgot I even had that," she said. "The license isn't from here, taxis around Pzerous are unregulated. And the answer to your question is that I'll take my cab with me. I just need to find out how much competition I'll have on the Miklat."

"I read that they spend almost as much time in Stryx tunnels as they do at stops," Henry said. "Can you make a living working just a couple of days a week?"

"Wait until you see what I charge you," she said straight-faced and then laughed at his expression. "I'll get another job. It's the main reason I want to move on from here. The local options for part-time work are limited to busing tables in the cafeteria or grading ore. My son left for Corner Station to attend the Open University a few cycles ago, and everything I own is in the cargo compartment, so I'm ready to go."

"I wondered if you were getting paid to make deliveries when I saw all the other luggage. What kind of job would you look for on the Miklat?"

"You are the curious one, aren't you? No, don't apologize," she cut him off. "I'd rather listen to you ask questions than watch you vomit in a sack. I've heard that the aliens who own the Miklat are willing to provide vocational training to anybody willing to work, but I might just go back into food service. There's always work for cooks."

"You're a chef?" Henry asked.

"Nothing so grandiose. My grandmother owned a diner, and I grew up helping with prep before I graduated to working the griddle. But my dad hated the food business, and my grandmother sold before I was old enough to take over. How about yourself?"

"Jack of all trades, master of none. I don't have anybody left on Earth and I lucked into a little scratch, so I thought I'd have a look at the galaxy. I'll take whatever work I can get."

"So you're planning to stay on the Miklat?"

"Until they stop somewhere better," Henry fibbed. "I don't know how people make decisions about where they want to live based on a brochure or a holographic catalog. I need to get my feet on the ground, talk to natives, get the lay of the land."

"You used to move around a lot on Earth?"

"I've been all over," Henry answered truthfully, then startled when his heads-up display suddenly came online without his invoking it. The text read, "Installation complete."

"Are you going to puke again?" the woman asked nervously.

"No, I feel fine now. I had an implant put in before I took the Frunge liner here and I guess the installation is finally complete. I'm just glad I never felt the nanobots crawling around inside my skull."

"I'll stick with my external translation device, thank you very much. I draw the line at putting alien technology inside my head. But that reminds me," she said, producing what looked like a pair of small blue fabric bags. "You need magnetic booties to walk on the Miklat's docking deck if you don't want to go head over heels."

"What will you wear?"

"I've got permanent magnets in my shoes that I can turn on and off by clicking my heels. A fare left these behind."

The Zero-G sickness never returned, even when they approached the Miklat along that ship's axis with the rapid spin displayed on the taxi's viewscreen. Henry was beginning to wonder if some of the food he'd grabbed off proffered trays in the casino had been human-safe, and made a mental note to ask in the future before eating anything he didn't order from an English menu. He didn't see any official customs or immigration control on the docking deck of the colony ship after exiting the taxi, but he did spot what looked like a small dragon staring down at him from its perch on some sort of conveyor that wasn't currently in use.

"What are you looking at?" a young girl with a pink backpack who had arrived with her mother in another space taxi asked.

"I've never been on such a big ship before," Henry replied, not wanting to draw any more attention to himself. "Everything on the opposite side is upside down."

"I see people walking. Why don't they fall off?"

"Come, Sheryl," the girl's mother said, ignoring Henry. "Your father will explain it when we find his cabin."

Henry couldn't help glancing up as he started shuffling forward again but the dragon was gone. The magnetic booties reminded him a bit of walking in mud, but he supposed it was better than making a fool of himself. He followed well behind the woman and her daughter for lack of a better plan, wondering at the lack of signage, and then it occurred to him to stop and try his implant.

"Welcome to the Miklat," a male voice said in his head as soon as he navigated to the information channel. "My name is Kruik, and I'm the ship's artificial intelligence. How may I help you?"

"Uh, I just came aboard and—can you hear me?" Henry interrupted himself.

"Perfectly well," Kruik replied. "Your implant's audio pickup and transmitter are functioning normally, though the ship is equipped with enough embedded microphones that I would be able to hear you in most locations regardless. Is your implant a recent acquisition?"

"Three days ago," Henry said. "I've been reading *Implants for Humans* but I haven't had time to check out all of the menus yet. It's impressive technology."

"Let me know if you need any coaching. Do you know how to send me your ticket?"

"Oh, right." Henry's ability to navigate his heads-up display with eye movements had improved greatly during the three days of practicing on the Frunge liner, so he quickly found the ticket he'd purchased and chose the sharing option.

"Excellent," Kruik said. "I see you've only booked passage to our next stop."

"I don't even remember where that is. I read about your ship when the Colony One movement was in the news with their lottery last year. I may want to stay long-term."

"We're always looking for residents, and if you find work and decide to remain on board, I can refund the ticket you've purchased."

"I'm also hoping to visit any alien worlds where you stop," Henry said. "I've never been on another planet."

"You've come directly from Earth?" Kruik asked and continued without waiting for an answer. "I'll put you on a corridor with Colony One lottery winners since most of them joined us at Earth. The permanent Human residents of the ship are almost evenly divided between refugees from the planet Bits, who joined us from Flower, and the Colony One members we picked up last year."

"But the Miklat isn't owned by humans," Henry said as he started walking again.

"Correct," the artificial intelligence told him. "The ship is wholly owned by the Zarents. They received it as a gift from Flower, who acquired it by way of salvage. I joined the ship less than two years ago myself, and I'm still mapping equipment failures and structural flaws."

Henry stopped walking again and looked around apprehensively. "Like leaks?"

"The entire ship is surrounded by an atmosphere retention field which is performing flawlessly. The Miklat is a very old vessel, and the Zarents were unable to maintain it properly during the long years it belonged to a Wanderer mob, so we're still working out the kinks. If you have an interest in ship's maintenance and repair, the Zarents are the largest employer on board."

"I'll think about it. Am I heading the right way for the lift tubes?"

"Yes. If I hadn't detected your implant, I would have activated directional lights in the deck," Kruik said. "You'll want to remove your magnetic booties once you're in the lift tube capsule or you'll likely stumble out on the residential deck where your weight will be almost ninety-two percent of what you experienced on Earth."

"You knew I had an implant before I talked to you?" Henry asked, wondering if all aliens or artificial intelligences could now track and identify him.

"Yes, and my scanners would have picked it up even if you disabled the transceiver, though that's the limit of what I would have learned. Humans don't have enough naturally occurring metal in their heads to hide implants from scans."

Henry shuffled into the open lift tube capsule and looked up as if he believed that Kruik resided in the ceiling. "Do I need to know the name of the deck and corridor with the cabin you're putting me in, or will I just ask you to take me home in the future?"

"Asking me to take you home will suffice," Kruik replied as the doors slid closed and the capsule began to move. "I can identify all of the Humans on board by their voices."

"Were you created by Zarents?"

"Dollnicks," the artificial intelligence said proudly. "I served in the military, but it turned out that my talents lay elsewhere."

Henry only spent a minute investigating his cabin before his stomach began growling again and he remembered that he had emptied it in the taxi. "Are there any restaurants open?" he asked out loud, curious to see if Kruik was still listening.

"It's the middle of the night on Human Standard Time, which is the clock we keep. There's an all-night diner in the food court on the bazaar deck, and several twenty-four-hour markets sell premade sandwiches and packaged groceries, though you'll have to wait until morning if you want to buy good produce."

"Is there an ag deck? I visited Flower once and the fresh produce was good as a farmers market on Earth."

"First Agronomist Miklat prides herself on keeping vegetables and salad makings in season throughout the year," Kruik said.

"Let's start with the diner," Henry said. He followed Kruik's instructions, and five minutes later found himself sitting on a stool at a counter where he was the only customer.

A man who looked to be in his late fifties was the only employee on duty, and he was engaged in cleaning the refrigerator and didn't notice the new customer arriving. After a minute, Henry spotted a metal counter bell next to the mini-register, so he went over and gave it a ding.

"Be with you in a minute," the man said without looking over his shoulder. "I just finished cleaning out the fridge and I have to put everything back in."

"Any pancake batter in there?" Henry asked as he returned to his stool. "I could save you putting it away."

"If you're placing an order, I have enough left for a full stack." The man used the promised minute to finish replacing everything in the fridge, save a pitcher covered with a bit of cling film. "Does that work for you?"

"You wouldn't have any fresh eggs to go with that, would you?"

"Two dozen left. It must have been a slow day for eggs. If they don't sell before the morning delivery, I'll hard boil them, and the lunch special will be egg salad."

"Give me two scrambled with the flapjacks," Henry said. "And I think I smell fresh coffee."

"Started the pot right before I began cleaning the fridge," the cook said as he began pouring pancake batter on the griddle in dollops which he measured by eye. "It's self-serve coffee during the graveyard shift. First time here?"

"Just came on board. It's going to take a while to get used to the time difference."

"Don't give in to sleep until tonight and that will help. Some people swear by spending the first day on the ag deck under the sun lamps to reset their internal clocks."

"That's an idea," Henry said. He took a mug from the rack on the counter, leaned over to remove the coffee pot from the maker, and poured himself a cup. There was a wicker basket full of dried creamer in foil envelopes, so he added the contents of two packets to his coffee and stirred until the black became light tan.

"Throw another brace of eggs on there for me, Marty," a man said from behind Henry. The newcomer continued to the rack of mugs and helped himself to a black coffee, no creamer or sugar. Then he took a seat at the counter, leaving an empty stool between himself and Henry as a spacer. "Haven't seen you before," he said with a sidelong glance.

"Just came on board," Henry said, and for some reason, he felt a surge of adrenaline. "What's your excuse for drinking coffee this late."

"My wife just left for the surface to talk to the Frunge governor and the bigwigs in the sovereign human community there. They aren't on our clock," he added.

"Is she in sales? Early bird gets the worm and all that?"

"Co-captain of the Miklat, along with her twin sister. They take turns visiting the authorities at our stops and pitching the Human Empire."

Henry turned his seat to the right to get a good view of his neighbor and found himself staring at the man's prosthetic arm. "Sorry," he said when he caught himself. "I haven't seen one like that with the mechanisms showing through the skin."

"Made by the Drazens. I'm Drake."

"Henry. So you're just going to stay up until your wife returns?"

"We try to live on the same schedule," Drake said. "Some people swear that the secret to a long marriage is to see as little of each other as possible, but what's the point of that?"

An enormous oval plate that was entirely covered by three thick pancakes with a couple of scrambled eggs on top appeared in front of Henry, along with a small paper cup filled with whipped butter. "I'm the people who our police chief was quoting on marriage," Marty said. "Do you want the genuine artificial maple syrup, or are you one of those crazies who eats pancakes dry?"

"Syrup," Henry said, taking the news about his neighbor's occupation without any outward show of emotion. "I didn't know that spaceships had police chiefs, but I guess it makes sense."

"Miklat is a colony ship, even though we aren't on a colony mission," Drake explained. "Colony ships are more like cities in space than ships. We also have a mayor, and the population was over sixty thousand at last count. Our capacity will be a half-million plus when all the restoration is complete."

"Did you, uh…" Henry motioned at the prosthetic arm with his fork and then winced when he realized how rude he was being. "Sorry, I'm just tired."

Drake laughed. "I'm not the thin-skinned type, and I lost the arm on a Drazen world working as a mercenary. If you were considering misbehaving, it's a bad bet on board a colony ship, and not because of my little police department. The ship's artificial intelligence controls everything, including a string of combat bots that he keeps in reserve."

"I met Kruik, I mean, I talked to him. He sounded like a nice guy."

"I love Kruik," Marty said, setting a plate with scrambled eggs, toast, and sausages in front of the police chief. "He always has time to chat about sports when the place is empty."

"I didn't order sausages," Drake said.

"Do you want to get back here and run the diner?"

"Message received."

Henry worked butter in between the pancakes, rearranged them as a single stack, and then cut them into wedges before pouring the syrup over the scrambled eggs and all. The cook and police chief both stopped to watch as he began to eat. "Good," he said after swallowing.

"Good," Marty repeated.

"You passed the first test," Drake said. "Anybody who complains about diner food is just looking for trouble."

They spent the next few minutes in silence, each man enjoying his food and chasing it down with sips of coffee while the cook began working on something that might have been a giant pot of chili. After Henry finished swiping the last bit of syrup with the final wedge of pancake, he glanced over at his neighbor to see the police chief staring back with a too-awake look.

"Have I been chewing with my mouth open?" Henry asked.

"You can tell a lot about a man from the way he eats," Drake replied. "Bit of a daredevil, aren't you? You're not big, but you didn't get those hands and wrists working at a desk. I'm going to guess that you've been a tree surgeon or a linesman, something that involves climbing and physical risk."

"You got me. I had a job painting towers for the electrical grid."

"Why?"

"To keep them from rusting," Henry said. It was one of the few legitimate jobs he'd ever taken because the pay was high and it was temporary work while the high-tension lines were shut down due to power plant maintenance. "I guess the new ones use alloys that don't need paint, but there are still older towers that work fine as long as they keep up with the maintenance."

"Funny, I didn't make you for a maintenance guy when I sat down," Drake said. "Your vibe is—are you planning to stay with the Miklat?"

"I bought the cheapest ticket that would let me see what the ship is like, just to the next stop. I want to see alien worlds too, but I won't know what that's like until I set foot on one."

"Our next stop is Farling Four," Drake said, getting up and refilling his coffee mug. "There's a sovereign human community with over twenty million members, which is how the Farlings got a tunnel exit connected, despite not being a tunnel network member. It's about as alien a world as you can visit, and it's becoming the main contact point for the Farlings and member species of their empire to the rest of the galaxy."

"Do we know much about them?" Henry asked. "I've heard rumors that the Farlings were somehow involved in the worldwide illegal drug network that got taken down six or seven years ago, and an even crazier one that they run Earth's pharmaceutical industry."

"Both have a grain of truth," Drake said. "I read quite a bit about the drug syndicate since it's in my line of business, and some of the drugs that the Horten pirates were supplying to gangs on Earth were designed by the Farlings. According to my wife, the second rumor is close to the truth. The Farling doctor who lives on Flower intended to take over half of Earth's pharma industry by producing better meds and overshot. He's the one who owns the next world we're stopping at."

"One guy owns a whole world?"

"Farlings live a long, long time, which gives the successful ones a chance to accumulate great wealth and attract followers. M793qK, the Farling who I'm talking about, can't visit his own world because the hierarchy of their empire has a price on his carapace, but everybody assumes it's just a matter of time now before he's reinstated."

"I can't even begin to digest that," Henry said. "Hey, I got a pretty good *For Humans* book that explained how my new implant works. Do you think they have one about Farlings?"

Drake shook his head. "I'd be a buyer of that one myself, but not much is known about them. It seems counterintuitive, but the older a species, the less public information you can find about them. It seems that young species like to brag while older species are better at keeping themselves to themselves."

Henry nodded. "I plan to spend the next few days learning my way around the Miklat, and then I'll go down to Farling Four when we get there. If it looks promising, maybe I'll stay for a while. When will this ship return?"

"We've been stopping three times a year, though not at precise intervals," Drake said. "But with the tunnel network connection, you don't have to wait for the Miklat if you want to leave. The artificial intelligences the Stryx hire to manage tunnel exits can send anything airtight through to a Stryx station, though it will take a few days to get there."

"Good to know," Henry said, standing up and stretching. "Hey, it was nice meeting you, both of you, and I think I know where I'll be eating for the next couple of days."

"Nice to meet you too," Drake said, but his eyes seemed to be boring through Henry's skull. "And just in case my first impression was correct, let's not have any trouble."

Ten

Jonah stood off to the side of the stage and listened as the children sang the theme song to the show in the slot before *Stone Soup* on the Grenouthian network.

Don't be a stranger, because I look funny,
You look weird to me, but let's make friends.
I'll give you a tissue, if your nose is runny,
I'm as scared as you, so let's make friends.

A few seconds later, the studio audience headed for the doors and the stage began its slow rotation to bring the kitchen set around to the front. Jonah walked alongside, reviewing all the last-minute notes from the assistant director on his heads-up display, and almost ran into Aisha, who was coming the other direction. The host of *Let's Make Friends* was practically glowing.

"Good show?" he asked her.

"That and a few other things," Aisha said. "The Verlocks finally finished their accelerated statistical analysis of *Let's Make Friends* camp and they gave the go-ahead to roll it out to other Stryx stations."

"Accelerated? It's been more than a year since the first full camp season on Union Station."

"I don't ask questions about alien math. I try not to ask questions of Verlocks in general unless I have a few hours free to listen to the answer."

"And what happened on the show?" Jonah asked since he couldn't remember the last time he'd seen Aisha so full of energy.

"Stryx Metoo co-hosted and he couldn't be more different from Jeeves. He told lovely stories about wandering around the multiverse and encountering strange lifeforms during the last twenty years. The children were so fascinated that Plurg's wandering tentacle stopped twitching. I'm going to have Metoo back at least once a month."

"That's great. I've got two co-hosts myself today and I plan to just sit back and watch."

"Two?" Aisha asked.

"Thomas and Chance," Jonah said. "The theme of the show is making food that's safe for humans. We're the most fragile species on the tunnel network and all the aliens can eat whatever we can without risking life or limb, so making our food is a useful skill."

"Isn't it a bit odd, having two artificial people cooking for humans? They only eat when they're undercover and trying to pass."

"Thomas is beta testing a new QuickU personality upgrade for chefs and I think he shared it with Chance. The cameras love both of them." He hesitated a moment, and then asked, "Any chance of getting you back for an encore sometime?"

"I'll have to check with my director," Aisha said. "I gave up being able to schedule appearances on other shows in the negotiations with the network to permit *Let's Make Friends* branding for the camp."

"Backburner then," Jonah said as the slowly rotating stage came to a halt. "I guess I'm up."

"Break a leg."

A furry paw reached down for Jonah and practically hauled him up onto the stage. "Last minute change," the assistant director said nervously. "This comes straight from the studio execs."

"Oh, come on," Jonah cried in exasperation. "I just went through all of your messages and there was nothing serious."

"It's not that bad. We just need to contextualize making safe food for Humans as hatching."

"Hatching? As in, eggs?"

The assistant director's eyes bulged comically. "There's something deeply wrong with Humanese. I said *hatching*, not hatching."

"Hang on," Jonah said in frustration, toggled his implant to verbose translation, and checked the last few words on his heads-up display. The best match for the word the Grenouthian used was labeled an anachronism. "You mean tailgating? That makes even less sense. We don't have tails."

"Haven't you ever gone to a festival on some world in a small ship, dropped the hatch, and shared food and drink with your neighbors who are doing the same thing? You know, *hatching*."

"I haven't gone to any festivals on planets," Jonah admitted.

The assistant director's eyes bulged again. "I keep forgetting how young you are. How old were you when you attended the Open University?"

"I didn't go. I went straight from school to work at InstaSitter. My sister went to the Open University."

"Forget I asked. You've talked about Live Action Role Playing on the show before and that's the important part. Just tell your guest co-hosts that they're making food for a mixed species party of LARPing fans, and now and then, throw in a line about leveling up or a boss fight. You'd better explain hatching for your Human viewers in the introduction."

Jonah spent the next minute reading about the ancient practice of tailgating at large sporting events on Earth and learned that floater pickup trucks for the consumer market still featured tailgates. He made a mental note to ask his wife if she'd ever heard of hatching or tailgating since Sephia had grown up in Floaters, a city on Chianga where the human community manufactured floaters for Earth under license from a Dollnick prince. When he finally looked up again, the Grenouthian assistant director had been replaced by the best-looking artificial people on Union Station, both dressed in sparkling white chef's garb.

"Union Station to Jonah," Thomas said, his voice crackling with simulated radio static. "Come in, please."

"I was just doing a little last-minute research," Jonah said. "Have either of you ever heard of tailgating?"

"Tailgating is the best," Chance said. "Not the food, the booze."

Thomas gave her a fond look and shook his head. "My wife is the only artificial intelligence in the history of Earth created by the Greeks. I'm talking about fraternities and sororities," he added for Jonah's benefit. "Not the nation."

"The thing is, the Grenouthians just made a last-minute change," Jonah said. "The show is still going to be about preparing food for mixed crowds that won't poison humans, but they want to, uh, contextualize it to LARPing. Specifically, hatching parties?"

"Great idea," Chance said. "That's the advanced species version of tailgating. I used to crash hatching parties at festivals to get free alcohol to recharge through my backup microturbine."

"Is it all finger food?" Thomas asked, not bothering to hide his disappointment. "I was looking forward to preparing a complex meal."

"On Earth, people used to show up a day early to do serious barbeque, and on some of the alien worlds where I tried hiding when my body mortgage was in arrears, they spent weeks cooking before a music festival."

"We're doing a live broadcast," Jonah reminded them. "Unless you brought a finished version of something that took hours in the oven, we won't be able to show the whole process."

Thomas sighed. "So much for real cooking. Switching to show mode."

"Is that a real thing?"

"The personality upgrade from QuickU has convinced me that most people eat with their eyes. If you don't have the time or ingredients to create something special, the next best thing is to pretend that you do."

"It's not just humans," Chance added. "Members of advanced species are equally good at creating reality through positive dialogue. We should try it on the show today."

"I'm not sure I understand, but if you lead, I'll follow," Jonah said, glancing out at the seating which was rapidly filling up with aliens. "Looks like a non-human crowd today."

"That makes sense since most humans already know how to avoid poisoning themselves."

There was a beep in Jonah's ear, and he checked his heads-up display for incoming messages. 'Just a few ideas for your introduction,' the long text from the assistant director read, and went on to present a polished monologue for the show's opening.

"Can we prep a few things before we go live?" Thomas asked Jonah. "I don't know why we didn't come in last night. I could have had a roast ready to come out of the oven by now."

"Go ahead, but you only have around five minutes," Jonah said. "I'm going to hide and do a little editing."

It seemed like only a few seconds had passed before Jonah was facing the primary immersive camera and watching through his peripheral vision as the assistant director counted down with a tapping foot. Behind him, he heard Chance say, "Oops. Don't let anybody eat that one."

"Welcome to *Stone Soup*," Jonah began when the status light on the camera showed that they were live. "As an avid amateur LARPer, I've attended faction parties where more than a dozen species were represented, and as a human, I pay careful attention to what I eat. But mistakes happen, especially with dips and seemingly harmless vegetables, and nobody wants to throw a party where the attendees leave in medical stasis pods. My guest hosts today will be demonstrating how to prepare food for your hatching party that won't kill humans. Our sponsor is the *All Species Cookbook*, and their latest magazine supplement features Frunge and Grenouthian quiche recipes that can be made human-safe with the appropriate ingredient substitutions. We'll be back in forty-two seconds with hatching ideas from Thomas and Chance."

The status light on the front camera blinked out as the booth switched in the commercial feeds which varied for every species watching, and Jonah went to see what the artificial people had been working up. To his surprise, the counter was covered with spatter from frenetic whipping, stirring, and chopping, but in just a few minutes, Thomas had prepped a dozen bowls of ingredients for—"Omelets?" he guessed.

"They're fast, flashy, and aliens like them as much as humans," Thomas said, pulling a handful of paper towels off the roll hidden in one of the cabinets and using them for a hasty clean-up of the counter. "Chance is working on cookies since the dough doesn't need to rise and they bake quickly."

"And cookies show up on a regular basis in LARPs," Chance added. "The hard ones are good for surprise-throwing weapons, and sometimes you can gain temporary powers from eating them."

"I've never run into that," Jonah said.

"It's a new thing. A Frunge consortium that produces grain-free flour became a league sponsor, and they're big on product placements."

"Ten, nine, eight," the assistant director called out loud to get Jonah's attention. The host of *Stone Soup* managed to get back in position before the Grenouthian, who switched to silent counting at five, got to one and the cameras went live again.

By the end of the show, Thomas had demonstrated a skill in making omelets that had the audience leaning forward in their seats for each new combination, and the smell of freshly baked cookies could have closed a hundred real estate deals had anything been for sale. Jonah bantered with the artificial people about his experience LARPing and helped Chance arrange cookies on plates that were handed out to the audience after the show. He sampled a carob chip cookie and almost broke a tooth before the taste caused his face to squinch up.

"I substituted salt for sugar in that batch and baked them hard for Verlocks," Chance explained. "And I used the fake flour made from quinoa in those molasses cookies, so pass them out to the Frunge."

Jonah nodded. "I guess that the chef upgrade from QuickU has kicked in because substituting recipe ingredients takes a lot of experience. I learned how to bake cookies from my grandmother when I was around eight, and I still treat the recipes like scientific formulas."

"Baking can be tricky that way. Too much sugar can also make cookies come out hard. Did you try any of the omelets that Thomas made?"

"Volunteers from the audience scarfed them all down. I guess it's true that most sentients eat with their eyes because I've tried all of the breakfast places in The Little Apple and I don't remember seeing any aliens lined up for omelets."

"It's the way he flipped some of them in the pan instead of folding," Chance said. "Look."

Jonah turned back to the set and saw Thomas demonstrating his technique for a gaggle of aliens, including an upper-caste Vergallian, who to the best of Jonah's knowledge would be vegan. The assistant director came up, put a paw on his star's shoulder, and filched a cookie from the tray. A second later, he spit it out in his other paw.

"Chance made them for the Frunge," Jonah said apologetically.

"The Frunge are welcome to them," the assistant director said. "They want to talk to you all in the booth."

"All three of us? They who?"

"Same big shots from the network who wanted the hatching tie-in to the professional LARPing league. Good show, and good luck."

Jonah distributed the cookies before huddling with the artificial people and explaining the situation. Thomas nodded as if he'd been expecting a summons and said, "Let me do the talking."

The show's director was waiting in the booth with a pair of briefcase-carrying Grenouthians, which in Jonah's experience was always a sign that the bunnies were about to go legal. To his surprise, the director simply muttered that the strangers had his full confidence and slipped out of the booth.

"Thomas," the bulkier Grenouthian greeted the artificial person. "And Chance. You have hidden talents."

"Thank you, Station Chief," Thomas said and tilted his head toward the smaller alien. "Is this your new assistant?"

"He'll act as our go-between and create a layer of insulation for Jonah."

"Have we met?" Jonah asked the larger alien.

"When you were too young to remember," the station chief for Grenouthian Intelligence replied. "I've known your father for decades. He told me that you'll be helping with the security contract."

"Then the whole business with working hatching into the show…"

"Was to give you a cover story to start showing up at the after-events for league matches. We'll put it out that you're thinking of making hatching food a regular feature on *Stone Soup*."

"And the targets?" Thomas asked.

The station chief elbowed his assistant, who drew what looked like some sort of throwing disc out of his pouch and tossed it in the air. It seemed to stick there, just over their heads, and then it began to spin rapidly, and the air suddenly smelled of ozone.

"We won't finalize the assignments until all of the contractors can agree on a meeting time, but I understand you want to get a head-start," the station chief said. "Our gaming analysts have identified thirty-four negative inflection points from the last season where a Human played a significant role in the outcome. Seven Humans were involved in more than one such negative inflection point, and four humans affected the outcome in three or more cases."

"That's a lot of impact coming from just four players," Jonah said before remembering that Thomas had asked to do all the talking.

The station chief turned to him. "Given that we're talking about Human players, I'm inclined to agree. But the professional LARPing league is new enough that we can't assign a probability to whether these players are accepting money to affect the outcome of matches, as opposed to being incompetent or unlucky."

"Will the Tharks be cooperating with our efforts?" Thomas asked.

"That remains to be negotiated. The Tharks have the best gambling investigators in the galaxy and their statistical models for competitive sports would make a Verlock weep. But that expertise gives them a competitive advantage in the bookmaking marketplace, and they're not going to give it away for no return." He elbowed his assistant again, and the younger Grenouthian produced a tab from his briefcase.

"Christopher Wray, Barbarian," the assistant read. "On two occasions, he slew a monster that appeared to be surrendering and may have been willing to provide important information under interrogation. In a third instance, the handle of his axe, which was slung crosswise behind his back, knocked a vase off its stand, causing it to shatter and wake a sleeping dragon." He looked up from the tab before adding, "The party subsequently wiped. In a fourth instance, Mister Wray, despite having no magical ability, attempted to read a scroll he'd looted from a chest which resulted in cursing all of those around him to lose half of their strength for five minutes. This occurred right as the dungeon boss resurrected."

"When you say—," Jonah began, and then glanced at Thomas, who nodded for him to continue, "—that the monster in the first two instances appeared to be surrendering, what does that mean exactly?"

"A panel of five professional LARPers reviewed the gameplay, and in each case, three of them thought the monster was surrendering."

"That's not very definitive, especially given that some monsters will surrender as a tactic to get opponents to lower their guard."

"Exactly," the station chief said and nudged his assistant. "Next."

"Athena, Huntress. In one instance, she was witnessed intentionally covering the tracks of a troll that her party was pursuing and instead leading them off in another direction. Twice she failed to make long-range bow shots where the odds of success, given her level, were better than three out of four, and in another incident, she fell into a chasm, leading her party to invest several hours in her rescue, which effectively removed them from contention."

"I could see not wanting to take on a troll if the party wasn't up to it," Jonah said. "Missed bow shots might have been deflected by magic or above-average luck stats on the part of the target. Did her fall into the chasm appear staged?"

"The ground at the lip was soft and the bush she grabbed had shallow roots," the assistant allowed. "If any of these were open-and-shut cases, the players would have been suspended and we wouldn't be investigating."

"I fell in a chasm once," Chance ventured. "Not LARP-ing, in real life."

Both Grenouthians waited a moment to see if the artificial person had concluded her bare-bones tale, and then the assistant continued.

"Vashti, Sorcerer's Apprentice. This is the new class introduced last season for players with limited innate talent who train to wield magic in LARPing space through the use of objects, potions, and scrolls that grant the user temporary power. In all five incidents, she was seen uttering an incantation and making complex hand gestures immediately before a negative inflection point for her quest party."

"Did she ever try invoking magic right before a positive inflection point?"

"I don't have that data," the assistant said. "The raters were only looking for potential problems, not ameliorating circumstances."

"Who else?" Thomas asked.

"Conan the Bard. He changed his legal name to match that of his LARPing character. On two occasions, Conan buffed his party with a martial song that made them appear, well, buff, thereby encouraging them to take on adversaries they couldn't hope to defeat. In another incident, he became so drunk on looted wine that he made an error translating the instructions of an ally, leading his party to attack friends. In the final example, he—" the young Grenouthian hesitated a moment, his eyes flicking to Chance, "—dallied at the inn with a member of a traveling dance troupe who ended up stealing the map he'd been entrusted to carry in his lute case."

"Sounds like a typical bard," Chance said.

"It's a starting point," the Grenouthian station chief told her. "It's possible that none of these examples were involved in match rigging, and a Human who wasn't associated with even a single negative inflection point has successfully altered the outcome of quests in ways we've yet to identify."

"I understand," Thomas said. "Thank you for the information. It helps to have a direction to aim our people while we're standing up the team. Is there a way that Jonah can contact your assistant without going through our channels?"

"I have a mailbox with the amateur LARPing league," the younger Grenouthian said. "The others in my party call me Whiskers."

"Whiskers," Jonah repeated. "I can remember that."

"Then we're done here," the station chief said. "I'll see you when the contractors agree on a sit-down date, and don't be surprised if you get pulled off Humans and put on one of the other species."

"I thought we'd been asked to participate specifically because of human players reaching the professional level," Thomas said.

"That's true, but it can be difficult to think the worst of your own species. Plus, investigating members of other species is good practice for the field agents."

Eleven

"Pava, wait!" Bethany called, sprinting to catch up with the Cayl hound. "You're going to make me late for work." Thanks to accompanying Pava to the park deck at least once a day, the young teen was in excellent condition and had finished the Union Station half-marathon for humans in second place for her age class the previous year, but Cayl hounds had been known to run down floaters. Bethany soon fell so far behind that Pava seemed to disappear into the ceiling due to the curvature of the deck.

"Incoming ping from Joe McAllister," the Stryx station librarian announced over Bethany's recently acquired implant. "Do you accept?"

"Yes," Bethany panted out loud, all her practice subvocalizing forgotten in the stress of the moment. "Mister McAllister?"

"If you're looking for Pava, she just ambushed Beowulf and knocked him to the ground," Joe said with barely contained amusement. "She must have known somehow that he was distracted by the Brunkie."

"The what?" she asked, coming to a complete halt.

"It's a small Drazen mammal, something like a cross between an otter and a wolverine, not that you're likely to have encountered either of those. Tourists to the Drazen homeworld buy the pups as pets, but the adults are aggressive, and somebody must have thought that setting it free on the park deck was the easy solution."

"Why do the Stryx allow people to bring dangerous animals onto the station in the first place?" Bethany asked.

"We're all dangerous animals," Joe said, and even over the implant, it was easy to hear the laughter in his voice. "Beowulf had the Brunkie cornered in a thicket and was racing around to keep it contained. He never saw Pava coming."

"What are they doing now?"

"They're, uh, you better not come. I'll bring Pava back to Mac's Bones when they're done fooling around and somebody can pick her up later."

"I'm working at the Galactic Free Press this afternoon. Can you host her until dinner?"

"Not a problem," Joe said. "It will keep Beowulf out of what's left of my hair for the afternoon."

The ping from the EarthCent Ambassador's husband disconnected, and Bethany began looking around for the nearest lift tube. The blueish grass and sculpted bushes reminded her of the section of the park deck maintained by Dollnick volunteers, but she couldn't spot the nearest spoke. "Libby?" she subvoced, this time pointing at her ear with good implant etiquette. "Can you tell me which direction to the closest lift tube?"

"Do you see the Foundation Tree?" the station librarian responded.

Bethany looked around again and spotted an immensely wide tree with smooth grey bark whose canopy went all the way up to the ceiling. "Yes. Is it behind there?"

"That's the spoke. The Dollnicks disguised it as a Foundation Tree. The doors don't open automatically when you approach because that would ruin the illusion. I don't think you could reach the four trigger knotholes even if you took off your shoes and used your big toes, so I'll open the door when you get there."

"Thank you." Bethany continued to study the disguised spoke as she approached, then pointed at her ear again and subvoced, "It's all holograms?"

"The foliage is natural," Libby replied. "The Dollnicks encased the spoke with scaffolding to support a biological substrate that accepts grafts. It's a nice bit of botanical engineering, but the maintenance requirements are too extreme to adopt the technique more widely. The only hologram is over the door." A section of bark at ground level seemed to vaporize, and the interior of a standard lift tube capsule appeared.

"Thank you," Bethany said out loud as she entered the lift tube. "Galactic Free Press, please."

Finalia was just grabbing her purse to rush off when Bethany arrived in the space set aside for ongoing *For Humans* projects. "Did I forget to ping you?" the harried editor asked. "Sorry. I have to get to a cosmetics conference on the Horten deck, it may be the first time they've allowed a human journalist to attend. We're back to waiting for the ambassadors to send in their draft chapters at this point anyway."

"That's okay," Bethany said. "I have an open invitation to shadow Bob Steelforth any time you don't have work for me."

"Then you might want to plan on doing that for the rest of this week," Finalia said, flipping open a compact to check her lipstick. "What am I doing? By Horten standards, I may as well have put my makeup on with a firehose."

"You look fine."

"Thanks. See you next week."

Bethany headed back to the reception area because it was easier for her to find her way to the Union Station desk from the entrance than working crosswise through the maze of desks and partitions. One of the part-timers told her that Bob was in a Gambling Commission meeting and that he didn't think it would be a good idea for her to interrupt. The teen started toward her father's office but she heard an excited babble of voices. She turned in that direction to investigate and ran into a crowd of people.

"There's a gryphon at the Freelance Desk," a woman who Bethany had never seen before informed her. "She's posing for selfies."

"Like a lion-eagle thing?" Bethany asked.

"An alien gryphon, Tyrellian."

Bethany wrestled with herself over going to her father to ask for something productive to do and getting a picture with the Tyrellian gryphon. By the time she'd arrived at the compromise of reducing the number of hours she put in for that week, the line had advanced to where she could see the gryphon. At the same time, she caught the eye of Roland, the Freelance Desk editor who she had met several times in her father's company. Roland gestured for her to drop out of the line and come over.

"Finalia didn't have any work for me today and Bob is in a commission meeting," she began to justify herself before being asked. "I saw the line and—"

"You can get a picture with Semmi later," Roland cut her off. "If you just admitted to having free time, you're mine for the day."

"Is there something I can do to help?"

"Ellen, our Earth Syndication Coordinator," Roland began, and pointed to a middle-aged woman who was sitting on the edge of his desk drinking coffee and chatting with a younger woman, "—finally got around to bringing us the membership list for the independent news syndicate we support. The data was compiled by asking all the journalists to fill out a postcard."

"Which software did they use to log the information?" Bethany asked. "I'm familiar with the spreadsheet that comes with the smartphone operating system used on Earth because I did a class project about protected technologies."

"They didn't get that far. Ellen brought us several shoe boxes full of postcards."

Ellen looked over while Roland was talking, and asked, "Did you find us a volunteer?"

"Bethany, this is Ellen, our Earth Syndication Coordinator, and a fine freelance investigative journalist in her own right," Roland made the introduction. "Ellen's sidekick is—where did she go?"

"Georgia's husband just pinged and said that she forgot her tab and he brought it to reception," Ellen said. "She'll meet us in the conference room." She examined Bethany closely. "Your face looks familiar."

"She's Walter's daughter," Roland explained.

"But I don't expect any special treatment," Bethany added.

"Don't worry, you won't get any from me," Ellen said and indicated the Tyrellian gryphon by lifting her chin in Semmi's direction. "One prima donna is all I can handle."

"Will Fiona be joining us?" Roland asked.

"She went to the wholesale market with John and Marco today. I suspect she wasn't enthusiastic about the idea of sorting cards and entering the data. It's not Semmi's kind of thing either, and the line for selfies is getting longer, so why don't we leave her here with her fans and get to work?"

"I've got a better idea," Roland said with a wicked grin and raised his voice. "We need volunteers for manual data entry. Please form a line in front of the gryphon to sign up and we'll meet in the conference room."

"Now she's mad at you," Ellen said with barely suppressed mirth as the line rapidly dispersed and Semmi turned to stare at Roland.

"She's not mad, but she's still not going to help with sorting cards or data entry," Bethany told them. "Hey, she's talking to me in my head!"

"You can understand her? Tyrellian gryphons are strong telepaths, and she can talk with Marco and Fiona, but they've spent years in close company with her."

"We have a Cayl hound who I can understand when she wants to tell me something. Maybe it's related."

"Then let's get to work," Roland said. He returned to his desk and picked up two shoe boxes, passed them to Bethany, and then took the remaining two boxes himself. "You bring Semmi," he told Ellen. "I reserved the shared conference room because we need the table space to get the cards organized."

Bethany followed Roland to the shared conference room that connected the offices of the Galactic Free Press and EarthCent Intelligence, with Ellen and the gryphon bringing up the rear. Roland had to chase out a half-dozen journalists who were taking advantage of the new coffee machine, a task easily accomplished by informing them that they were welcome to stay and help with data entry. Semmi curled up in the corner, fished a smartphone out of her flight pouch, and began watching anime.

"Are these in any particular order?" Roland asked Ellen after all four boxes were on the table.

"None that I could see," Ellen said. "We should be thankful that they distributed pre-printed postcards so the names and other information are arranged the same way for everybody."

"Did the syndicate members fill the cards out in their native language or English?"

"The instructions said to use Humanese, which I hope everybody understood to mean English."

"Why didn't you request English in the instructions?" Bethany asked.

"We don't spend all of our time on Earth," Ellen explained. "I got the cards printed at an open world where my husband was trading and Humanese is how they refer to English in places like that."

"So far, so good," Roland said, shuffling through a short stack of cards. "Everybody used pen and the writing is legible. Let's start by laying out all the cards that fit on the table, which may be a whole box."

"What for?" Ellen asked. "I thought we'd all sit down with a stack of cards, our reporter tabs, and start transcribing the data."

"I'm going to use the room's holo system to capture a high-resolution image so we have a backup that doesn't involve my keeping four shoeboxes of postcards on my desk forever. I don't have the space."

Bethany opened a box and began laying the postcards out in columns on the table while Roland demonstrated the capabilities of the new coffee machine to Ellen. A few minutes later, Georgia came in and joined Bethany in laying out cards.

"Are you a freelancer too?" Bethany asked while they worked.

"When I have the time," Georgia replied. "I always wanted to do investigative journalism, but the last couple of years I've mainly been back to food writing because it's easy for me to fit in with trading, travel, and parenting."

"We had a career day at my school and lots of the kids said they wanted to become independent traders and see the galaxy."

"Not you?"

"I get sick in Zero-G, and I want to be an editor, like my father," Bethany said. "Have you seen the galaxy?"

Georgia laughed. "Not as much as I'd like. My husband got stuck as the Human Empire's Minister of Trade, so I've visited some of the alien homeworlds. But we spent almost a whole year on Earth managing the Human Empire's exhibition for the New Worlds Fair. It's also easier to make a profit trading in places you know, and my husband doesn't like operating at a loss." She paused with a card in her hand and said, "Here's Gerald."

"You know him?"

"He's a freelancer who works out of Manhattan. Ellen always holds a teleconference with the syndicate members when she goes to Earth to tell them what stories the Galactic Free Press is interested in acquiring. Gerald usually comes to those in person."

"A teleconference is like a holoconference but with smartphones," Bethany surmised.

"Everybody on Earth has a smartphone," Georgia confirmed. "Sometimes two or three."

"So why didn't you ask the syndicate members to submit their information through an app?"

Georgia glanced in the direction of the coffee machine and whispered, "Ellen isn't exactly a smartphone expert."

"What was that?" the Earth Syndication Coordinator demanded. "Compared to John, I think I do very well. The only functions he can use are the walkie-talkie and the navigating thing. He has to ask Semmi to make calls for him."

The gryphon looked up from her phone, snorted, and returned to the anime she was watching.

"Have you had any thoughts about how you want the names organized?" Bethany asked to smooth over her smartphone faux pas. "Will you want a quick way to look at which journalists are available by geographical region, or by their reporting specialty, or their availability?"

"I'm not a technologist," Ellen admitted. "Georgia does all the database research when we're on Earth. What do you think, Georgia?"

"It's a good question," Georgia said. "If we just stuff all of the information into spreadsheets or database records, it will be easy enough to search on any of those attributes, but if you want to produce a report that you can just browse—"

"That one," Ellen interjected.

"—we should decide upfront which information to key off. I mean, it's not a lot of data when it comes down to it, so even on your smartphone, it would be easy to generate custom reports. But if you want a simple reference—"

"Yes."

"—then just tell us what you care about the most."

"Alphabetical order?" Roland suggested.

"You're worse than me," Ellen said. "I might remember the names of a few dozen syndicate members at most, and that's when I see them in a byline. What good would a list of names be?"

"It's traditional," Roland replied as he began rummaging through an upper cabinet looking for something crunchy to go with his coffee. "Does anybody else like Harry's Digestive Biscuits?"

"No thank you," Bethany and Georgia chorused.

"I'll try one," Ellen said, joining the Freelance Desk editor back in the coffee machine corner. "Are they new?"

Georgia rolled her eyes at the obvious ploy to avoid working with the postcards and Bethany had to suppress a giggle. She listened in to Roland and Ellen discussing the relative merits of cookies and biscuits, and soon placed the last postcard from the shoebox they were emptying.

"First batch is ready for imaging," Georgia told Roland.

"Great," he said and picked up the universal remote for the conference room's holographic technology. "Now, how does this work again?"

"Can't you just tell it what you want?" Ellen asked.

"That's an idea." Roland pressed the microphone button and said, "Give me an image of the table."

The holographic system lit up and projected an image of the conference room table that was almost as large as the real thing. Unfortunately, it was a catalog image, not real-time.

"I want to see the cards on top," Roland corrected himself.

The hologram was instantly replaced with what looked like a still shot from a poker game. No faces were shown, but several pairs of hands and alien appendages were shown holding cards.

"Let me try," Ellen said, taking the remote control from her boss and holding it like an old-fashioned microphone.

"Please provide a hologram with the postcards laid out on the table."

The hologram wavered, almost like the control software was hesitating, and then it displayed an image with stacks of picture postcards laid out on the table.

"Where did that come from?" Georgia asked as she studied the picture postcards. "These are from all over the galaxy."

"I know what it is," Bethany blurted out. "My dad told me that the paper has been experimenting with an old Earth technology, something about Large Language Models, that can answer basic questions and gets better with training. But it has a little problem with hallucinations."

"Why would you be playing with something like that?" Ellen asked. "You could get a real artificial intelligence to answer your questions or run all of your technology."

"I'd forgotten about this, it's a cost control thing," Roland said. "We used to pay the station librarian to take care of all of our technology and information needs, but she's been raising her prices to encourage us to find our own solutions."

"Is there a manual for that?" Bethany asked, pointing at the remote.

Roland shrugged. "No idea."

"I can capture an image with my implant for the backup," Ellen said. "I think the resolution is high enough. I'll just have to stand on a chair."

"Maybe you could do half of the table at a time just to be safe," Georgia suggested.

While Ellen was putting her plan in motion, Bethany began to giggle.

"Do I look that funny?" Ellen asked. The teen pointed at Semmi, who was using her smartphone to record a video of Ellen teetering on a chair. "Don't you post that," she warned the gryphon.

"Maybe an image wasn't a great idea to start with," Roland said. "I don't need to keep the boxes on my desk. The paper has storage space for archival materials, and I could put the postcards in there."

"Or run them through a scanner, like GenePost does," Bethany said. "If the postcards are the same size, maybe you could use the same scanner."

"Could the scanner read the printing and fill in all the data fields so we don't have to transcribe the information?" Georgia asked.

"I think so. It's not something I've ever had a reason to try, but, Libby?"

"Yes, Bethany," the station librarian responded through the room's audio system.

"Do we have access to any scanners at school that could read data from a whole batch of hand-filled postcards, like, a few thousand?"

"It's not the sort of hardware the school needs, but batch scanners aren't uncommon for certain business applications, and the Galactic Free Press could rent one that handles a wide range of sizes from one of the Dollnick office supply distributors."

"Would it understand English printing?" Bethany asked.

"All of their office equipment sold locally has been updated to support standard Human languages, and if there's a problem with a particular postcard, it would store an image and prompt you to transcribe the information manually," Libby explained. "You can select any of the standard data formats and pour it into the database or spreadsheet of your choice after the fact."

"Then that's what we'll do," Roland said, obviously relieved to be free of the task. He took out his company programmable cred and gave it to the girl. "Why don't you take care of the rental, Bethany? Make it your afternoon project. But first, let's get these postcards back into the box."

Georgia winked at Bethany and started scooping up cards as Roland and Ellen began a new conversation at the coffee machine, this one about the Ladies in Waiting. As soon as the postcards were all back in the box, Semmi rose, stretched, and returned her phone to her flight pouch.

Bethany blinked in surprise, then said, "Your gryph—I mean, Semmi, wants to come with me to the Dollnick distributor."

Ellen hesitated. "Are we going to get a delivery of Tyrellian gryphon treats that takes up half the hold? We already have enough for the next year."

"Scraw," Semmi said noncommittally. The gryphon stalked out the door, then turned back and beckoned to the teen.

"It was nice meeting you both," Bethany said to Ellen and Georgia. "If the Dollnicks at the office supply distributor are like the rest of their species, I won't be long."

Ten minutes later, Bethany finished describing her needs to the four-armed alien wearing a transparent green visor below his crest who nodded along with her description. Then he let out a long whistle that her implant failed to translate, and added, "Forty-three creds includes delivery and pickup for a thirty-one-hour rental. Universal batch scanners aren't light."

Semmi placed her front paws on the counter, stared at the Dollnick, and said, "Scraw."

"I didn't catch that," the Dollnick replied.

"Oh, she wants a frame," Bethany translated the image the gryphon was projecting in her mind. "A metal frame—is that chrome?" she asked, turning to Semmi.

The gryphon nodded, sat back on her haunches, and held her paws apart like she was describing the size of a fish she'd caught.

"Is that the width or the height?" the Dollnick asked.

"Both," Bethany said when an image of a square appeared in her head, the sides clearly labeled with equal numbers. "She's telling me it's eighty point two—what are the units?"

"Grops," the Dollnick said, "Assuming that's the same as the space she's indicating with her paws. We'll have to cut it down to size. Do you want Horten glass and backing?"

Semmi nodded again and produced a programmable cred from her flight pouch. Then an image of a gryphon hiding behind a spaceship with a picture and then jumping out and startling a group of people appeared in Bethany's mind.

"I think she's saying it's a surprise."

Now it was the Dollnick's turn to nod in understanding as if he dealt with such requests every day. "No problem. She can pick it up here when she's ready. We never close."

Twelve

Henry woke screaming from a nightmare in which he was falling from an office tower in Manhattan. A gryphon accompanied him on the way down, but rather than saving him, she was recording his impending death on a smartphone. It took almost a full minute for him to realize that he was safe in his cabin on the Miklat.

"What time is it?" he asked out loud.

"Just past four in the morning, Human Standard Time," Kruik's voice informed him. "Did you have a nightmare about falling?"

"How did you know? Do I talk in my sleep?"

"It's not that," the ship's artificial intelligence replied. "Nightmares about falling forever are common with Humans who are sensitive to jumps and tunnel transitions."

"Next time I have to be in a ship that jumps I'll plan on staying awake," Henry said as he got out of bed.

"That would likely cause you even more distress. We intentionally schedule these things for when the majority of the Human population is sleeping because those who are sensitive to the transition sometimes become dizzy and disoriented, even to the extent of fainting."

"Then it's a bad bargain either way. How about people traveling in stasis?"

"I haven't seen any negative reports, but the people may be having nightmares and forgetting them," Kruik said.

"Well, I'm up now, and I'm not going to get back to sleep," Henry said, beginning to pull on his clothes. "Can I move my ticket up to the first shuttle? Will it depart after breakfast?"

"The first shuttle to the surface departs in fifteen minutes. It's mid-morning on Farling Four, though the day is approximately thirty-five hours."

"That's almost fifty percent longer than Earth normal," Henry said. "How do the twenty million people living there manage?"

"I have limited experience with disrupting your circadian rhythms since the Miklat runs on Human Standard Time, but I've seen a draft paper by a Farling which claims that rather than adapting by sleeping longer at night, most Humans employ what he calls a 'siesta' strategy, taking a long nap in the afternoon," Kruik said. "G32FX, the author, claims that he hasn't observed any adverse health effects."

"Why does that name sound familiar?"

"He's also the administrator of the planet. If you want to catch the first shuttle, I recommend packing your things and proceeding directly to the docking deck."

"I pack every night before I go to bed," Henry said, slipping into his shoes and making sure the magnetic booties were in his jacket pocket. "I'm ready to go."

As soon as the lift tube capsule started to move, Henry sat on the floor, stretched the booties over his shoes, and secured them with a magnetic strap. When the doors opened on the docking deck, he shuffled out like an old pro in low-gravity environments and made a beeline for the shuttle whose body was about the same size as a large sub-orbital passenger craft on Earth, though the wings were mere stubs by comparison.

Nobody asked for his electronic ticket as he climbed the ramp, and since Kruik hadn't said anything about assigned seating and the shuttle was almost empty, he chose a whole row to himself near the front. But when he went to put his bag in the overhead compartment, he found that he couldn't reach the latch.

"You can stand on the seat, though you may have trouble retrieving the bag when we land if it slides back in the compartment," a woman's voice informed him. "But I'm sure your bag will fit under the seat in front of you and you'll still have space for your feet. The shuttle was designed for Dollnicks."

Henry thanked her without looking around, stuffed his bag under the aisle seat in front of him, and was about to sit, when the woman said, "May I?"

He turned and managed not to flinch at the alien's appearance, that looked a bit like somebody had been experimenting with variations on the proportions of human faces. All the parts were present and easily identifiable, but the result would require very low lighting or a fog of alcohol to be mistaken for a human.

"Of course," he said, stepping back into the aisle to allow the alien to scoot in and take the middle seat. Henry wondered why she chose to sit next to him when they were surrounded by empty seats, but he was happy to have a neighbor who might be able to tell him something about the planet. "Is this your first trip to Farling Four?"

"My fourth," the alien said, fastening her safety harness. "I visit the surface every time we stop, and you need to buckle up." She twisted toward him and offered a handshake. "I'm Belle, a journalist for Gem Today."

"Henry," he said, fumbling with the lap and shoulder belt. "Wait. Does that mean you're a clone?"

"Yes," she replied with a half-smile. "I'm surprised you don't recognize me. You haven't met any of my sisters?"

"I thought you looked a bit familiar, but I've never been so close to a Gem," Henry said, and then he shook his head in disbelief. "I just got my implant recently and I can't get over how good they are. I'm sitting with you talking in English and you're replying to me in Gem and we understand each other perfectly thanks to—what?" he cut himself off when he saw she was shaking her head.

"I'm speaking your language," Belle said. "I've been on board the Miklat for over a year and spent some time in Human communities before that, so I picked it up."

"Do any of us speak your language?"

"Not fluently that I'm aware of. Are you interested in clones?"

"I'm on my first trip away from Earth and I'm interested in everything," Henry said. "I came into a small inheritance, and I've always wanted to see something of the galaxy, so here I am."

"You picked an interesting place to start," Belle said. "Farling Four has only had its tunnel network connection for a year, and the mix of species on the surface is more diverse than a Stryx station."

"I thought everybody lived on Stryx stations."

Belle shook her head again. "Stryx stations attract large populations from local tunnel network species, and for practical reasons, the oxygen-breathing species mainly keep to themselves. You may encounter small numbers of other oxygen-breathers from around the galaxy, primarily tourists or businessmen, but most biologicals prefer to live in places where there's a healthy population of their own species."

"Got it," Henry said as the shuttle began to move. "But then why are there so many different species on Farling Four?"

"It's an intersection point between the tunnel network and the Farling Empire, which has a dozen oxygen-breathing species as members. Right now, it's a hotbed of commercial activity as species who previously had limited access to each other's markets are trying to figure out if there's a profitable trading opportunity. It's also a magnet for journalists since we can find ample material for stories that will be new to our audience. I imagine that half the intelligence agencies in the galaxy are trying to establish a presence on the surface."

"I don't know anything about that stuff," Henry said, wondering if the clone had somehow intuited his purpose for coming to Farling Four. He was about to ask her whether it was possible to rent a floater at the spaceport when a woman in her mid-to-late twenties wearing a fancy uniform danced down the other aisle, somehow maintaining her balance, and plopped down in the seat next to the clone. Then Henry's stomach dropped through his magnetic booties as the shuttle performed a complicated corkscrew maneuver to exit the docking deck and establish its own inertial reference frame while accelerating toward the planet.

"Hey, Belle," the newcomer said. "Got any plans for breakfast, or can I treat you?"

"Don't think about food, don't think about food," Henry muttered to himself like a mantra, and for the next few minutes, he couldn't sort out what his neighbors were saying from the rushing in his ears.

When the universe finally settled down enough for him to pay attention again, Belle was saying, "—then we'll have lunch on Farling Four. I was planning on visiting that bakery in Humantown, and it's my turn to treat."

"That's where I'm going," Henry managed to say to let the women know that he was still alive and part of the conversation. "Maybe we could share a taxi."

The uniformed woman leaned forward a bit to take a good look at him, and her stare made Henry feel like he'd fallen under a microscope. "Who's your new boyfriend?" she asked Belle, the teasing tone in her voice not matched by her eyes.

"Captain Katya, this is Henry," the Gem made the formal introduction. "We just met on the shuttle. It's his first time away from Earth."

"I think I met your husband at the diner the other day," Henry said after taking another deep breath. "He mentioned that his wife was the captain and that he waited up for her when she visited stops at night."

"Co-captain," Katya said. "You must be talking about my brother-in-law, the Miklat's police chief. My husband isn't a diner fan, and he follows the Verlock academy tradition of keeping to a sleep schedule unless there's an emergency."

"And I appreciate your offer to share a taxi, but I'm afraid I have a few other places to go before I get to Humantown," Belle told Henry. "Maybe next time."

"So," Katya said, still leaning forward against her safety restraints. "Your first time away from Earth and you chose Farling Four. There aren't any beaches or tourist attractions that I've noticed."

"I'll need to find work if I stay," Henry said. "I wanted to see the planet before I make up my mind. Kruik told me that I'm welcome to come back and there's no shortage of cabins or jobs on the Miklat."

"Do you have an implant?"

"I got one on the way here when I made a connection through a Stryx station."

"Most people try to avoid getting implants, especially if they grew up on Earth," Katya said. "You must be very comfortable around aliens if you plan to seek them out for conversation."

"I don't have that much experience—" Henry gripped the arms of his seat and the color fled from his face. "How long are we going to be in Zero-G now?" he gritted out.

"There are sick-up bags in the seatback," Belle told him, shifting slightly toward Katya in the roomy seat. "Do you think you'll need one?"

"Maybe? I had a light dinner yesterday and haven't eaten since."

"Try to keep talking, it will help distract you," Katya said, and for the first time, Henry detected a hint of warmth in her voice. "We'll only be weightless for a minute before the shuttle hits the atmosphere and starts braking. We left the Miklat right after I boarded and have been accelerating toward the planet since then. Where are you from on Earth?"

"All over, but most recently, the New York city-state," Henry said. "I've been living on the road since I was a kid, and after coming into a little money, I thought I'd try the same thing in space. I didn't know about Zero-G sickness."

"I've read about the colonization of what people used to call the New World back on Earth when the only way to make the trip was by ocean-going ships," Belle said. "People used to die from seasickness, or maybe it would be more accurate to say that they were killed by dehydration that resulted from seasickness."

"Ixnay on the motion-sicknessay," Katya hissed at the Gem before addressing Henry in a cheery voice, "Do you like sports?"

"Mountain climbing," Henry gritted out. "But I have a problem with altitude sickness. Is there any oxygen on this thing?"

"Hang in there. How did you enjoy your time on the Miklat?"

"It was different, especially how the ship's artificial intelligence was always willing to help with questions. I found a great diner and—" Henry blanched at the thought of food and reached for the pouch of the seatback in front of him. Just then, a shudder ran through the shuttle, and weight began to return.

"Kruik must like you," Katya commented. "That's the fastest insertion into a planet's atmosphere I can remember him doing."

Henry took a few deep breaths and let the sick-up bag fall back into the pouch. "Kruik came along to pilot, or does he send a copy of himself?"

"He flies the shuttle remotely," Belle said. "Ironically, cloning artificial intelligence is more difficult than cloning biological life, or so I'm told."

"That sounds backward."

"In some ways, sentient artificial intelligence is more of a mystery than biological life," Katya said. "Don't ask me for details, though. I'm more of a general picture person."

"Humantown is only a two-hour walk from the spaceport," Belle said. "I would recommend against taking a taxi before you get the lay of the land because they aren't automated."

"You mean they have drivers?" Henry asked. "Even Earth stopped using taxi drivers before I was born. Is there something wrong with Farling technology?"

"It's not a technology thing, it's a guild thing. You need a special license to drive a hack on Farling Four, and self-driving taxis and rentals are prohibited. The result is that they're expensive, and if the driver is having a slow day, he'll take you the long way around."

"I could try to negotiate a lower price."

"The drivers aren't humans. They're—what's the species again, Katya?"

"You're asking me? They're snaky things with armored bodies that look like they evolved in a desert somewhere," the co-captain said. "I only remember the names of the species that M793qK includes in his crest."

"Will I understand them with my implant?" Henry asked.

"Which one did you buy?" Katya inquired.

"Trader grade."

"That's as good as it gets for languages short of a diplomatic implant. It should work for any of the species in the Farling Empire, and if it doesn't, make sure you download the latest translation tables the next time you have Stryxnet access."

"You might do it now while you still have connectivity through the shuttle," Belle suggested.

"That's a good idea," Henry said. He invoked his heads-up display, began navigating his way through the menus, and then his head began to spin. "Stop the world. I want to get off."

"Maybe you should lay off navigating with eye tracking until we land," Katya suggested. "Just relax and breathe. We'll be on the ground soon enough."

Much to his surprise, Henry woke up still wearing his safety restraint, so either he'd somehow fallen asleep, or the shuttle had hit an air pocket and the drop had knocked him out cold. His neighbors were gone, and he felt a sense of betrayal, even though he had just met them. Then he heard Kruik's voice over his implant, "Belle and the co-captain asked me to wait as long as possible before waking you so you could shake off your motion sickness before exiting the shuttle," the Dollnick artificial intelligence said. "How do you feel?"

"Better," Henry admitted. "Sleeping is the only thing that works for me when I get motion sick, so I guess they did me a favor. How much time do I have before you lift off?"

"Five minutes. This was my second attempt to wake you without sending a bot."

"I didn't notice. Sorry."

He unwedged his bag from under the seat and made his way down the wide aisle of the shuttle, noting that quite a few people already occupied the seats on either side for the return trip to the Miklat. Then he hit the ramp and almost fell on his face when his feet refused to move properly, and he realized that he was still wearing the magnetic booties. After a quick check to make sure he wasn't blocking traffic, he sat down and took them off.

If the other arriving passengers had proceeded to an immigration or customs line, he had no idea where it was. Henry didn't see any other shuttles on the tarmac, just trader ships of various types, and a couple of mid-sized freighters. The elevator stalk was visible behind the cityscape, but there was very little sign of life in the immediate area. On a hunch, he invoked his heads-up display and checked the information channel. The result was a hierarchical catalog listing that apparently included every product or service available on the planet, but choosing 'maps' brought up an interface that might have been copied from a smartphone.

"Uh, Kruik?" he ventured.

"My shuttle will be departing in three minutes and then I'll be unable to hear the transmissions from your implant," Kruik replied. "Do you want to return to the Miklat already?"

"No," Henry said hastily, more because he was unprepared for another trip in space than out of dedication to his mission. "I don't see a terminal building or customs."

"The Farlings aren't worried about border control or customs for individual visitors at this point. If I was bringing down a load of immigrants, they would have sent somebody to keep count, but you're free to proceed to the city or wherever you decide to go."

"I was going to try Humantown."

"My suggestion is to rent a bike," Kruik said, and there was a quiet thud as the shuttle's ramp raised back against the hull where it served as a hatch. "There's a Two Wheels franchise at the maglev station."

"Where is that?" Henry asked.

"You'll see it as soon as the shuttle lifts off."

The promised maglev station appeared as soon as the shuttle was out of the way, so Henry dismissed his heads-up display, slung his duffle over his shoulder, and hiked over to the little cluster of buildings. The tracks were invisible and the magnetic coils must have been buried, but he could make out a straight line heading off to the horizon which must have been the right-of-way into the city. A small shop manned by a kid who was engrossed in watching something on a tab sat catty corner from the ticket office.

"I'm interested in renting a bike," Henry said loudly to get the kid's attention. "Do you take programmable creds?"

"That's what the mini-register is for," the kid said, pointing vaguely into the dark shop, and then correcting his aim. "There it is."

"And can you recommend a bike, or do I just pick one out?"

"All the same thing, aren't they? Not that anybody ever rents them. Stupid idea, bike rentals at a spaceport train station. Everybody has luggage and they either take the maglev or order a taxi."

"Then why did you open here?" Henry asked.

"Didn't, did I? Da bought the place. Must have been on a bender."

"Well, I'll take one," Henry said, bringing out his programmable cred. "How much a day?"

"Four creds, but we put a hold of fifty creds against your coin to cover the bike."

"I can live with that. Are the bikes that inexpensive?"

"Made by the Frunge," the kid said, slotting the programmable cred into the mini-register, ringing up the transaction, and waiting for Henry's voice approval. "Cheap and indestructible, but some people lose them."

Henry took the nearest bike off the rack, made sure the tires were fully inflated, and mounted with the duffle still slung over his shoulder. "Is there somewhere in Humantown I can drop it off when I'm done with it, or do I have to bring it back here?"

"Da has another place across from the maglev stop in town. If you had gotten off the shuttle a few minutes earlier, you could have taken the train with everybody else."

"When's the next one?" Henry asked out of curiosity.

"Half an hour maybe? But it won't stop for one person. If there isn't a shuttle on the ground, they just keep going. Whatever business we get comes from small ship owners who park around here."

Henry found that pedaling the bike chased away the last of the queasiness he still felt, and after a few minutes, he stopped and moved his duffle to the luggage rack over the back wheel. Fifteen minutes on, the path began to slope uphill, and he decided to give his legs a break and use up some of the battery, but he couldn't find the switch to engage the electric motor. After trying everything he could think of with the brakes and shift, it dawned on him that what he had assumed was an eBike was a purely mechanical bicycle.

"Welcome to Farling Four," he said to himself.

Thirteen

"Donna," Sephia greeted her husband's grandmother. "You're early. We don't need to leave for another fifteen minutes."

"Stanley will come and join me at the official starting time, but I made some cookie dough that I didn't have time to bake at home. I thought I'd do it here if that's okay with you."

"Of course, but you'll have to ask Jonah where he keeps the cookie sheets. I've never been much of a baker."

"Who is it?" Jonah called from the bedroom.

"He's getting deaf in his old age," Sephia said with mock despair. "Your grandmother," she shouted back. "She came early to bake cookies. Where do you keep the cookie sheets?"

"In the skinny cabinet next to the oven, but it's packed. Wait a minute and I'll get them out."

"And where's my favorite great-grandson?" Donna asked as she set the bowl of dough on the counter.

"At the neighbor's," Sephia said. "Birthday party for a three-year-old, and I was on my way to get Adam when you arrived. Why don't you do whatever it is that people who cook do to make the oven hot and I'll be back with my bundle of hyperactivity in a minute."

"Has he been bad lately?"

"Not really, but I imagine that being with a half dozen other little terrors will wind him up pretty good."

After Sephia left, Donna ignored her grandson's instruction and opened the cabinet that was indeed jammed with cookie sheets and baking pans to the point that she couldn't pull one out without removing them all. She was still trying to replace the unneeded baking pans in some semblance of order when Jonah came into the kitchen, smelling of soap from his shower.

"You didn't need to do that, Grams," he said and bent to kiss her on the cheek. "Besides, I had them in order."

"Order my foot," Donna replied. "Where's the vegetable shortening?"

Jonah made a face. "Adam got into it, so I had to throw out the whole container. Here," he said, extending a ceramic butter dish. "Use butter."

Donna shook her head in mock despair. She rubbed the bar of butter with a paper towel and then used that to grease the first cookie sheet. "I told your grandfather to bring his special neck pillow so don't worry about rushing home. We're good until at least midnight."

"We shouldn't be anywhere near that late, and if we are, just call InstaSitter," Jonah said. "We get a hundred percent discount, you know."

"It's all well and good that InstaSitter made your mother and aunt so rich that they can use the money to help move humanity forward, but I'm not too old to stay up late for my great-grandson. I must have babysat for you and your sister a hundred times when you were around Adam's age, and the two of you were terrible."

"The reason you babysat for us so much is that InstaSitter blacklisted me and Viv for tag-teaming the sitters. When I was training alien teens on what to expect when babysitting humans, I used our home videos to prepare them for the worst."

Donna laughed. "No, leave the dough alone or you'll get it on your clothes. Is that a new suit?"

Jonah glanced toward the living area to make sure that his wife wasn't back yet. "Sephia bought it for me, so I figured I better wear it at least once. She's not a big fan of cooking or sewing but she knows how to shop."

"Never mind that. I want more great-grandchildren."

"Promise not to tell anyone?"

"Sephia's pregnant?"

"You have to promise."

Donna scowled and then offered her hand with a pinkie extended, which Jonah solemnly clenched with his right pinkie. "She's about two months in, but don't say anything. The racing season has another month to go, and she doesn't want her parents or you guys nagging her about safety."

"But the floaters pull such strong acceleration in the corners that I've heard of drivers passing out," Donna said. "Surely she—"

"—has consulted with the best medical professionals and knows what's safe for her and the baby," Jonah spoke over his grandmother. "I promised to support her when we got married, and that's what I'm going to do. *You* just promised not to tell anybody, and that includes letting on that you know before Sephia's ready to tell you."

Donna scowled and used a spoon to distribute balls of cookie dough on first one sheet and then the next. The Dollnick oven only required a few seconds to pre-heat, and she had just put in the trays when Sephia returned with a little boy who looked like he had fought a pitched battle with a heavily frosted cake.

"Gran-gran," Adam piped and made a beeline for his great-grandmother, arms spread wide for a hug. He ran across the room before Donna had a chance to crouch, and collided with her legs hard enough that it might have knocked her down if she hadn't braced. "I had cake!"

"And now I have cake too," Donna observed dryly, looking down where Adam had buried his face in her skirt. "Where's Bodie?"

"Grandma takes."

"Blythe said that Clive has been working too much lately so she borrowed Bodie to keep her company," Sephia said. "Of course, if you asked Clive, I'm sure he'd say the same thing about Blythe. Your whole family has the workaholic gene."

"I suppose Blythe and Clive both feel the years adding up and they want to do what they can while they still have the energy," Donna said with a sigh. She absent-mindedly wiped the frosting off her skirt with a crumpled paper towel before remembering she had used it to grease the cookie sheets. "Oh, well. And where was it that you and Jonah are going tonight?"

"It's a Live Action Role Playing match in the professional league. We've been invited to watch from the commentator's booth, and then to attend the after-party with the players, what the aliens call hatching," Jonah added as he took several plastic containers out of the fridge and put them in a bag.

"I know what hatching is. Don't forget that Stanley was working for Earth's biggest gaming concern before your mother was out of diapers."

In the lift tube on the way to the LARPing studio, Sephia asked Jonah, "Do you think your grandmother knew about hatching, or was she just saying?"

"She usually watches *Stone Soup*, so she might have known about it from the show a couple of weeks ago, though she may have forgotten where she'd heard it," Jonah said. "The weird thing is that the human version of hatching on Earth, tailgating, happens before sporting events rather than after."

"I guess when the aliens call us a backward species, they mean it literally. Who would want to load up on food and drink and then sit in a packed stadium for hours? The bathrooms must have been a mob scene."

"That's exactly what I was thinking." The lift tube doors opened, and Jonah steered his wife to the left when she started in the direction of the main entrance to the LARPing studio. "The observation lounge is this way."

"Those idiots better not say anything about my dress," Sephia muttered.

"You look beautiful, and that's just the way commentators are," Jonah said. "Their job is to talk constantly, and when they run out of things to say about the action, they babble."

A beefy Grenouthian was working security at the door to the observation lounge, but he recognized Jonah and let the couple pass without asking for identification. Sephia had never been in the lounge before and couldn't help feeling disappointed when she saw the small desk from which the Drazen play-by-play announcer and the Horten color commentator did their broadcast.

"It's just a little desk in front of a blue wall," she said. "Where are all the staff and the racks of LARPing equipment I always see in the background?"

"That's added by the engineer in the booth," Jonah told her. "Bunk and Poga could do their thing anywhere as long as you gave them a holographic feed of the LARP to watch. I've seen them—uh-oh."

"Uh-oh, what?"

"Bunk looks like he's been on a bender," Jonah said in a low voice, his eyes on the Drazen who had just entered from the dressing rooms. "His tentacle is practically dragging on the floor."

"They're professionals," Sephia said. "I'll bet you twenty creds that he's fine when the cameras go hot."

"I can't gamble on anything related to LARPing. It's part of the contract EarthCent Intelligence signed."

A Horten entered from the other dressing room, his skin a cheery shade of brown, and he didn't lose a second in going after his co-host. "Hey, Bunky. Was there a sale on Divverflips, but only if you drank them on the spot?"

"You're looking a bit petrified yourself," the Drazen growled in return, but it was clear that his heart wasn't in the weak jibe.

"Bunk, Poga," Jonah said, moving forward to get between them. "Thanks for inviting us to your show. We're both looking forward to the match."

"Bunch of adrenal freaks chasing around in a hologram beating up robots with fake weapons," the Drazen grumbled, and then he noticed the bag that Jonah was carrying. "Is that what I think it is?"

"Cold snacks," Jonah confirmed, producing two containers. "The red one is sardines in hot sauce, and the white one has those rice balls you like, Poga. I already ran them through a sterilizer."

"What's in the container with the blue lid?" Bunk asked. He pulled the red lid off the container he'd been handed and then tilted the whole thing up to his mouth to sip off a bit of the hot sauce. "Just the pick-me-up I needed."

"I'm not sure. I found it in the fridge on set after I had your ambassador as a guest the other day and—"

The Drazen grabbed the container with his tentacle and ripped off the lid. "Lugunkies," he practically purred. "And the mold is still fuzzy. I can't believe Ambassador Bork would forget them."

"I mentioned to him that I'd be in your studio, so I think he left them behind on purpose," Jonah said. Crossing his fingers behind his back, he added, "He's probably a big fan."

The two commentators both fished eating implements out of the drawers on their respective sides of the broadcast desk and made short work of the gifts. That they managed it without getting any food on their clothes or messing up their makeup was a testament to their professionalism.

A bored-looking Grenouthian assistant director waved a few floating immersive cameras into place in front of the desk, and the large open space in the lounge was replaced by a hologram that showed a mixed-species party of adventurers warming up for the action by stretching or meditating. Jonah and Sephia found seats that gave them a view of both the broadcast desk and the hologram and settled in for the intro. Then the match began, and Bunk was off and running.

"They're trying to fast-track through the jungle, and that rarely ends well," the Drazen said. "Two rogues out front checking for traps, followed by the big Dollnick barbarian, and a pair of Frunge rangers with nocked arrows watching the canopy. That Vergallian healer will probably be busy soon enough, especially the way the Human rogue with the axe is using it as a machete to clear a path. Did you ever have any players in your party incapacitate themselves when you were in the league, Poga?"

The Horten color commentator chuckled in the manner of his species, and his already brown skin tone grew deeper. "There was the Drazen with the tentacle accident, but you don't want to hear about that," he began on the usual note. "Nobody in any party I was part of ever did a serious self-injury with their weapons, unless—" he said, glancing at the Grenouthian assistant director who was diagramming some sort of complex procedure with both paws, "—you include magical mishaps. I went on a quest once with a Fillinduck assassin whose handwriting was so bad that she couldn't read the labels she'd written on the potions she'd bought at the apothecary. When we were approaching an ambush point and she wanted to add a quick boost to her stealth, she accidentally drank the poison she'd bought to coat her daggers." He bowed his head.

"Probably delegated all of the writing in the family to the third member of the trio," Bunk said. "And it looks like the Human rogue has discovered the hidden entrance to the target cavern."

"Are you sure he didn't activate a cloak of invisibility?" the Horten asked, staring at the volume of the hologram where the rogue had been scouting a moment earlier.

"Let's see it again in slo-mo." The booth engineer took the hint to bring up the holo-in-holo feature, so the live action continued, while in the bottom right corner, a replay of the missing human began. It clearly showed the rogue dropping below the surface, a surprised look on his face as he made a futile grab at the surrounding vegetation, which tore off and disappeared with him.

"That was an inflection point," Jonah murmured to his wife. "It looks like falling down the shaft came as a surprise."

"And it benefits his party," Sephia said. "I thought you're supposed to be looking for players trying to throw matches."

"Maybe taking himself out of the action to reduce the party's strength was the goal." His wife shot him a skeptical look, and then the hologram divided in two, indicating that the party had split. The rogue was seen putting away his tinder box in the glow of a torch.

"Never write off a rogue," Poga said. "We had a Grenouthian pathfinder who was practically indestructible in our championship year. I saw him drown, get crushed under a rockslide, fall into a volcano, and get swallowed by a boss dragon, but every time he just came back stronger."

The end of a rope dropped right in front of the rogue, and he immediately grabbed hold and gave one firm tug. A few seconds later, the second rogue appeared, followed by the barbarian and then the rest of the party, one by one. As soon as the last member of the party disappeared below the ground, the hologram returned to a unitary view.

The next hour was full of the usual combat as the monsters tried to defend their dungeon while Bunk and Pogo attempted to make it sound like something truly exceptional was happening. Jonah was concentrating on the sole human member of the party, who despite a marked limp, continued to contribute at a high level. When the assistant director froze the action for a long commercial break, Sephia nudged her husband.

"Never mind the human," she told him. "Watch the spellcaster."

“The Verlock?” Jonah asked in surprise. “They’re the last species I would suspect of trying to fix a match.”

“I don’t think she’s cheating but she’s really good. She should be on *Mage Search*.”

“I’ll mention it to Dorothy so she can tell Dietro, but I’d be surprised if the Grenouthians haven’t already scouted her.”

The action started again, and including commercials, another two hours flew by before the party defeated a giant rock creature in the final boss fight, winning the right to continue to the next dungeon.

“I didn’t see anything suspicious,” Jonah said. “You?”

Sephia yawned. “No. It was all pretty pedestrian LARP-ing if you ask me, but I suppose they have to play conservatively this early in the season and not waste any new tricks they’ve learned. It reminded me a bit of the first three or four races of the year on the floater circuit where all the drivers are just trying to get around the track quickly without running into each other.”

“Isn’t that always the objective in floater racing?”

“You of all people should know that you can’t make an omelet without breaking some eggs. Defensive drivers don’t have any place on the competitive circuit.”

As soon as Bunk and Poga finished the post-LARP wrap-up, the Drazen came out from behind the desk and hailed the human couple. “Thanks for the eats,” he told Jonah. “I wouldn’t have made it through without them. And you look great in a dress, Sephia. Why don’t you wear it racing?”

“Regulations,” she said with a forced smile. “Are you coming to the hatching?”

“Not unless I’ve lost my mind,” the Drazen said. “One Divverflip hangover a week is enough for me.”

Jonah and Sephia headed back toward the lift tube, and then continued into the LARPing studio, since the after-party was taking place at the virtual reality tavern. The players were still in the showers or changing rooms, but the Dollnick who operated the tavern recognized Jonah and insisted on showing off an omelet-making technique that supposedly stretched back millions of years. The alien employed two pans at the same time, flipping the omelet from one to the other, and used his other pair of hands to add a variety of vegetables and a handful of Sheezle bug larvae.

"Reminds me of home," Sephia said when she saw the finished product. "It used to drive me and my brother nuts that we couldn't eat any of the food we saw advertised in the Dollnick restaurants."

"Those fish eggs the Dollnicks use work great for omelets," Jonah said. "They're a little oily, and that probably accounts for why they fluff up so well."

"Remind me again what we're supposed to be doing here. Chatting up the players and asking if they happen to have taken any payoffs from gamblers lately?"

A familiar-looking Grenouthian entered the tavern, looked at Jonah, and gave the side of his nose a furtive rub before heading off into a dark corner.

"Hold that thought," Jonah said. "I think my contact just signaled that he wants to have a chat."

The Grenouthian lived up to his working name as his whiskers could be seen twitching from five steps away. He tapped a furry foot impatiently as Jonah approached, and greeted the human with, "Well?"

"We didn't notice anything suspicious, if that's what you mean," Jonah replied.

Whiskers blinked. "You didn't see the switch?"

Jonah shook his head. "I don't know what you're talking about."

"When the party was ambushed by reincarnated ghouls. The Frunge rangers were fighting back-to-back with their short swords, and somehow the Ring of Bzael moved from the female's hand to the male's hand."

"I was concentrating on the human rogue," Jonah admitted. "I didn't see a thing. Did it affect the outcome in some way?"

"No," Whiskers said. "But I can't figure out how they did it. I've rerun the holo at the slowest possible rate and the ring just vanishes from the female's finger and appears on the male's."

"Are you saying they have some sort of cheat code? The station librarian runs the LARPing studio, and there's no way that the Frunge can hack a Stryx."

The bunny looked at Jonah like he'd suddenly grown a second head. "What do the Stryx have to do with it? The point is that the Frunge don't have any magic in their stats, I triple-checked. If they can pull off something like teleportation in LARPing space, what else can they do?"

"But why would they use magic to swap a ring in the middle of a fight?" Jonah asked. "If you noticed, I'm sure that some Frunge fans noticed, and—" he broke off because Whiskers was nodding. "You mean they did it on purpose to send a message?"

"Hi, we're open for business," Whiskers said, and the voice Jonah heard through his translation implant was a reasonable impersonation of a Frunge. "If we can do this, imagine what we can do for your betting line."

"Or maybe it was just a stunt, showing off to their friends."

"That is more likely."

"Then why are you so excited?" Jonah asked.

"This is my first investigation, and I had to come up with an excuse to talk to you if I'm going to have anything to report," Whiskers said. "The last projection from our analysts suggested that there's less than a thirteen percent chance any of the players in the league will try to fix a match this year. It's going to be a long season."

Fourteen

"No, this won't do at all," Finalia announced. "Either Ambassador Czeros is trying to be funny or there's something wrong with the translation."

Bethany tapped the sentence she'd just finished reading on her tab to mark the place and looked up. "It's a little hard to follow, but he is writing for Frunge."

"The entire chapter is about the history and culture of winemaking on Earth. The Roman Empire waged war on the known world and kept men, women, and children as slaves, but the only fault he finds with them was storing amphoras of wine in a fumatorium to add a smokey flavor."

"Maybe he's trying to avoid condemning us so he's focusing on something that wouldn't be important to most readers."

"Either that or he's as much of a lush as the rumor mill claims," Finalia retorted. "The problem is that there's nothing technically wrong with his submission, other than his choice to focus on wine."

"I liked the helpful hints about how to re-cork a bottle and remove wine stains from natural fibers," Bethany said. "I'm not sure about the picture of people crushing grapes with their bare feet, though. It sounds like something he might have seen in a Grenouthian documentary that only happened for a short time in some backward place."

"Treading on grapes barefoot is traditional. But how is it going to look when all the other ambassadors give us chapters that delve into human science and philosophy, and then in the middle of it all, ten thousand words about alcohol content and acidity?"

"Have you seen any of the other chapters yet? I thought we were still waiting for them."

"We're waiting for the other ambassadors to send in their drafts, but they all submitted synopses, so I have a pretty good idea of what..." A funny expression came over her face as she trailed off and began swiping at her tab. A few seconds later she said, "We could be in trouble."

"What's wrong?" Bethany asked.

"I found the synopsis that Czeros submitted for approval. "The language is a bit flowery, but he wrote about taking a deep dive into the pillars of human civilization and focusing on one of our greatest achievements as a species. When he talked about core knowledge that survived despite the rise and fall of languages and cultures, I thought he was talking about philosophy or advances in mathematics. When I read it now, it's clear that he intended to write about wine all along."

"I still don't see a problem with having a chapter about wine. My mom let me have a glass at her birthday and it wasn't bad, though it made me sleepy."

"All of the synopses the ambassadors turned in are equally vague," Finalia practically wailed. "I just assumed that they intended to reframe our highest learning in the context of their own intellectual systems and that it couldn't be condensed into a paragraph or two. But what if they all do the same thing?"

"Write about wine?" Bethany asked. "Do they all like it that much?"

"Not wine, necessarily, but what if they all focus on some minor facet of our culture that happens to interest them? The goal of the *For Humans* series has always been to provide a comprehensive guide to a subject that's accessible to people with limited educations."

"But this book isn't for humans, it's for aliens, and compared to us, all their children are highly educated before they finish primary school. Maybe Ambassador Czeros knew that there was no point wasting his chapter on some basic concepts that every Frunge with an interest in humanity would already know. Instead, he's trying to pass along his enthusiasm about what he sees as one of our cultural highpoints."

Finalia swiped at her tab again, and her face fell. "Listen to what the Verlock ambassador proposed," she said. "Since the first Human looked up at the night skies and beheld the planets and stars, mankind has been attempting to construct mathematical systems to explain celestial motion. Philosophical and theological constructs placing Earth at the center of the universe gave rise to elegantly complex models which, while sufficiently accurate to explain phenomena observable by the naked eye, were saddled with fatal flaws." She skimmed ahead and bit her lips. "I didn't understand what he was saying the first time I read it either, but now I'm worried."

"If Verlocks want to read about the history of our progress in astronomy, I don't see the harm," Bethany said. "One of the first lessons that Libby taught us is that there's never a reason to be ashamed of learning. The advanced species know that we only discovered the scientific method a few hundred years ago, and maybe seeing how far we've come in a short time will make them think better of us."

"Your optimism almost puts your father to shame, and that's saying something," Finalia said with a sour smile. "It's too late to ask the ambassadors to submit more detailed synopses since we're expecting the rest of the finished drafts by the end of the month."

"Do you want me to mention it to my dad?"

"Yes. No. It's my responsibility. I—" she broke off to point at her ear and appeared to be puzzled by whatever she was hearing over her implant. Then the editor gave a slight shrug, looked at Bethany, and asked, "Would you be willing to go to the Dollnick embassy and hear what Ambassador Crute has written? He interpreted our guidelines to mean that the material should be accessible to a fourteen-year-old human, and he wants to make any tweaks before he submits his draft."

"Sure," Bethany said, though the butterflies rose in her stomach. "Do you mean now?"

"Yes."

"Okay."

Finalia passed along the girl's reply and then lowered her hand. "I'll hold off on talking to Chastity and your father until you tell me how it goes with Crute," she said. "Answer his questions honestly and don't worry about sparing his feelings if he reads you an engineering treatise that only Hep would understand. And make sure the ambassador knows that you have to be home for dinner in a few hours. It's already midafternoon."

Although she had been casually introduced to all the Union Station ambassadors at one time or another thanks to frequent invitations to the EarthCent Ambassador's picnics at Mac's Bones, going by herself to an embassy was an entirely different affair. During the brief trip in the lift tube, Bethany peppered the station librarian with questions about Ambassador Crute, and she was shocked when Libby refused to answer on the grounds that it would amount to unfair sharing of competitive business information.

"You teach us all about the ambassadors in class," Bethany protested.

"Today you're acting as an employee of the Galactic Free Press, and what would the journalists working for Gem Today, the Drazen Shipping News, or the Grenouthian Network think if they knew I was helping you?"

"But how is asking whether or not the ambassador understands English without his implant competitive information?"

"It's not something he's on the record answering one way or the other," Libby explained. "You could ask Ambassador McAllister next time you see her."

"Now I really don't understand," Bethany said. "You know that she'd tell me, so why can't you tell me?"

"Because I'm not her," the station librarian replied as the lift tube doors opened. "The Dollnick embassy is to the left."

The ambassador must have informed his staff that a youngster from the Galactic Free Press was expected because a Dollnick intern was waiting at the embassy doors to escort her into Crute's presence. The Dollnick ambassador rose as they entered his office, but Bethany wished he had remained seated as he was easily two heads taller than her father and towered over both her and the intern.

"Shoona will remain as a chaperone," Ambassador Crute informed Bethany. "Editor Finalia informs me that your age correlates with that of average Human students at the level for which the *For Humans* series is targeted. It wouldn't be appropriate for me to entertain Dollnick fledglings at an equivalent educational level without a chaperone present."

"Uh, thank you, Ambassador," Bethany said. "I've never had a chaperone."

Crute indicated a chair with one of his lower arms and frowned when Bethany's feet were left dangling well off the deck. "There's a hassock under the reading desk," he told the intern who was serving as chaperone. "Please bring it for our guest."

"I don't mind," Bethany said, but the Dollnick ambassador waved aside her words and waited until the chaperone had installed the hassock below the human's feet before retaking his seat.

Ambassador Crute leaned forward, the elbows of his lower arms on his desk, the hands supporting the elbows of his upper arms. His upper hands formed a bridge on which he rested his narrow chin in a pose that reminded Bethany of a famous Dollnick sculpture from her art appreciation class.

"Did you read my synopsis?" Crute inquired.

Bethany blushed. "I didn't know you had submitted one until today, but I should have sought it out," she immediately amended herself, knowing that aliens didn't think highly of humans making excuses.

"I was asking because I decided to go a different direction with my chapter." The ambassador fluidly shifted into a new pose, this one freeing up his left upper arm to hold a large tab. He let out a barking sort of whistle that Bethany's implant left untranslated, perhaps the Dollnick equivalent of clearing his throat, and then began to declaim in English that sounded a little too high-pitched and reedy for someone of his bulk. "Building A Better Can Opener. A uniquely Human approach to science and technology." He paused and looked at Bethany, obviously waiting for her reaction.

"It sounds very interesting, Ambassador," she said.

"And you understood all the words? The vocabulary isn't too advanced."

"No, ambassador. I mean, yes, I understood. No, the words aren't too advanced."

"Excellent," Crute said. "I was afraid I would have to start from the beginning and explain the function of a can opener, which is my chosen allegory for Human technology. Have you ever used one?"

Bethany felt the butterflies in her stomach dissipate when she realized that the ambassador was asking something she knew quite a bit about. "My grandfather runs Kitchen Kitsch in the Shuk, and my mom used to work for him. We have a collection of at least twenty can openers in a kitchen drawer, and sometimes I think my mom buys stuff in cans just to have an excuse to use one."

"Do you have a favorite?"

"Maybe the one that doesn't seem to be doing anything when it goes around the can, but when you're done, the whole top lifts off because it was cutting just below the lip around the outside."

"Ah, yes. I have several versions of that model in my collection," the ambassador said. "Did you know that Humans invented the can before they invented the can opener?"

Bethany blinked. "I never really thought about it."

"Imagine the audacity. The early history of canned food on Earth is rife with stories of people being injured while attempting to stab a sharp implement through the lid."

"But what would be the point of inventing a can opener before you have cans to open? Does anybody do it that way?"

The Dollnick ambassador let out a cheerful whistle that Bethany's implant translated as more of a chuckle. "Of course. With us, the goal of engineering is to create cost-effective approaches to solving problems. Not to create problems and then to look for cost-effective solutions. Xule's Rule is named for the inventor of the metal canning process, giving him an immortal place in our engineering pantheon."

"Dollnicks like canned food that much?" Bethany asked.

"It's been replaced by stasis-field storage in most applications, but Xule's Rule is one of the core concepts of good engineering practice. To paraphrase, 'Don't design half of a product and stop there.'"

"I guess that makes sense."

"Excellent. I'll start again from the beginning." The Dollnick ambassador struck his speaker's pose, but this time he didn't find it necessary to clear his throat. "Building A Better Can Opener. A uniquely Human approach to science and technology. The first bridge on Earth may have been a tree fallen across a stream, or it might have been a path on top of a dam constructed by beaver. It's fascinating to note that Humans went on to create stone bridges that spanned rivers and soaring cathedrals featuring impressive domes without first developing the mathematics to explain how the structures remained standing." He paused again. "Am I keeping the vocabulary at your level?"

"Yes, Ambassador," Bethany said. "But aren't you describing how all engineering works? Libby taught us that most technologies on Earth advanced through building on previous successes."

"But without any—" Crute began in an excited voice and then restrained himself. "When Dollnicks or any of the other advanced species create a product, be it a can opener or a space elevator, we start with material science, chemistry, and physics, and establish a range of possible solutions. Then our engineers, building on that foundation, apply the techniques passed down from generation to generation to create a cost-effective solution. Does that make sense to you?"

"Yes. That's not what we do?"

"Humans traditionally skip the basics and attempt to jump to the end. Floaters based on our technology have now replaced the old forms of ground transportation on Earth, but imagine for a moment that you're living at the dawn of the automotive age, and you've purchased a vehicle with an internal combustion engine that's as powerful as twenty horses. Yet when you take your marvelous new toy out for a drive and it begins to rain, you have to keep stopping to clean off the windscreen."

"The what?" Bethany asked.

"Human engineers at the time had no access to advanced field technology so they enclosed the passenger compartment to keep out inclement weather," the Dollnick ambassador explained. "For the driver to see out of the cabin it was necessary to make sections from glass, but it took another Human generation to develop a means to automatically wipe the glass clean."

"That doesn't sound right. The engineers who created a whole new vehicle must have been able to figure out a way to keep the glass clean."

"You would think so, but that's not the way Human technology progresses. The engineers saw themselves as improving on the design of the horse-drawn carriages with which they would have to compete in the marketplace, and horse-drawn carriages didn't have windshield wipers."

"Because the horses could see where they were going in the rain?" Bethany asked.

Crute seemed to deflate a little at this question. "I don't believe the drivers relied on the horses for navigational aid unless they over-imbibed at the local tavern and fell asleep on the way home. The carriages didn't require windshield wipers, in some instances because the driver sat outside the compartment, and otherwise because the glass was vertical and the carriage moved too slowly for the view to become completely obstructed by rain."

"Oh. Is your whole chapter about automobiles?"

"I started with ground transportation for the sake of context and because it gave me a natural segue to suspension bridges, but from there I move on to flight and—did you know that Humans developed heavier-than-air flying machines by studying birds and experimenting with gliders before the mathematical models for aerodynamics were fully developed?"

By the time Bethany escaped from Crute's office, she was sure of two things. First, the Dollnick ambassador meant well, and he genuinely admired the pluck of human engineers who developed technological innovations without necessarily understanding the underlying science. Second, while she could understand the vocabulary and the individual examples, there was just too much engineering in the chapter for her to wrap her mind around. As she was entering the lift tube, her implant pinged with 'Mom.'

"Yes," Bethany replied, pointing at her ear even though she was alone in the capsule.

"If you're done at the paper for the day, come by the cookbook office," Brinda told her daughter. "We had a visit from a chef representing a sovereign human community on a Frunge world that's making a push into producing grain-alternative flours for traditionalists. She cooked up a storm, basically all their feature recipes, but she said the quality deteriorates after refrigeration."

"On my way."

When Bethany entered the offices of the *All Species Cookbook*, there were so many people crowded in that she had to stand on her toes to spot her mother, who was speaking with the host of *Stone Soup*. Bethany had known Jonah since childhood, thanks to Pava being the mother of Bodie, the Cayl hound that had chosen Jonah's family as a puppy, and she saw him even more frequently now that the cookbook was sponsoring his show.

"Beth," Jonah greeted her. "When are you going to sign up with InstaSitter? It's the best way to learn about aliens in their homes."

"I've already got a job working for your aunt's paper, and I still have to do homework for school," Bethany replied. "Did you come for the cooking demonstration?"

Jonah confirmed her guess with a nod. "You didn't miss much. The chef was too much of a factory rep to make baking look like anything other than a lab experiment, but the food more than makes up for the lackluster performance. I recommend the sushi ravioli."

"Gross."

"Then the faux macaroni and cheese. It tastes as good as the baked mac n' cheese that my grandmother makes. You'd never know that the pasta isn't made from wheat flour."

Fifteen

After months working as a bicycle courier in Humantown, Henry knew his way around the maze of alien architecture better than most people who had been living there since the sprawling section of the city had been turned over to humans. He also felt fantastic and wondered why he hadn't ridden a regular bicycle back on Earth.

"Henry," a woman called from one of the trapezoidal doorways that were typical of Farling construction. "I have a package for the factory district. Are you done for the day?"

"Not even close, Mona," Henry replied, bringing his bike to a halt with an artistic skid. He tapped his oversized wristwatch to change the display from showing the time to the dispatch page of the delivery service that employed him and didn't see any open tickets. "Cash and carry?"

"You know me so well," Mona said, handing over a small package wrapped in protective cling film that was used for everything from preserving food to patching broken windows. "Will five Dibels cover it?"

Henry reflexively translated the Farling currency into eBucks, rounding at one decimal place, and grunted his acceptance. The woman handed over a light metal coin with a ceramic insert showing a beetle-like face with multifaceted eyes and the English letters 'G32FX.'

"Is there a delivery deadline?" he asked. "I was thinking of grabbing dinner and then working until the sun sets."

"Did you just get out of bed?"

"I took a nap in the park," Henry said. "My body seems to have adjusted to the longer days provided I keep feeding it and close my eyes for a bit when I get tired."

"You be careful," Mona warned him. "I came to Farling Four directly from Earth with the first batch of immigrants almost a decade ago. At least half of us ended up with light exhaustion before we'd been here three months. It can take a long while to catch up with you, but humans aren't engineered to work twenty-four-hour days. And it would be best if you could drop the package and then eat."

Henry didn't ask whether the recipient would soon be closing shop for the day, or if Mona was worried that the longer the package was in his hands, the more likely something might go wrong. He put the coin in his belt pouch, the package in his messenger bag, and asked for the exact address.

"Go to the Blue Arch and an Oosh carrying a black umbrella will be waiting there to collect it from you," she said. "I'll send her a message now."

"I've never seen an Oosh with an umbrella," Henry said. "Aren't they basically fish out of water?"

Mona paled and lowered her voice. "Don't ever let one of them hear you say that. They may look like sharks that swapped their tailfin for a stubby pair of pseudopods, but they've been walking around on land longer than we have, and they're prickly about their appearance. If she invites you back to her place for dinner, I'd take a hard pass."

"Pass on becoming fish food, got it. The street market traffic should be winding down by now, everything but the food vendors, so tell the Oosh to figure on my being there in fifteen minutes."

When Henry coasted to a halt under the blue arch, he saw a couple of large spidery-looking aliens playing some sort of game on a stone checkerboard that was worked into the plaza like a giant mosaic, a few Quadies, a four-legged species that also sported four arms, one set of which were twice as long as the other, and an enormous dragon variant that was sunning its long snaky body and leathery wings. He spotted the Oosh with the black umbrella approaching from the other side of the dragon and noticed that she left a wide margin while skirting around the wingtips.

"Ugly," the Oosh declared as soon as she was within speaking distance. "Can you understand me?"

Henry bit back his initial impulse, which was to pretend that she'd introduced herself with the name 'Ugly,' and replied, "I understand. Who sent me?"

The Oosh bared shark-like teeth in a mouth that stretched almost the whole way across her face, though given her streamlined torso and lack of a chin or neck, it was hard to say exactly where her face began. "Mona sent you."

He got the package out of his messenger bag and held it out for the Oosh, whose upper appendages didn't quite match his definition of arms and hands, but served the same purpose.

"Do you have something to give me?" he asked.

The mouth stretched even wider if that was possible. "Did Mona imply that something was owed?"

"No, no. I was just asking to be polite," Henry said. He hoped that all the notes he was making about his interactions with the client species of the Farling Empire would be appreciated by EarthCent Intelligence, which was why he intentionally pushed a little beyond the boundaries of propriety in every encounter. "Then we're all set."

"Have you eaten?" the Oosh asked unexpectedly.

"Yes," Henry lied, suppressing a shudder. "I'll just be going then." When he checked the bike's mirrors before turning back through the arch, the shark-like alien was still looking after him, like he was the fish that had gotten away.

No new tickets had appeared on the wrist comm that had become the standard personal tech for humans on the planet, and as he rode back to Humantown, he dictated notes about what he had seen and heard that day. When he'd protested to the EarthCent Intelligence agents who had come to recruit him on Earth that he knew nothing about being a spy, Chance had suggested he start keeping a journal of everything he saw and heard. In addition to helping him later recall facts that he didn't think important at the time, by recording absolutely everything, the journal was more likely to be accepted as an innocent pastime or psychological compulsion should a counter-intelligence agency get their hands on it.

When Henry put his bike in the rack in front of Café Bronx, he was surprised to see that all the outdoor tables were taken. He reluctantly entered the restaurant, took a seat at the counter, and gave his order. It wasn't until after he took a sip from his iced coffee that he realized he couldn't see either of the regular cooks. The next time the counterman passed, Henry flagged him down. "Hey, Todd. What happened to Jeremy and Sheila?"

"Left to open their own place, didn't they," Todd said.

"Then why is it so crowded?"

"Deb hired a new cook, didn't she. Makes all the same dishes only better."

Henry peered through the large horizontal opening to the kitchen area where patrons could normally see the two red-headed cooks working, which was one reason he normally preferred eating outside. It seemed whenever he ate at the counter he noticed Jeremy mouthing "Oopsy," at his wife, or Sheila tasting something by probing with her finger and licking.

"Is the new cook on break?"

"Short, isn't he," Todd said, holding his hand flat about halfway up his chest to indicate the new cook's height. "Spidery dude."

"Deb hired one of those spider-dudes to cook?" Henry asked, at the same time half standing with his feet on rungs of the stool to get a better viewing angle into the kitchen. Sure enough, one of the aliens that looked like an arachnophobe's nightmare was wielding two frying pans and a spatula with different limbs and appeared to be stirring something with a fourth. "It knows how to cook human food?"

"Better than Jeremy and Sheila, doesn't it."

"Feel like company?" a voice to Henry's left inquired, and the local reporter for the Galactic Free Press took the stool next to him. "I had breakfast and lunch here today and I couldn't help myself from coming back. And I'll have the special, Todd."

"That good?" Henry asked Robin, who was the one person in Humantown he'd gone out of his way to cultivate when he learned the man's profession. "How long has it been cooking human food?"

"I asked Deb if I could interview the new cook, but it turns out that the L'meuf don't communicate audibly, and my implant doesn't do telepathy," the reporter said. "I tried a little sign language, but it just ignored me."

"L'meuf are way in advance of us," Henry pointed out. "I've delivered to one of those workshops where they make levitation belts that work like Dollnick floater technology, and somebody told me that they're the ones who developed our wrist comms. Why would one of them want a job cooking in a restaurant?"

Robin shot Henry a sideways look. "You know that there's only work for so many scientists and engineers in any culture. Even the Verlocks have jobs for a finite number of mathematicians. Our cook could be smarter than Hep, the guy who heads Earth's interstellar jump drive program, and not even be average at math in his own species."

"Do you mean that he's so smart that he could learn to cook in a few hours by following recipes?" Henry asked. "I've only been here three months, but I haven't heard of any spiders working as cooks."

"Deb said that he didn't understand what she meant when she asked for his work history, but once she saw him in the kitchen, she knew that he was a professional. Maybe he cooked on a Stryx station, or in one of the outlying farming communities where the original people brought here from Earth were growing seed crops."

Todd took a large plate off the ledge that framed the bottom of the opening to the kitchen and placed it in front of Henry. "Bon appetit."

"Eggplant parm," Robin said. "Good choice. I had it for lunch."

Henry poked suspiciously at a mound of vegetables topping some unfamiliar-looking rice on the side of the large plate. "What happened to the dinner roll and the little cup of canned green beans?"

"That's spaghetti squash and basmati rice," Todd told him. "Spidey has taken some liberties with the old menu, but nobody has complained yet. Just try it."

"Or you can give it to me and take my special when it comes," Robin said. "The parm was so good that I could eat it twice in a day. In fact, I already regret that I didn't order it myself."

Spurred on by their comments, Henry sampled the rice and squash first since he didn't want to burn his mouth on the eggplant, and his eyes went wide. "This is the best thing I've tasted since leaving Earth," he said. "Longer than that, and I wasn't afraid to spend money in restaurants before I left. I guess the aliens are better than us at everything."

"Wait until you try the eggplant. You'll understand why there weren't any open tables even though the dinner rush was hours ago."

By the time Robin's special arrived, a fresh farm-raised fish with asparagus and young potatoes, Henry had finished his dinner and found himself fighting the urge to order a second serving, even though the first had been if anything, too generous.

"Spidey bakes a mean dessert," Robin told him between bites. "I had the vegan banana bread with chocolate chunks with lunch. I felt so guilty that I rented a bike to go look at the new wholesale showroom the Oosh set up to sell weapons to traders."

"Weapons?" Henry forced his mind away from food for a moment. "Advanced tech?"

Robin began laughing, started to choke, and coughed out a bit of potato. "If you're going to do that while I'm eating, wait until we're somewhere with lousy food."

"Sorry, but what's so funny?"

"The Oosh have a warrior culture, kind of like the Cayl, but without the academic side of the coin. They can use advanced weaponry, of course, and they're generally considered to be the enforcers in the Farling Empire, but they believe anything with greater range than bows and arrows to be unsporting. The showroom might have been copied from a Frunge blacksmith's display, or better yet, from the armory for one of those historical reenactment dramas the Drazens and Hortens are always producing."

"Can I get you anything for dessert?" Todd asked as he took the empty plate.

"Do you have any of the banana bread left?" Henry asked.

Todd smiled and shook his head. "That was gone by mid-afternoon, and I thought that we'd be pushing it for days. He made another batch of desserts for supper, but all I have left is a salted caramel éclair."

"I'll take it."

"Split it with me and I'll get you into the Riverboat Club," Robin said as soon as the counterman turned away. "It could be the only chance you get in life to rub elbows with real-life spies."

"How would you know that they're spies?" Henry asked, his internal caution lights flashing red. "I can't imagine they would come out and tell anybody."

"The way Bluve, a Dollnick spy explained it to me, intelligence agents have two choices," Robin said. "They can register with the authorities on the planet they're visiting, which allows them to work in the open, or they can try to stay undercover and risk all sorts of nasty alien consequences if they get caught. Farling Four is an open world so there's no need to sneak around. The reason I know

Bluve is a spy is that he tried to recruit me as a source before I told him I work for the Galactic Free Press."

"Why did that stop him?"

"There's a family connection between the paper and EarthCent Intelligence, they were founded by sisters. Bluve said the other intelligence services see recruiting our reporters as akin to soliciting double agents, which I guess is rude. Anyway, he apologized for trying."

Henry fought an epic but brief battle with himself when the salted caramel éclair arrived, but professional pride won out over gluttony, and he cut the éclair in half.

"You won't regret it," Robin said, hurrying to transfer half of the éclair to the saucer that had come with his tea before Henry could change his mind. "The Riverboat is the only place in Humantown where the aliens from the Farling Empire mix socially with humans. If you've never seen a drunk Oosh singing karaoke, you're in for a treat."

"That, I think I could pass on," Henry said. He took a bite of the éclair and immediately regretted his deal. "Are all of the aliens affected by alcohol?"

"To varying degrees, at least all the oxygen breathers I'm aware of. Some people think that the Stryx engineered it into all our genes to provide a path for bridging the cultural divide, but I don't think that jibes with evolution. And it's the gambling that draws them in, not the booze."

Henry took another bite of the éclair and decided that he'd rather be a food critic than a spy. "I think of myself as a decent card player. I've made it to the final table in a pretty big field, but I imagine that the aliens see us as easy pickings."

"Strangely enough, gambling is one of those areas, like gaming in general, where humans can be competitive," Robin said. Then he took a bite of his half of the éclair and fell silent for a good thirty seconds. "It depends on the game, of course, but we can usually make a respectable showing at the ones we were playing before the Stryx opened Earth. I even took a pot off a Verlock in a poker game when I caught him bluffing."

"Good to know," Henry said, filing the information away. "Are there any cardsharps working the casino?"

"It wouldn't be a real casino without professional gamblers. If you ever see a woman who's too beautiful to be real, she's from the Vergallian upper caste, and you don't want to bet against them in any games that involve bluffing. Some of those upper-caste women are truthsayers, and it's a passive type of telepathy, so it can't be detected."

Henry finished his half of the éclair and sighed. "That was a three-Dibel dessert if I've ever had one, maybe even four. What do they charge?"

"All desserts are one-and-a-half Dibels," Robin said. "The last I saw, Dibels were near parity with the Stryx cred. It makes you wonder if the Farlings target the exchange rate even though they aren't members of the tunnel network." He fished out a ten-Dibel coin and left it on the counter. "Supper's on me. I'm going to get a good bonus for the Oosh weapons showroom since I captured images as well as writing the story."

Security at the Riverboat Club consisted of a bored-looking Oosh with a sword whose blade was almost as long as Henry was tall and a scrawny human who somehow gave off the aura of being more dangerous than the landshark.

"Who's your pal?" the man asked Robin.

"Henry, from Earth," Robin replied. "Been here over a month, and he just shared his éclair with me at Café Bronx."

"You're a fool," the man said to Henry's face. "But they like fools with money in this place. Show me a hundred Dibels and you can walk through the door."

"I'll show you, but from over here," Henry said, checking through his pouch by feel for some of the largest denomination Farling coins, equivalent to a week's pay on Earth. "I may be a fool, but I'm not an idiot."

Henry never felt as many alien eyes on him as when he entered the casino for the first time. Eyes that assessed his intellect, eyes that measured his physical shape and extrapolated fighting ability, eyes that could see the programmable cred in the secret compartment of his belt pouch. And it all happened in an instant during which he would have sworn that conversation and the sounds of clattering chips came to a halt, but then the instant was over, and he may as well have been invisible.

"Did you catch that?" Robin asked, a half-smile turning up the side of his mouth.

"Everything really stopped for a second? I thought I imagined it."

"You've been cataloged, categorized, and probably x-rayed if any of the aliens can see wavelengths that short. There's Bluve waiting for a seat at the poker table. Want me to introduce you?"

"Sure," Henry said, suddenly understanding why the reporter had been willing to pay for dinner and invite him along. Robin must have learned a few tricks from alien journalists and was working a side gig. The reporter probably picked up a commission from the Dollnick intelligence agent, and perhaps others, for steering promising sources their way.

The two men made their way across the crowded floor of the casino to the poker table where all eight of the players were aliens. As they approached, a L'meuf who might have been the brother of the spider cooking in the Bronx Café pushed all his chips into the center of the table.

"Fold," grunted a Drazen who was one of the two surviving players in the game, though it came out like a groan.

The Horten who remained glared at his hole cards like he was willing them to change suits even as his skin color became blotchy and showed signs of strobing. "Fold," he hissed, throwing in his cards. "If I find out that you can read my mind..."

"Don't make threats you can't back up," one of the Oosh at the table commented significantly.

"But he's never been in here before, claims he's never even played poker, and he's making us all look like amateurs," the Horten protested.

"Then let somebody else take your seat."

"Not until I win my money back." The Horten picked up one of the gold-streaked chips at the end of his diminished hoard and pushed it toward the croupier. In return he received so many stacks of lower denomination chips it was clear to Henry that the Horten was the whale at the table.

"The way they're going I'm never going to get in," Bluve complained to Robin immediately after being introduced to Henry. "It's enough to drive a Dollnick to drinking."

"Can I get you something while I'm at the bar?" Robin asked immediately, confirming Henry's suspicion that the pair were used to working together.

"A piece of Harry's Fruitcake if they have it, but not if it's dried out," the Dollnick said as the reporter began turning away. "It's not good if the alcohol all evaporates."

"Do you play cards here often?" Henry asked for the sake of sounding social.

"Every night that I don't have somewhere else to be," Bluve said. "It makes it easy for people to find me so I can give them money."

"That's pretty nice of you."

"I'm not running a charity. Did Robin explain what business I'm in?"

"He said you're a spy, but I have a hard time taking him seriously," Henry said.

"Intelligence agent sounds much nicer when it's translated into Humanese," the Dollnick said. "Does your implant capture images?"

"That's a kind of personal question."

"I pay twice as much for information that's backed up by visual evidence. What do you say?"

"You're trying to hire me?" Henry asked, surprised by the bluntness of the approach even though he'd known it was coming. "But you don't know anything about me."

"And I'm not interested in knowing anything about you," Bluve told him. "I can pay for hard facts on what's filling up the warehouses in town and how long it's there. Any pricing information is worth a bonus."

"You know that I work as a bicycle messenger."

"And get into warehouses on a regular basis. Who do you think paid for your supper?"

"Who decides what my information is worth?" Henry asked. He was genuinely interested in how such things worked, even though he had no intention of spying for the Dollnicks while still trying to figure out how to earn his keep with EarthCent Intelligence.

"We negotiate," Bluve said. "Before you go home tonight, the Horten on the big stack and the Grenouthian over there at the roulette wheel will try to recruit you, and I wouldn't be surprised if one of the Oosh turns out—did you see that?"

"See what?"

"The L'meuf just showed his hole cards after I thought he bluffed everybody out of the ante. He had the goods."

"Then that was a pretty dumb raise," Henry said. "He should have played possum."

"Classic intimidation tactics. He's taking advantage of the cards he was dealt to get the other players to associate his raises with strong hands."

"Does his species play a lot of poker?"

"None that I'm aware of. I don't associate the spiders with gambling at all." A disgusted-looking Frunge swept his remaining chips off the table into a pouch and rose from the table. "That's my cue," Bluve said. "You know where to find me if you come across anything worth selling. And welcome to Farling Four."

Sixteen

Thomas stepped out of the his-and-hers charging bays, ran a quick self-diagnostic, and did a precise stretching routine to test that his body's actuators weren't submitting spurious data. Then he tapped on the frame of Chance's charging bay and his wife opened her eyes.

"Sure you don't want to come along?" Thomas asked. "All of the other species will be sending senior agents."

"If you were going to be talking about LARPing quests or combat, I'd be there with bells on," Chance replied with a simulated yawn. "But it's going to be a bunch of statisticians arguing about the probability that the betting line may have been impacted by actions or lack of actions on the part of players who probably never had a fraudulent thought in their lives. I'm stopping by the training camp for a few hours to make sure that my replacement isn't going too easy on the recruits, and then I promised Dorothy I'd visit SBJ Fashions and test some active-wear designs for her."

"A new product line? I thought Jeeves was keeping Dorothy busy with management to put a lid on her new product expenditures."

"He gave up trying after bringing Metoo on board. From what Dorothy tells me, they only see Jeeves in weekly meetings now, and he doesn't always come." Chance stepped out of her charging bay and started her own stretching routine. "I hope Metoo is up to keeping Baa in line. I like her, but she's overpowered to be working in the fashion business enchanting purses and a few odds-and-ends for LARPing."

Thomas grabbed a soft cloth off the shelf, and standing on one leg alternately like an ostrich, gave each of his shoes a quick buff. "Clive thinks that having an apprentice is good for Baa and she won't do anything to ruin that in a hurry. We know next to nothing about Terragram mages, and the other species aren't talking. One of the analysts that I assigned to scour the alien media for LARPing news that could affect our security contract came back with an interesting tidbit. A retired Sharf champion wrote an editorial demanding that his species recruit a Terragram mage since we have one."

"We have Baa? She'd be surprised to hear that." Chance began shadow boxing, her version of a post-recharge warmup. "Are the Sharf one of the advanced species who made it through their early development without getting traumatized by a pantheon of Terragrams playing gods?"

"They seem to have gotten past it, which makes me suspicious about Baa's rehabilitation roughly coinciding with Live Action Role Playing taking off again with the cooperation of Stryx station librarians," Thomas said.

"Don't you get started on Convergence Theory," Chance said. "It makes my processors ache, and there's no way to prove it one way or the other."

"Fair enough. I have to get going to meet Jonah so we can arrive together."

"Have a good day, and ping me if you can free up a couple of hours later to make a new dance training holo for the series Marcus is producing. If you can't make it, maybe I'll just dance with him," she added with an exaggerated wink.

"Be careful dancing with Marcus," Thomas said, pausing on his way to the door. "He's coming up on fifty, and if you break him, Chastity won't forgive you."

Jonah was waiting in the food court of the Empire Convention Center nursing a coffee when Thomas arrived. They were both a little too early to go to the reserved conference room, so the artificial person took a seat.

"I don't feel like I'm making any progress," Jonah said after a quick check to see if anybody was eavesdropping. "Sephia and I have gone to a half dozen matches, and players are starting to take it for granted that I'll do a little cooking at hatching parties, but nobody talks about gambling."

"Do they talk about the gameplay?" Thomas asked. "If a player is doing something subtle to affect the outcome, the other party members are the most likely to notice. They're in the moment together, which you can't replicate by watching holos, whether live or recorded."

"I can't, but how about you?" Jonah asked, coming alive as if the coffee had just hit him in one shot. "Is there a personality upgrade for Live Action Role Playing that you could get from QuickU and tweak for different players? My sister is always telling me about the personnel system they're trying to set up for the Human Empire, and she said that some of the advanced species can simulate the reactions of their employees to hypothetical changes or perturbations. Their managers can model the results of policy changes before rolling them out."

Thomas remained silent for a moment. "That's an interesting idea and one I should have thought of myself," he eventually said. "QuickU does have a personality upgrade for LARPing in development, and you've just given me a reason to make a trip to Earth for the beta package, but I'm not sure about the tweaking aspect. The other species might have enough information about their players to do it, but we don't. Not for humans, and certainly not for alien players."

"I guess I'm a bit frustrated that I'm spying on people who see me as a friend. If we knew for a fact that one of our players was trying to fix matches and that humanity's reputation was at stake, it would be different."

"I understand how you feel, but there's a reason that the professional sporting leagues hire people like us to provide security before problems appear," Thomas said. "We're as much a deterrent as we are an investigative force. The league makes the players all sign privacy waivers that give us the right to look into their assets, but I wouldn't be surprised if the real purpose of the waivers is to put the players on notice that they're being monitored."

Jonah tilted his cup way up to drain the last of the coffee and made a face. "As long as they don't ask us to start running sting operations. Libby didn't show many Grenouthian documentaries in school, but one that she made sure we all saw before leaving was titled 'Guilty Until Proven Innocent.' It was about how domestic intelligence agencies all over Earth would assign agents and informants to approach targets and try to recruit them for illegal activity."

"We show that one in the training camp," Thomas said. "As a technique to entrap enemy noncombatants into acting as agents, it's acceptable, if not ethical. But putting temptation in front of your citizens and manipulating them into breaking the law is just a way to inflate arrest statistics."

Jonah checked the time on his implant. "We better go in if we want to be early. Where did you say they're holding the conference? The Meteor Room?"

Thomas rose and shook his head. "Across from the Meteor Room on Sales Row. The smaller rooms are usually reserved during conferences by salesmen who want to make a private pitch without dragging prospective clients back to their hotel rooms. The convention center is booked for the week by a multi-species home furnishings liquidator, so the small rooms were available."

"A whole week for a retail show, and they took the rest of the convention center?"

"It's a Dollnick operation. I wouldn't be surprised if the same prince who operates the Empire chain owns the liquidator as well. They're based out of a Class Two cargo carrier that does a round of Stryx stations selling, and then hits all the major manufacturing hubs to restock on close-outs, seconds, anything they can buy for centees on the cred."

"Oh, no," Jonah said. "Sephia told me that she, my mother, and my grandmother were planning to do some shopping together today. I just assumed she meant they were going to visit the boutiques on the Vergallian deck."

"You should be pleased," Thomas said. "I've heard that the liquidators are offering unbeatable prices."

"Where are we supposed to put home furnishings? Our home is already furnished, as are my mom's and grandmother's. The money they save on new stuff is going to be spent paying to store the old stuff for the rest of our lives."

"You could sell the old stuff, or donate it to charity."

"But there's nothing wrong with it," Jonah objected, and then he made a slicing motion in front of his neck with one hand like the Grenouthian assistant director on his set calling for a cut. "I'm done. Thank you for helping me get that out of my system so I can pretend to be enthusiastic about whatever new furniture awaits when I get home."

"Where did you learn that trick?" Thomas asked, replicating the slicing gesture in front of his own throat. "Is it something programmed into your genes that you uncovered?"

"It's from the InstaSitter training program. All our sitters go through a course on dealing with stress. The 'cut' gesture is just something I picked up from the assistant director on my set. When I took our course, the instructor was a Frunge who taught us to associate a physical gesture with deep breathing and meditation as a shortcut to reaching a relaxed state. It's not a perfect solution, but it helps."

The room reserved by the Professional LARPing League for their gambling security contractors was around half full when Thomas and Jonah entered, meaning that they had timed their arrival perfectly. Some of the alien agents recognized the artificial person and offered a variety of head bobs and limb twitches to acknowledge his entrance, but Whiskers, the young Grenouthian assigned by their station chief to work with Jonah, was the only alien to follow them to their seats.

"Exciting, isn't it," Whiskers said. "I've never been in an all-species security meeting before. Have you found any signs of match-fixing yet?"

"Nothing," Jonah replied. "I've been attending hatchers with the players, and I haven't heard anything to suggest there's cheating going on."

"We've been working the financial records angle. I can't believe how much top players earn through endorsements and personal appearances. I'm going to try to up my game and go pro myself. Even the support characters can pile up enough to marry a century early."

"Will your station chief give you permission?" Thomas asked. He was always on the lookout for insights into Grenouthian behavior, as the species was notorious for avoiding direct questions about how the pecking order worked in their government and businesses.

"If I can go pro, I'll quit, and then it won't matter what he thinks," Whiskers said. "If I've learned one thing during a cycle of sorting through badly encrypted financial statements, it's that if anybody wants to bribe a top player, it's going to take such a large bet to earn out that it would set alarm bells ringing in the warren."

A tentacle settled over the excitable Grenouthian's shoulder, and Herl, the Drazen Intelligence chief, joined the group. "Thomas. Jonah. Whiskers," he greeted them one by one. "I see that my presentation today will be right on point."

"You're going to talk about spotting oversized bets?" Jonah asked.

Herl wiggled both thumbs on his left hand in the Drazen version of a noncommittal gesture and then decided there was no point in being coy. "I've worked gambling security for a dozen professional leagues over more than two hundred seasons," he said. "It was my specialty before they promoted me to my top level of competence. When a player goes bad, the motivation is much less likely to be greed than fear. Professional gamblers try to corrupt players by taking advantage of their weaknesses, introducing them to expensive vices that take more than a legitimate income to satisfy. The—"

"If you'll all be seated, it's time to begin," a Dollnick announced in a loud whistle that Jonah's implant translated with a tone of impatience. "We have a lot to get through today, and somebody only reserved the room for eighty-two minutes."

"That's ridiculous," Herl said, spinning toward where the Dollnick was employing all four of his arms to point at individuals and gesture for them to be seated. "My presentation is timed for exactly ninety-seven minutes and there's no fat to be cut." Then he curled his tentacle around as if to shield his eyes from the overhead lights and took a closer look at the speaker, "Lume? What are you doing here?"

"If you'll all be seated, I'll answer your questions," Lume said, continuing to point and pat down the air. "I only have a brief window of time myself as I need to get back in the tunnel to Chianga to catch Flower before she leaves or I'll be playing catch-up for the next deci-cycle. Grule," he added with a sharp whistle. "Park it."

The younger Dollnick flinched on being called out by his senior and dropped into the nearest chair, and the rest of the intelligence agents in the room followed suit. There were a few grumbles along the lines of, "Who died and left *him* in charge," but Lume was well known in the business, and nobody wanted to challenge an alien who could juggle a dozen knives while chopping ingredients for a salad at his lunch counter.

"Thank you," Lume said once they were all seated. "To answer Herl's question first, the Professional LARPing League asked me to coordinate your efforts because rumors have reached them that some of you were having difficulty playing on the same team. I've been working in close cooperation with intelligence agents from all your species on Flower for the last six years, and the league's lawyers believe that my experience can help extract the signal from the noise some of you have been making."

"Is there an issue with the work assignments?" Thomas asked.

"Excellent question. I've reviewed all the forum messages related to the division of responsibilities. My conclusion is that the addition of your team from EarthCent Intelligence for the current season is at the root of the disputes. I'll only remind everyone that change is difficult and the time to put away childish things arrived when I walked into this room. Now, are there any serious questions about priorities for the season, or can we give our guest speaker enough time to complete at least eighty percent of his presentation?"

"Is your presence here a one-off, or will you, and by extension, Flower, be involved in gambling security for the league this season," the Horten station chief demanded.

"I've accepted a retainer to return and troubleshoot any interagency disputes that may arise, but my strong preference is not to generate any more billable hours," Lume said. "Anybody else?"

"I'll – keep – it – short," the senior Verlock agent present said, using up more time than the entire exchange that had just taken place. "Our – current – model – indicates – a – one – in – three – chance – that – a – match – has – already – been – fixed – this – season."

"You believe the outcome may have been altered, or are you talking about point shaving that affects the ranking of parties and members," a scholarly-looking Frunge asked.

"Shaving," the Verlock replied tersely.

"Point shaving is always two orders of magnitude more likely than outright match-fixing," Lume said. "Is there any other urgent business? No? Herl, the room is yours."

The Drazen spymaster rose from where he'd sat with the humans and made his way to the open mouth of the

'U', which was comprised of seven identical tables covered with a continuous roll of white tablecloth that had been folded to make the corners. He stopped in front of the two Drazen agents assigned to work the security contract and handed one of them a tab before continuing to the position where everybody could see him without twisting their necks.

"Blackmail," Herl began in a deep tone. "Think of Live Action Role Players as trusted financial advisors who have worked with your family for years. Why would such an individual sacrifice their honor and your trust to embezzle funds?"

"Gambling debts," the Horten who'd spoken earlier stated confidently.

"Rinty addiction," a member of the Fillinduck trio present suggested.

"Trying to cover up bad investment decisions by borrowing from Aadisha to pay Andille," a Vergallian agent said.

"Blackmail?" Jonah ventured.

"Thank you," Herl said. "All of your examples are reasons for an individual to lose their moral compass, but if a professional gambler of the criminal persuasion finds out, the result will be blackmail."

"But giving in to blackmail would just make the player's position worse," Whiskers objected. "Throwing a match won't help with a drug problem or a scandal."

"This is how the blackmailer gets his hooks in the victim," Herl said. "Whatever the player needs to make it through to the next match, be it drugs, covering debts for another cycle, or keeping a moral failing out of the news, the blackmailer will offer a temporary fix. Never a permanent fix, mind you, lest the leverage disappears, but stringing the player along with promises that it will all end with just one more score."

"Then it's not the initial failing that brings them down, it's the attempt to cover up," Jonah said. "I've heard news reporters say that's often the case in government scandals as well."

"Are you suggesting we need to get to the players before the blackmailers can move in?" one of the young Drazen agents asked.

"If only it were that easy," Herl said. "When sentients run into the sort of trouble that they don't want to confess to their families or close friends, they often turn to more distant acquaintances, a description which characterizes the professional gamblers who hang around players and try to ingratiate themselves. Other than young Oxford there, how many of you have ever socialized with professional LARPers?"

"I have," said the younger Vergallian agent, who looked like she might still qualify to compete in junior dance competitions, in addition to taking the crown at any beauty pageant on Earth. "I started hanging around the tavern in the LARPing studio in my elf dancer outfit, and some of the male players like being seen with me, especially if there's any media present."

"Are you even old enough to be drinking in a virtual tavern?" one of the other female agents groused.

"I drink juice," the girl said, sounding scandalized by the very notion of poisoning her body with alcohol. "And I'm planning to audition for the league at the next open trials."

"That's the perfect cover to get closer to players," Herl said. "Jonah. Have you considered trying for the league yourself?"

"I'm nowhere near good enough for the professional level," Jonah said. "I'd have to drop everything else I'm doing and practice full-time for a few years just to get to the point of failing with dignity rather than being laughed out of the studio."

"Then we'll target getting Alinka on the inside, keep you on the hatching circuit, and if somebody could embed in the studio—"

"Me," Whiskers offered eagerly. "I interned on the Grenouthian News, so it won't look strange if I drop-ship into the LARPing league broadcast."

"Drop-ship?" Alinka asked.

"It's an expression Grenouthians use for when somebody in upper management creates a job for a young relative or clan member without opening it to competitive applications," Jonah explained with a suppressed sigh. "Most of the assistants to assistants on *Stone Soup* are nepotism deals."

"Speaking of family relations, is your participation in this contract a way of announcing that you'll be deputy director to Thomas after your father retires?" the Fillinduck inquired.

"I only agreed to do this because EarthCent Intelligence didn't have somebody else with LARPing experience and a bit of local celebrity who could get into the studio and spend time around the players. It's not a career move for me."

"You should consider it," Herl said seriously, "We're all a bit nervous about the speed with which the Human Empire is moving toward autonomy. They haven't established a track record or built the kind of inter-species relationships at the departmental level that help keep the tunnel network on an even keel. Given your lifespans, multi-generational points of contact are the best bet to preserve trust."

"Don't tell me that Clive is retiring already," the Horten station chief complained. "When did he start the job? Forty years ago?"

"Less than thirty," Jonah said, betting that the number would be better received than closer to twenty. "It's less an issue of age than that he doesn't think it would look good for the Director of Human Empire Intelligence to be the father-in-law of the First Administrator."

"Who?"

"Emperor McAllister," the older Vergallian agent said. "Humans have a thing about inventing new job titles for old jobs."

"Continuity – is – key," the Verlock station chief intoned. "We – need – time – to – gather – data – to – model – the – behavior – of – aliens. Tweaking – for – generations – is – much – less – data – collection – intensive – than – starting – from – scratch."

"You want my father to remain in his job when the Human Empire replaces EarthCent, and me to start training for a Deputy Director role under Thomas to save you the trouble of building a new model?" Jonah asked, trying to keep the sarcasm from his tone.

"Yes," the Verlock said. "Thank – you – for – understanding."

Seventeen

"Is today the deadline?" Brinda asked her daughter.

Bethany sighed and set down her spoon. "We haven't received drafts from any of the ambassadors since Finalia tried editing the chapter that Ambassador Czeros submitted and returned it to him for comments. The next afternoon, Ambassador McAllister visited the Galactic Free Press offices and practically begged us not to do that again. I guess the Frunge don't take kindly to editing."

"I'm not sure I've ever met Finalia. Is she a dinosaur like your father, who edits on paper with a red pen? I could see how that would cause a diplomatic incident with the Frunge."

"She edits on her tab, with change tracking to make it easy for the author to see what she's altered," Bethany said. "Ambassador Czeros sent back the draft with all of her changes rejected."

Brinda scraped the bottom of the sundae glass with a long-handled spoon to get at the last bit of now-cold fudge. "He sounds just like most of the aliens I've done business with over the years. They aren't shy about disagreeing, and they don't favor compromise solutions where neither side is happy."

"We expected all the ambassadors to submit their chapters early. I know that the Dollnick Ambassador finished his at least a month ago because he read it to me, but he's sitting on it."

"Maybe he's revising."

"Finalia thinks that Czeros warned the other ambassadors and they all decided to wait for the deadline and submit together so we wouldn't have time to suggest edits," Bethany said. She took a sip of tea, and feeling very much like an adult, asked her mother, "How are things at the cookbook?"

"The usual," Brinda said with a smile. "Shaina tries to boss me around because she's my older sister, and then I remind her that Pava is Queenie's mother, so I win."

"Seriously."

"The *All Species Cookbook* is generating so much money that our main challenge is not letting it go to our heads. The monthly supplement magazine takes most of our time, and your cousin Mike was a big help finding us alien students from the Open University to act as beta readers and catch the obvious cultural faux pas."

"Volunteers?"

"We pay them a token amount for their time, but they're really in it to be able to have an internship at the *All Species Cookbook* in their work history. The students are studying art, like your cousin, and there aren't too many good opportunities to get professional experience." Brinda glanced at the antique gold wind-up wristwatch that Walter had given her on their last anniversary. "You better leave now if you don't want to be late."

Bethany shot to her feet like the last trumpet had just sounded. "Thanks for lunch, Mom. I'll get it next time." Then she ran for the lift tube, looking every bit of the coltish young teenager that she was.

Finalia looked up sharply when her assistant entered the *For Humans* room. "Oh," the editor said in disappointment. "I thought you were a courier."

"Just me," Bethany said. "Nothing yet?"

"I received a query from the Vergallian ambassador this morning confirming that the deadline for her submission was today, then nothing. I'm sure that it's queued up and ready to go, but she's waiting for the last minute."

"I never would have guessed that the alien ambassadors would be afraid of an editor. Aren't they all hundreds of years old? It seems kind of childish."

"They aren't afraid of me," Finalia said. "They aren't even concerned that I'll insist on changes because their contracts all give them editorial control. They're diplomats with extensive experience in avoiding unnecessary unpleasantness."

Bethany almost missed landing on her chair out of surprise as she sat. "You gave them editorial control? I thought my Dad told me that publishers never give writers editorial control."

"With one exception."

"Jeeves," Bethany guessed. "All right, I can understand not trying to edit what a Stryx has written since he'd just wave his pincer and it would revert back, but why did we give the ambassadors the same contract?"

"Clerical error," Finalia said, and then corrected herself. "My fault, I should have double-checked. I requested a standard contract for all the ambassadors and then I signed them without reading every paragraph because I thought I knew what was there. Our administrative assistant accidentally pulled up a Jeeves contract for the template."

"Mail call," a co-op student from the Open University announced as he walked into the room. "You hit the jackpot today. I've got eight certified deliveries for you, and they all require signature confirmation before I can release them." He handed a bonded tab to Bethany, who passed it to Finalia. The editor suppressed a shudder, pulled the stylus out of its holder on the edge of the tab, and scribbled her signature eight times on successive forms. The co-op student produced a handful of disposable memory chits, laid them out on the table, took his tab, and departed.

"I can't look," Finalia said. "You do it."

"Which one should I check first?" Bethany asked.

"It doesn't matter. Just pick one."

Bethany inserted a random chit into the desk's data slot and a holographic text was projected at the closed end of the room. "The Best Justice Money Can Buy. A history of Human jurisprudence by Ambassador Aleeytis, Empire of a Hundred Worlds."

Finalia read silently, and then said, "Next page," before Bethany had finished three-quarters of the first. This pattern repeated throughout the chapter, and when the editor finished the last page, she looked like she had bitten into a lemon.

"I couldn't keep up with you, but what I read wasn't that bad," Bethany said. "The ambassador kept pointing out that we only had writing for a few thousand years before the Stryx opened Earth, so we didn't have time to establish much of a legal corpus."

"Her grammar is better than mine," Finalia practically snarled. "And I can't argue with any of her observations, which as near as I can tell are both fair and true. But anybody who reads this will think that Earth would be better served to replace its judiciary with Vergallian princesses."

"Was she being serious about the advice for Vergallian tourists visiting Earth?"

The editor nodded glumly. "I can't argue with her there. Any alien tourist who gets caught up in legal proceedings on Earth would be wise to leave as soon as possible and not waste money defending themselves unless they intend to return one day. She also reminds them that while Earth remains a probationary member of the tunnel network, the treaty allows alien tourists to request a trial at their embassy with the ambassador acting as judge."

"I didn't see that," Bethany said. "Was it always in the tunnel network contract? I know that the Stryx reserve the right to change some sections of it as circumstances require."

"That's an interesting question. I wouldn't be surprised if it's a revision that was put in to help Earth's tourist business, since it wouldn't take many bad experiences with the local courts to put aliens off visiting. But the hardest part of the chapter to swallow is where she goes into detail about how being able to afford a top lawyer impacts the outcome of legal actions. I can't help wondering where she found all those statistics."

"Do you want me to try to locate the source?"

"Let's see what else we have to deal with first," Finalia said and gestured at the remaining memory chits.

Bethany replaced the Vergallian memory with a new one picked at random, and the title page popped up in the flat hologram, "Games Humans Play. Ambassador Ortha, Horten Empire."

"Well, this isn't so bad," the editor said before requesting the next page. "He's complimentary about Chess and

Go, though he seems to be saying that the real accomplishment is that we developed games that we're so bad at playing."

"I didn't quite finish that part before you turned the page."

"It's an argument I've heard before. As soon as Earth's computer science reached the point that they could produce limited artificial intelligence systems that were capable of self-learning, it turned out that even our grandmasters weren't as good at our games as we thought they were. And that's an interesting observation."

"What?" Bethany asked, skimming a little to try to keep up with Finalia's reading speed. "His story about playing poker with the EarthCent Ambassador, Joe, Stryx Jeeves, Maker Dring, M793qK, and the Thark ambassador?"

"I'm sure he included the anecdote for the sake of name-dropping, but can you imagine when Joe called, and it turned out that Jeeves, M793qK, and the Thark ambassador were all bluffing? Ortha writes about it as a sort of high-water mark for human civilization." Her smile faded immediately after she called for the next page and saw the helpful hints in the margins. "He's giving betting advice for poker!"

"I've never played. What does he mean by investment odds?"

"I'm not a gambler myself, but we're going to have to slap a disclaimer on the book or every bad card player in the galaxy will be lining up to sue us when they follow Ortha's system and lose."

The pair read on silently, with Bethany figuring out that she could keep pace with her boss by skipping every third line, though she often lost the thread of the ambassador's meaning. After poker, Ortha moved on to discuss first-person-shooter games and the development of something called Massively Multi-Player Online Role Playing Games, which sounded a little like LARPing without holograms, though the MMORPG acronym was less pronounceable.

"All right," Finalia said when she finished, reaching for her cold coffee and then pushing it away. "I suppose from the point of view of a species that's been obsessed with games for the last half million years or more, none of our efforts will look particularly original. I've never really thought about presenting humanity to an alien audience as the sum of the games that we play, but maybe it's as legitimate as looking at our art or music. Let's see the next one."

Bethany swapped memories again, and the title page of the new chapter read, "All The World's A Stage. The Shakespeare Species, by the Grenouthian Ambassador to Union Station."

"The whole first page is a speech taken directly from 'As You Like It,'" Finalia said a few seconds later.

"Wait, let me finish it. I've never read it before."

"Fine, tell me when you're done. I can't believe he just labeled us the Shakespeare Species. It's the sort of thing that could go viral."

A tear rolled down Bethany's cheek, and she repeated the last three lines out loud:

"That ends this strange eventful history,
Is second childishness and mere oblivion;
Sans teeth, sans eyes, sans taste, sans everything."

"Don't take it so hard," Finalia said, reaching across the table and patting the girl's hand. "It comes to all of us eventually, even Grenouthians, and the play is a comedy. Next page."

"To be or not to be?" Bethany read.

"Next page," the editor barked and then repeated the command. "That's a relief," she said when a page of regular prose appeared. "For a second there I thought the whole chapter was going to be speeches from plays." She read to the bottom and then leaned back in her chair rather than calling for a new page turn.

"Do you want me to take over running the projection?" Bethany asked when she reached the bottom.

"I'm curious to hear what you think," Finalia said. "It's supposed to be written for your age group, or whatever that translates to in Grenouthian grade levels."

"He seems to be suggesting that Grenouthians who want to understand humanity should read Shakespeare out loud, and if possible, stage the plays," Bethany said. "He suggests in the helpful hints that they use blunted practice swords and forgo fake blood. But didn't Shakespeare write these plays before electricity was invented?"

"Electricity was discovered, not invented, and Shakespeare lived before the Age of Enlightenment. The ambassador is suggesting that humanity hasn't advanced at all in half a millennium."

"But that's not true!"

"I'm not so sure," Finalia said. "It's been a while since I read Shakespeare myself, but there's a reason he's remembered. You probably know that the Grenouthians opened theme parks all over Earth for the alien tourist trade. They restore historical sites and hire local reenactors to portray life in the past. I always thought they were laughing at us, but maybe the Grenouthians respect what we managed before developing modern science and becoming obsessed with maximizing leisure time."

Bethany wrestled with the concept for a moment and tried applying one of her father's lessons about generalizing alien behavior from a single species. "Maybe the point is that we're so far behind in science and technology that the ambassadors don't see the need to mention it when trying to explain us to members of their own species."

"Let's see the rest of the essays and then go talk with your father," Finalia said. "Do you know how to tell the projector to send copies to our tabs?"

"I think so," Bethany said, removing the Grenouthian memory chit and picking a new one. "Do I just ask out loud?"

"You can, but then the station librarian bills us a cred for a special request. I'll show you how to do it manually when we're done."

"A cred? Just for sending a couple of files? Libby?"

"Are you making a file transfer request?" the station librarian responded immediately.

"No," Finalia said sharply. "Bethany was just asking."

"Is this related to your school work?"

"I might write a paper about Shakespeare," Bethany hedged.

"If you want me to transfer the Grenouthian ambassador's chapter to your student tab, there will be no charge," Libby said.

"Maybe later," Bethany said, wilting a little in her chair. She inserted the next memory chit and read off the holographic projection, "Human Foods Worth Tasting. Ambassador Bork, Drazen Empire."

"I hope he isn't going to replicate the forward he wrote for the Drazen section of the *All Species Cookbook,*" Finalia said as she began to read. "Hmm. He seems to have enjoyed himself at the New Worlds Fair."

"My mom says that Ambassador Bork stops in the new office of the *All Species Cookbook* as often as the Gem ambassador, though she shows up for dessert tastings and he never misses barbeque."

"They hold barbeques in their office?"

"There's a sort of fume hood that comes down from the ceiling," Bethany replied while skimming the text. "He knows a lot about chili peppers. I'm turning red and starting to sweat just thinking about them."

"You got that from your father," Finalia said. "Our former food editor brought a spicey soup to our last potluck and told him that it wasn't hot."

"Dad fired him?"

"Her, and she quit a few months later to open a restaurant. I wonder if the ambassador drew the illustrations himself."

"They look awfully familiar," Bethany said, squinting at the holographic projection even though her vision was excellent. "I know where I saw them. Mom brought home a Drazen Foods catalog the other day."

Finalia huffed out a deep breath. "I don't want to be the one to accuse the Drazen ambassador of plagiarizing. Maybe he got permission."

Two pages later, Bethany ventured, "It's not as well written as the other chapters we've seen. He's repeated that line about the best way to a Human's heart being through the stomach three times already."

"Four, but there's a sort of rhythm to it, so he may be using the line as a mantra. I've been to Drazen poetry performances and repeating a line central to the theme is quite common."

"But is the chapter about the food we eat or the foods he thinks Drazens will like?"

"The latter, I think," Finalia said. "The title was something like 'Earth Food Worth Trying.' What I don't understand is the emphasis on price. The aliens I've interviewed about their travels to Earth always say that everything is cheap."

Bethany hesitated for a moment, and then she said in an uncertain voice, "I think the prices might be from the Drazen Foods catalog too."

"Skip to end," the editor instructed the projector. "Maybe he gave credit to—there."

"Special thanks to my old friend Glunk, the founder and principal stakeholder of Drazen Foods, for allowing me to use facts from their eponymous catalog, and for providing samples of current products," Bethany read. "What does eponymous mean?"

"It's an adjective expressing 'of the same name' though I wouldn't have used it in this situation myself. And thank you for not knowing. It gives me an excuse to open a conversation with the ambassador and maybe I can talk him into dropping the prices."

The next chapter was by the Verlock ambassador, who started with the mathematical discoveries of the ancient Greeks and presented several geometrical proofs complete with illustrations. He gave half a page to the development of calculus, quoting Bishop Berkley's line about "ghosts of departed quantities," and then laid out a comprehensive program by which Verlocks who felt the call to assist a primitive species could find ample volunteering opportunities on Earth teaching math to the needy.

"There's another one?" Finalia asked in surprise after the Fillinduck ambassador's chapter. "I thought we already reviewed all eight of the submissions."

Bethany placed the memory chit in the data slot. The projected text began, "Humans For Aliens. A Forward by Ambassador Kelly McAllister, EarthCent."

"She's not one of the authors," Finalia said with a frown. "I wonder if your father or Chastity asked her for a Forward and forgot to tell me."

"My colleagues asked me to write a Forward to *Humans for Aliens* in case any humans purchase the book and wonder at the choice of subject matter," Bethany read out loud. "I want to assure human readers that the ambassadors of the advanced species took their task very seriously and chose subjects in which they have first-hand knowledge and experience. It can be difficult for aliens to empathize with some of humanity's self-inflicted problems, but I believe that the ambassadors have all succeeded in putting a human face on humanity for their native audience."

"Look at the helpful hint in the margin," Finalia said.

"When translated into alien languages, the idiom 'human face' will appear as 'Vergallian face, Drazen face, etcetera,'" Bethany skimmed forward a bit and asked, "Do you want me to continue reading this out loud?"

"I already finished it, unless there's another page," Finalia said. "Let's go see your father, and he can decide whether or not we need to ping Chastity."

Walter was just returning from EarthCent Intelligence where he'd attended a meeting with Thomas and Wrylenth which left his head spinning. He intercepted Finalia and his daughter in the reception area and ushered them into his office.

"Are you okay, Dad?" Bethany asked. "You look upset about something."

"I just learned that entertainment companies on Earth have been stealing the work of artificial intelligences for over a century," Walter said angrily. "If Thomas, Chance, or any of the other artificial people we know wrote a novel or a screenplay, anybody on Earth could produce it without paying them a cred or acknowledging their authorship."

"But why?"

"Wrylenth explained that in the early days of artificial intelligence development on Earth, before any of the machines achieved sentience, everybody involved in the arts, from writers and actors to musicians and mimes, was concerned about losing rights to their creations, including holograms of themselves. They managed to narrow the definition of copyright so it didn't apply to any work created by artificial intelligence based on the assumption that artificial intelligence couldn't *create* anything, only imitate and extrapolate."

"Which is how most human novelists I've read operate," Finalia interjected.

"Exactly," Walter said. "All creators stand on the shoulders of the artists who proceeded them, but the decision was made that artificial intelligence wouldn't be afforded that right. Where else did they think the machines would learn? Artificial intelligence was already contributing new insights into the sciences when the Stryx opened Earth, and for all we know, that may have been one of the triggers that got us connected to the tunnel network. But the idiots back home never updated the copyright laws and don't want to be bothered."

"Is the Galactic Free Press going to take a public stand?" Bethany asked.

"I think so. If anything, Chastity was even madder than I was. She went directly for a swim after the meeting to cool down." As he took the seat behind his desk, it finally registered that Finalia and Bethany had come to see him about the book. "Did the ambassadors decide not to submit their chapters after all?"

"They arrived on time, including an unsolicited forward from Ambassador McAllister, which she wrote at the behest of her colleagues," Finalia said. "I have to admit that none of them need editing in the normal sense of the word, though Ambassador Bork went a little over the top in promoting the Drazen Foods catalog."

"He's friends with Glunk," Walter said. "You know how aliens are."

"I do now. I haven't read all the chapters word-for-word, but I can say without hesitation that the ambassadors wrote for their native audiences and the result will make little sense to humans."

Walter tapped a pencil on his desk and glanced at his daughter to see if she had anything to add, but Bethany remained silent. "I'll have to read the chapters myself, but it sounds like you're saying that publishing with a parallel English translation may be pointless."

"Unless your idea is to create a Rosetta stone for English, and I can think of better candidates for translation in that case," Finalia said.

Eighteen

Henry pulled up on the handlebars, leaned back, and popped a wheelie. He continued pedaling and tried to maintain his balance, but a few seconds later the front wheel dropped back down with a thud. The ten-year-old kid riding alongside him who had sustained a wheelie since the last intersection casually held out a hand. Henry dug in his pouch and brought out a Dibel which he flipped into the air. The kid swerved to catch the coin and then peeled off down an alley, all while keeping the front wheel of his bike off the ground.

"Showoff," Henry grunted, then braked hard to avoid a floater delivery van that dropped out of the sky without warning. "Get a license," he shouted as the alien driver stepped out without checking traffic.

The driver made a rude gesture with a secondary limb that required no interpretation.

"Just saw a new type of alien," Henry dictated to his wrist as he rode. "Reminded me a little of a Dollnick, except the lower set of arms is replaced by something between a flipper and a tentacle. And half of its face was hidden by hair, which might explain why it can't drive worth a—Watch it!" he interrupted himself as another bicycle messenger cut in front of him. Then he saw the dark green hair vines peeking out from under the helmet and started pedaling furiously in pursuit. "Gzinka. Wait up."

The Frunge female who sometimes ran messages for Henry's primary employer pretended not to hear him and continued at top speed. Despite being in the best shape of his life after four months of spending half of his waking hours on a bicycle, Henry couldn't close the gap and was breathing hard when she skidded to a halt in front of the Riverboat Club.

"Oh, Henry," Gzinka said with a mysterious smile that always left him feeling that he was missing something in her meaning despite his high-quality implant. She removed her helmet and asked, "Where did you come from?"

"Earth," he replied, mainly to keep the syllable count down until his breathing could return to normal. "Delivery?"

"If you're asking whether I'm working, I'm not, and if you're making a pass at me, I don't go in for any of that kinky interspecies stuff."

Henry reddened as her hair vines rustled with suppressed laughter. "I was looking for you," he said. "I delivered a package to the Frunge armorer with the forge near the dam, the one with the giant drop hammers. He looked so angry that I was afraid he was going to pick up one of his broadswords and cut me in two."

"You want to pick my brain for confidential cultural information," Gzinka surmised. "That will cost you a drink."

Henry checked his wrist comm to make sure no new jobs had come in, then stood his bike in the rack next to her custom-made messenger model, which featured large saddle bags and an overdrive sprocket that could generate ridiculous speeds for riders with the muscle power and stamina. While she waited for him, the Frunge pulled a quick-trellis out of her seemingly bottomless purse and captured her hair vines in an updo without taking the time to weave them.

"Women on Earth would kill to be able to do their hair that fast," Henry said, struck by the transformation in her appearance. "You just went from grungy messenger girl to elegant club lady."

Gzinka's hair vines flushed dark green with chlorophyll. "Cultural lesson Number Seventeen," she announced sternly, despite the twinkle in her eye. "Complementing an unmarried female Frunge on her appearance is a good way to get your head stove in by the blacksmith in her family."

"What if she doesn't have a blacksmith in the family?"

"Cultural lesson Number Eighteen. *ALL* Frunge have a blacksmith in the family."

The pair of bouncers at the door passed the two messengers without comment, and once inside they made their way to the bar, which was relatively empty due to the early hour. Henry paid an exorbitant amount for Gzinka's drink, which took the L'meuf bartender several minutes to make. He drained his free water before ordering himself an iced can of the tomato juice drink that was manufactured locally.

"The delivery was some sort of machined gear which I could see through the plastic wrapping," Henry said, returning to his original question and ticking off items on his fingers. "No paper, no grains, there weren't any female Frunge in the area for me to accidentally look at and cause offense. I didn't stand around waiting for a tip or anything.

I just checked his identity, handed him the package, and got back on my bike."

"Did this all happen inside the gate posts of the smithy?" Gzinka asked.

Henry thought for a moment. "I don't remember seeing any gate posts, unless you're talking about the pair of poles with the string tied across the top where you turn off the main road."

"Those are temporary gates. A Frunge blacksmith will always create showpiece gates, usually wrought iron with fancy filagree work in precious metals, but it's considered pretentious to do so before a business is established and proven. The poles and the string are erected where the finished gate will eventually stand."

"You're saying that I rode my bicycle into the smithy proper and that's an insult. But I remember seeing those trip hammers from a distance the first week I was on the planet. How long does it take for a business to be considered established?"

Gzinka took a long sip from her multi-layered drink and regarded Henry over the brim of the goblet. "How old did you say you were?"

"Twenty-eight. Old enough that you can tell me the facts of business."

"But not old enough to have created an established business, even if you began working while you were still in diapers. A Frunge business isn't considered a going concern until it's been running at a profit for over five decades, say, twice your age." She took another sip, and amended her statement, "Except for restaurants, which come and go. A restaurant is doing well if it can keep the doors open for seven years without a change in ownership."

"If they sell drinks priced like the one you just ordered, I imagine the original owners can retire after five years."

"Don't be *that* Human," Gzinka said, and then held her drink up to the light, studying the layers that remained in suspension. "I didn't think the L'meuf would know how to make it. He only started bartending here a couple of weeks ago, and there aren't that many Frunge who come here."

"There's a spider cooking at the Bronx Café who could open his own place in the New York city-state back on Earth and make a killing," Henry said. "I guess they're fast learners."

"They share what they know."

"A hive mind? If they're that high-powered, why isn't it the L'meuf Empire rather than the Farling Empire?"

Gzinka sipped off another layer of her drink and smacked her lips. "Do I look like an expert on the L'meuf? Ask him."

Henry looked over to where the bartender was standing on three legs, polishing two glasses, and possibly playing a game or sending a message on his personal communications device. "Excuse me?"

"I can't serve another drink until you finish the first," the spider replied through an external device that must have translated thoughts directly to speech. "House rules."

"I was just wondering—" he felt a movement beside him and noticed that Gzinka was sidling away, "—never mind."

"Good decision," the Frunge said after she returned to her place. "They spit acid, you know."

"I didn't, actually. Is there anything else you've neglected to tell me?"

"I don't know how the L'meuf share knowledge, but it's not a hive mind," Gzinka told him. "You owe me another drink."

"You have expensive tastes for a bicycle messenger," Henry groused, and then it struck him all at once that she was the only alien working in a business dominated by humans. "What did you say your last job was?"

"I didn't," she said, and surprised him with a conspiratorial wink that as much as said, 'You tell me yours and I'll tell you mine.'

Henry was on the verge of asking her straight out if she worked for the Frunge government when he saw a man with heavy facial tattoos enter the bar. They spotted each other at the same time, and the man immediately ducked out.

"Watch my drink, it does tricks," Henry said to Gzinka and then walked as rapidly as he could to the exit. The tattooed man was waiting for him outside.

"It wasn't me," the man said before Henry could open his mouth. "I don't want to spend the rest of my life looking over my shoulder, and I'm not a killer, so you have to believe that I wasn't the one who ratted you out."

"Then how do you know I was ratted out?"

"It was in my contract to watch you go after the item. I didn't know that our employers had already extracted what they needed and no longer required our services. All I got out of the job was the upfront payment, and I spent that on making my way home. Even with the tunnel open, it's not easy to get to this place."

"You live here?" Henry asked. "I thought from the tattoos that you were from the Free Republic."

"Call them pirates, that's what they are, and five years ago, I jumped on the chance to move here to get as far away from them as possible. I should have stuck with farming, I'm pretty good at it, but then a Farling who recognized me from back in the day made me an offer that was too good to turn down."

"I was working for the Farlings?"

"I don't think so," said the man who had hired Henry to break into QuickU. "The Farling I'm talking about only came up to my waist and I doubt he had two letters in his real name. He was a cut-out for someone, just like I was a cut-out man for him. I only met with him once after he approached me, to get the money and the tech that I passed to you and the other guys who I was instructed to contact."

"You met the Farling on Earth?" Henry asked.

"Here. At the labor exchange plaza, and that's all I know." He took a deep breath and looked straight into Henry's eyes. "Are we square? I had to travel as supercargo with an independent trader to get home and I almost died from dehydration after being sick in Zero-G for a week. I'm never going to space in a small ship again."

Henry nodded slowly. "I believe you, but I'd rather not run into you again."

"I'm going back to the human farming province tomorrow. I've been working in a warehouse since returning and I realized that I never should have left the farm. I was going to have a drink at the bar and put my savings on the wheel before boarding the maglev, but that was just another stupid idea. I'm off to catch the night train." He started to turn away and then offered Henry his hand. "I'm sorry I got you involved, and I'm glad you beat the rap."

"Beat it like a drum," Henry said, returning the handshake. Then he went back into the Riverboat Club and was almost surprised to find that Gzinka had waited for him.

"Who was your friend?" she asked bluntly.

"Just a guy I met on Earth."

"Who happened to be from here?"

"How did you know he was a local?" Henry asked, feeling the hair on the back of his neck stiffen. "With all those tattoos, he looks like a pirate."

Gzinka studied him over her drink as she drained the last layer. "Haven't you heard that looks can be deceiving? In some professions, it's an advantage."

"What are you getting at?"

"I was here the night that Robin brought you in and introduced you to Bluve. It's cute the way that you buy me drinks to try to get information to sell the Dollnick, but wouldn't it be more efficient if I buy the drinks, and you bring anything interesting you come across to me?"

It took Henry a few seconds to realize that he hadn't blown his cover. "You and Bluve are competitors in the same business."

"It's a friendly competition," Gzinka said. "We know each other from conferences."

"I didn't know that people in your profession attended conferences."

Gzinka let out a long sigh that sounded a bit like wind blowing through the fens. "Too many conferences. And I just know I'm going to get tapped to talk about Farling Four at the next one. What do you say?"

Henry gave her a wicked smile. "If I didn't know it would poison me, I'd have what you're having, but I guess I'll have to settle for another juice."

"So," Gzinka said after signaling to the bartender to come over when he had a moment. "About your friend who was hired a few months back by 2E, a low-rent

Farling who's known for his willingness to sell his intermediary services to the highest bidder."

"You just happened to see that too?"

"When I don't have anything else to do, I tail 2E just for practice. He must be the least perceptive two-letter Farling on the planet. Now tell me something to pay for your refill."

"As it happens, 2E hired that tattooed fellow to act as a middleman for some less-than-legal activities on Earth," Henry said, recalling Chance's offhand advice that the closer he stuck to the truth, the easier it would be to remember his story. "Tattoos hired me to, uh, facilitate a shortcut in the normal purchasing process. The job didn't proceed as planned. Tattoos and I both suspect that 2E was using us as the backup team and decided to cut bait after the varsity squad delivered."

Gzinka gave a knowing chuckle as if she'd just heard the oldest story in the galaxy. "Sucks to be you," she said.

"I can't get over how good this implant is with slang."

"Read my lips, Henry. I'm speaking Humanese."

Henry felt his jaw drop and snapped it shut. "You learned our language just to recruit me?"

The Frunge laughed out loud, and a few of her hair vines shook so much that they pulled free from the quick-trellis. "I learned Humanese because it's so easy. Half of the young professionals in our business must know it by now. Most of our employers require that we attain fluency in at least two alien languages before working in the field, and Humanese is the new gimme."

"I always thought that English was tough for foreigners because of all the irregular verbs."

"The whole language is irregular from our standpoint, but there isn't enough of it to matter," Gzinka said. "Did you know that your word 'set' has more than four hundred different meanings? What's the matter with you people? You couldn't have come up with a new word and split the difference?"

"Above my pay scale," Henry said. "And if I'm going to earn my keep, I better get back to work."

"Following up on what Tattoos told you? You haven't received any new jobs since you came in here."

"How do you know that?"

"I keep an eye on the spectrum," Gzinka told him. "If you don't come up with anything worth reporting, I can pay you to bring a story to Bluve."

"You want me to feed him false information?"

"True. False. Who can tell the difference? The galaxy isn't so black and white, my Human friend." She laid a finger along the side of her nose and added, "Follow the money."

"Follow the money," Henry repeated. He left the bar without waiting for his refill, made a quick circuit of the casino floor just to check for high rollers, then retrieved his bike from the rack and rode out in the direction of the labor exchange plaza. There were only a few hours of daylight remaining, and even the most die-hard jobseekers had given up and gone wherever the unemployed spent their time. He rode a lazy loop around the plaza, dictating to his wrist comm and trying to put together the pieces.

The ground floor spaces of the surrounding buildings were taken by retail shops or businesses offering services to job seekers, including several stores renting uniforms and professional garb. There were even a few one-room vocational schools, offering crash courses in various in-demand skills. Henry noted several beauty parlors in a row, and he had to smile when he saw a woman sitting under a hair dryer next to a Frunge sitting under a misting machine for hair vines. There was even a storefront where the spiders had their hairy bodies fluffed and dried while watching whatever passed for entertainment with them on personal holographic projections.

Henry jammed on the brakes and skidded to a halt just past the L'meuf beauty parlor. Could the short Farling he'd seen at the back be 2E? It seemed too much of a coincidence, yet what would he have thought a few hours earlier about the chances of ever encountering the tattooed man, even if he'd known they were on the same planet? He rode back around to the other side of the plaza and pulled up the text of *Implants for Humans* on his heads-up display. Five minutes later, he sat down at one of the stone tables for board games, propped his chin on both hands, and activated the implant's telephoto mode.

A spider was just entering the beauty parlor through the low door, and Henry watched as it did some sort of complicated limb-slapping greeting with the proprietor, at one point involving six of their legs. Then the customer climbed onto one of the webbed chairs, positioned the conical grooming unit over the bump that passed for a head on top of its disk-shaped torso, and activated the personal holographic screen, which appeared backward to Henry since he was seeing it from the opposite side. EarthCent Intelligence's first true covert operator tapped his wrist comm and began to describe what he was seeing.

"A sword, no, it's a large knife, and something is using it to chop up—carrots?" At the risk of getting motion sick, Henry accessed the control slider for the zoom and pulled back until he could confirm that he was indeed looking into the right storefront, then zoomed in again. "It's definitely a carrot, and now I can see the hand holding the knife. Must be a Dollnick, because another right hand that looks just like the one with the knife is scraping the carrots into the bowl and handing them to a human guy. Wait, a commercial just started, and—are they selling maggots?"

He looked away from the squirming larvae and noticed a faint sheen, almost like the Northern Lights, playing in the space between the styling device and the spider's head. He gambled on switching back to *Implants for Humans* again and read how to change the view from the visual spectrum to radio wavelengths, which according to the helpful hint, was a good way to check for leakage from a microwave oven or find a lost smartphone. The resulting image looked like a waterfall of bright light. He did an image capture, zoomed again, and saw that the brilliant white was a patchwork of pinpoints of light spaced by random—or was it data? He recorded several more samples before a message flashed across his vision that he was nearing ninety percent of his implant's storage capacity, at which point he switched back to the visual spectrum just as the holographic projection the alien was watching returned from another commercial break.

"*Stone Soup*?" he read off the backdrop of the set. "Why would a spider be watching a show about..." a chill ran down his spine and he let his eyes move back to the customer. The spider's jerking limbs reminded him of a dreaming dog until he realized that the L'meuf was dicing vegetables in pantomime. He zoomed out just enough to be able to move his head a little to see further into the shop. The next personal holographic projection he saw from the wrong side was showing a poker tournament. A quick look at the viewer showed the spider's limbs dealing imaginary cards.

Henry hesitated and began reviewing the protocols Thomas and Chance had explained for emergency extraction should he stumble upon information that he believed was worth risking his cover. "Four months with nothing, and now this," he mumbled to himself. "When it rains, it pours." He reflexively checked the sky as he spoke and saw that the planet's rotation had brought the tunnel back in sight and a large ship was just coming through. "The Miklat!" Henry exclaimed, taking the old colony ship's appearance as a sign. He got back on his bike and pedaled furiously toward his rooming house to collect his belongings.

Nineteen

"Doctor's orders," Chastity explained to Chance in the dance studio's dressing room. "Marcus set the maximum heel height for all of my SBJ Fashions tango shoes to seven."

"Seven centimeters?" the artificial person asked as she swapped her tango shoes for sneakers.

"Seven out of ten. There's a limiter in the menu and he locked it out. I think Marcus asked Jeeves for help because he didn't have my password."

"It doesn't seem fair," Chance commiserated. "You're the owner of the largest English language newspaper in history and you can't make your own decisions about the height of your heels."

Chastity sighed. "It's not worth getting divorced over, and I guess I was limping around with sprained ankles a bit more often than makes sense for a woman my age. Does Thomas ever try to interfere with your choices?"

"Every day, but he can't help it. It's just his core personality."

"I don't know how the two of you do it," Chastity said, slipping her tango dress onto a hanger and reaching for the Frunge business suit she'd picked up at a boutique that morning. "With all the personality upgrade testing the two of you do for QuickU it must be like living with a stranger every other day."

Chance laughed as she pulled on her ripped blue jeans. "The personality upgrades don't turn us into strangers. It's more like if you came home and found out that Marcus had a new hobby and it turned out that he was a natural. Take sewing. Dorothy always made fun of me because I couldn't run a straight line of stitches to save my life, even with a machine. I tested the combined seamstress and fashion designer personality upgrade from QuickU, practiced for a few days, and took the SBJ Fashions contractor test in disguise. I got their highest score ever, and Dorothy wanted to hire me as her assistant."

"You weren't interested?"

"I already have a job, and besides, I love shopping for clothes. Thomas would nag me about spending most of my income on fashion if I could do it all myself, and then he'd want me to make his clothes as well."

Chastity started to reply and broke off to point at her ear to indicate an incoming ping. The conversation went on for almost a minute, her throat barely moving as she subvocalized her replies, and then she said out loud, "Drat."

"Anything I can help with?" Chance asked as she tied the laces of her retro basketball sneakers that would cause Thomas to suffer an electrical breakdown if he ever found out how much she'd paid for them.

"The Grenouthians just scooped us again. The Vergallian princesses who recently started arriving on Earth at the request of the Ladies in Waiting are holding a conference to set their priorities for the coming year. How can the bunnies have better news sources than we do on our own planet?"

"That question has come up at EarthCent Intelligence. Our analysts think that the Grenouthians create a lot of goodwill with the historical theme parks they run all over the world, both for helping preserve historical buildings and practices, and for employing millions of people as reenactors. Those millions of people have family and friends, and then there's also the possibility that the alien intelligence agencies are pooling their information on Earth like they do on Flower."

"I've always suspected that the Grenouthian News has a direct pipeline from their intelligence service, but I can hardly complain when we share a conference room with EarthCent Intelligence."

"Whose director is your brother-in-law," Chance added as she straightened up. "Did the Grenouthian story say anything about the priorities the princesses are focused on?"

"It was mainly humorous speculation, like starting a surveillance program to increase handwashing among doctors and restaurant staff," Chastity said. "They did mention the princesses will try to get all the legacy countries and city-states to agree to update intellectual property laws. I'd be in favor of replacing Earth's copyright law with the tunnel network version, which is an average of what all the member species have settled on. The same for patents and trademarks."

"Thomas would be in favor of that," Chance said. "He wrote a book that he didn't bother publishing because as an artificial person, he couldn't assert copyright on Earth." She grabbed her five-feather Baa's Bag from the shelf, then realized it belonged to her friend. "Hey, twins," she said, holding the two purses side by side.

"I'm going to have a word with Baa. She told me that my purse was one of a kind."

"When did you buy it?"

The publisher of the Galactic Free Press slid on her loafers while searching her memory. "Was it last year, or the year before?"

"I bought mine two months ago after I donated a few older ones to the embassy's charity sale," Chance said. "Yours was probably unique when you bought it."

Thomas and Marcus were both long gone when their dance partners emerged from the changing room. Chastity reflexively checked the time on her heads-up display and realized that she'd been talking with her friend for almost twenty minutes. "Back to the grind," she groaned. "See you next Tuesday morning? Marcus found some old Argentinian Tango albums on vinyl in the Shuk so he sent his antique turntable out for repair. It should be back by then."

"We'll be there," the artificial person answered for herself and her partner.

At the very moment that his wife was making commitments on his behalf, Thomas was doing his best to convince Jonah to consider making a long-term commitment of his own.

"Can you see yourself hosting *Stone Soup* in another twenty years, or another forty?" Thomas asked. "You'll run out of recipes long before then."

"There's no such thing as running out of recipes, and we have all of the alien tribute dishes from human communities on open worlds," Jonah said, but it was clear that he was wavering. "And I'm not worried that I'll end up working for Viv and Samuel if everything goes ahead with the Human Empire taking over from EarthCent. I just don't think I have an aptitude for intelligence work."

"Thanks to your training under Tinka at InstaSitter, you had more experience managing an interstellar business with millions of part-time employees by the time you were twenty than all but a handful of humans in the galaxy," Thomas pressed his point. "Even though we're working toward becoming a more traditional intelligence agency, the job for the foreseeable future will be maintaining and expanding our subscription database for business information, and most importantly, building on our relations with other intelligence agencies."

"What about you? You've been with EarthCent Intelligence longer than anyone, and everybody knows you're going to take over from my dad. Why should you give up the director slot to me in twenty years? I thought the advanced species prized continuity above almost everything when it comes to cross-species cooperation."

"You won't be angry if I tell you?" Thomas asked, suddenly sounding a little tired.

"Of course not," Jonah said. "I just want to know the truth."

"The advanced species don't discriminate against artificial intelligence, but they try to avoid relying on it overmuch. They feel the same about artificial people, which is why there are so few of us in most cultures."

"But all of the colony ships and orbitals are controlled by artificial intelligence, not to mention the tunnels, the Stryx stations, and every warship I've ever heard of."

"Which is just another reason for us not to hog the top roles where biologicals are competitive," Thomas said. "The reason artificial intelligences far more capable than myself ended up in all of the roles you just mentioned is that they can make decisions and take the necessary actions faster than any biological in the same role could act."

"But this is a job that you've been preparing for your whole career," Jonah pointed out. "Can't the aliens cut us a little slack?"

"They already do. It's a bit like the aversion that all the advanced species have toward the Gem for being clones. The advanced species don't agree about much, but cloning is held in universal disdain. Employing artificial intelligence in government roles is a little less controversial. The Sharf are a good example of a species that doesn't differentiate between biologicals and artificial intelligence for most jobs, but they aren't even members of the tunnel network."

"You'll have to give me time to talk it over with Sephia and think about whether I can give up the show when my contract ends. There might have been something in the small print that allows the Grenouthian network to replace me with a hologram under some circumstances."

Thomas leaned back, considering the battle more than half won. "You don't have to leave the show altogether," he said. "Didn't you say that the Grenouthians are looking into doing mini-seasons on open worlds with human populations so you could survey alien-inspired cuisine? There's no better cover in the intelligence business than traveling as a performing artist."

"You don't think the Grenouthians would catch on?"

"The Grenouthian agents embedded in your crew will be too busy recruiting their own local sources to care what you're doing. Working as support staff for a performing artist is also excellent cover for an intelligence agent in the field."

Jonah rose and topped off his coffee from the machine that his aunt had installed in the shared conference room. "Since we're having the meeting here and our electronic security leaves much to be desired, I'm going to assume that you don't have a problem with the other species finding out that you're pitching me to take over at some point."

"Knowing that I plan to hand the reins over to you when you're ready will make it easier for them to work with me when I take over from your father," Thomas said and then frowned. "I wonder what's keeping him."

"Dad *is* kind of late," Jonah said. "It's a good thing there aren't any aliens waiting." He took a sip from his coffee and walked over to the holographic projection system, where he slid in a reusable Horten holo-memory. "Maybe we should just get started. I know that Dad isn't interested in LARPing. He only suffers through it because it's part of the gambling security contract."

"Gentlemen," the station librarian's voice came over the room's audio system. "Director Oxford has asked me to inform you that he won't be available, and he requested that Thomas meet him for lunch."

The artificial person rose from his seat and gave Jonah a significant look. "It's almost lunchtime and I don't want to make your father wait. Let's plan on doing this another time."

Jonah retrieved the Horten memory he'd just slotted into the projector and followed a few steps behind Thomas until they reached the nearest lift tube bank. He heard the artificial person request Mac's Bones before the door slid closed.

When Thomas climbed up the ladder to the bridge of the waiting Sharf two-man trader in the Tunnel Trips lot, he wasn't surprised to see John sitting in one of the command chairs, because he'd spotted the senior agent's Grenouthian four-decker parked in the camping area for independent traders. But he did a double take on seeing that the other command chair was occupied by Henry, the agent he'd recruited on Earth and sent to Farling Four.

"Ready," John said, and the ship lifted off under the control of the Stryx station's owner, who used manipulator fields to send it through the bay doors and out into the core. "We may as well wait until we're clear since we've gone to this much trouble," he added.

"This is the first time Clive has invited me to a lunch," Thomas made air quotes around the word, "that he hasn't attended himself."

John held up both hands and then began folding fingers down one at a time, curling his right thumb into his palm just as the rental ship flew clear of Union Station.

"I know these precautions are likely futile, but I thought I'd go through the motions for Henry so he can see how it should be done," John said. "Joe acted as the cut-out, carrying my message to Clive, and Clive decided to stay with our original idea of limiting contact for Henry to you, me, and Chance."

"Did you ping Chance?" Thomas asked.

"Yes, but she said you could fill her in later using a secure infrared link under a thermal blanket."

Thomas nodded, the built-in magnetic cleats in his feet holding him firmly to the deck as the ship went into a tight spiral around the station to produce weight for the travelers. From the look of relief on Henry's face, the maneuver was highly appreciated.

"Let me fill you in on my part of the story and then Henry can tell you why he pulled the fire alarm," John said. "I had just brought Ellen back to Earth to meet with her news syndicate when the ship's controller spit out a tunneling network telegram from the Miklat telling me that my package was ready for pickup. The next rendezvous opportunity with the Miklat was at Long Trench, the Drazen mining world that's less than two days in a tunnel from Earth. I left Semmi and the kids with Ellen since we'd just got there and popped through to meet the Miklat. I was expecting to find an envelope with some holo-memories or hand-written notes waiting for me, but Henry thought that his news was important enough that he'd better make sure it was delivered by coming in person."

"You didn't have a code phrase to cover the situation?" Thomas asked.

"I used the wrong one," Henry spoke up. "I was supposed to tell John that his cargo was ready for pickup if I was requesting extraction. Cargo versus package—I chose the wrong word."

"I would have come directly in either case because of the timing, so no harm done," John said. "I met with Henry on the Miklat and he passed me a handwritten note explaining the bare bones of what he'd learned, which is what decided me to bring him directly here. On my way back to the ship, Co-captain Zerakova's husband, Drake, pulled me aside for a little chat. It seems that he'd spotted Henry as somebody operating outside the system and wanted to make sure that I knew."

"Did you tell him that Henry is working for us?"

"Not in so many words, but Drake is a sharp guy. I'm sure he figured it out for himself."

Thomas waited a moment to make sure that John was finished with his story, then turned to the undercover agent. "You must have made the right decision calling for extraction or John wouldn't have spent another three days in the tunnel bringing you here. What did you learn?"

Henry took a deep breath and launched into the summary of facts as he'd arranged them in his head. "There are more than twenty million humans living on Farling Four and the largest concentration is in Humantown. The place is growing so rapidly that there are always jobs going begging for workers, especially skilled positions. Right around when I got there, those job openings started filling up with members of the L'meuf species, sort of giant hairy spiders. And the thing is, they were all good at their jobs, better than the average professional. I think everybody just assumed that the spiders had learned the skills working with humans in the rural areas, though I also heard of a few setting up as chiropractors and dentists."

"Not the sort of skills that small groups of human ag workers would have been likely to pass on to an alien species they'd never encountered before."

"That's what I thought. And then I ran into the cut-out man who hired me for the QuickU job where John caught me," Henry said. "He claimed to have come out of the deal in worse shape than I did and spilled the beans about his employer, a local two-letter Farling who's basically a street hustler. The cut-out told me where he'd met 2E to get the money and kit, and on a hunch, I rode by to see if anything jumped out at me. Lady luck must have thought she owed me for leaving a casino without placing a bet because I saw 2E meeting with a spider in an employment agency, which I initially thought was a L'meuf beauty parlor."

"This is starting to sound like either a case study for field work or an example of why field agents require training," Thomas said. "Go on."

"I parked across the plaza and used my implant's zoom to try to see what the Farling was doing with the spiders. 2E was already gone, but then it struck me that all the L'meuf who I thought were there to get their hair fluffed were watching how-to holograms for skilled work. Then I switched from visible light to radio frequency, and what I assumed were hairdryers were some kind of teaching device. I saved images of the data stream, but I haven't downloaded them from my implant yet because I don't have anything to put them on."

Thomas looked back to John, who nodded that he believed Henry was being straight with them. "Do you think anybody figured out who you were and will notice your absence?" the deputy director of EarthCent Intelligence asked.

Henry made a face. "There's a Dollnick intelligence agent who thinks I'm on retainer with him because I couldn't figure out a way to say 'no' and maintain my cover. And a Frunge who worked for the messenger service where I was employed pulled me aside right before I ran into the cut-out man from the Earth. She wanted to hire me away from the Dollnick or pay me to pass him misinformation. I didn't give it much thought at the time, but while I was on the Miklat waiting for John to come, it occurred to me that the Dollnick and the Frunge might have both been playing dumb."

"What do you think, John?" Thomas asked.

"About the aliens being on to Henry, or about the L'meuf combining personality upgrades from QuickU with the deep learning technology he described to teach professional skills to job seekers?"

"Both."

John shrugged. "I never believed we'd have much chance keeping undercover agents a secret from the intelligence agencies of the other species. On a world like Farling Four where half of the sentients walking or crawling around are probably on retainer to one spy agency or another, the chance of Henry working there without one of the alien agents getting suspicious was approaching zero. But maybe by agreeing to work for a couple of them, he bought some time."

"Do you want to send me back?" Henry asked. "It was an interesting place, but I had the feeling that most of what was going on there was so far over my head that the aliens could have discussed their secret plans with me sitting at the table and I wouldn't have noticed. And the Dollnick wasn't the only alien intelligence agent in Humantown who wasn't hiding anything. Verlock Intelligence has a storefront where they sell educational math puzzles and buy information, and somebody told me that the Astria's Academy of Dance franchises are a front for the Vergallians."

"They always are," Thomas said. "I wonder how well Vergallian Ballroom will translate to the species of the Farling Empire when most of them aren't humanoid."

"The Oosh have short legs but they're more graceful than you would think."

"What I don't get is why the L'meuf went to the trouble of hiring Henry to break into QuickU to steal the chef personality upgrade while it was still in development," John said. "I can't imagine there are that many job openings for spiders who want to cook human food in the Farling Empire, and I've never come across a L'meuf on the tunnel network."

"We know they have some form of group telepathy, and that's often a sign of a species where individuals don't function well on their own," Thomas said. "But if human food is the lowest common denominator in the Farling Empire as well, it could be that the L'meuf plan to open Earth-style restaurants for other aliens, or even for themselves. I'll check and see how well the *All Species Cookbook* sells in their space."

"How about the other skills the spiders are learning?" Henry asked. "I saw another one in the same employment agency who was cramming to be a dealer or a casino gambler, and there was a L'meuf bartender at the casino who could mix any tunnel network drink, including all the alien ones. I went by the employment agency a final time on my way to catch the shuttle up to the Miklat and shot an image of the pricelist that was posted in the window. My implant couldn't translate the text, maybe there just isn't enough demand for the L'meuf language yet, but it looked like they were offering around a couple hundred different skills."

"If they're getting them all from QuickU, that would be the whole catalog," Thomas said. "I can copy the files directly from your implant if you navigate to the security menu and temporarily set your storage to open access. If you don't want to do that, I won't think any less of you."

"I'm game," Henry said and invoked his heads-up display menu. "Hey. Is there any chance we could run this thing backward and I could learn new skills from QuickU like a spider or an artificial person?"

"If any of the advanced species have figured out speed learning, they've kept it quiet to protect their education industries. The idea of a biological species using QuickU personality upgrades this way never would have occurred to me, and it could turn out that the L'meuf's ability is a rare thing."

Thomas stopped talking to focus on the storage capacity of Henry's implant when it became available and downloaded the image captures to his own, much larger, storage area.

“I just got a ‘transfer complete’ message, but I still see the images in my storage,” Henry said a few seconds later.

“You’ll have to delete them manually. The memory is protected from outside alterations, and you should wait a couple of days until I give you the word,” Thomas said. “Are you staying on Union Station, John?”

“I have to get back to Earth or Ellen and the kids will start to worry about me,” John said. “I can bring Henry along if we want to keep him off the radar on Union Station for now.”

“Keep him away from Myort or he’s as good as blown.”

Twenty

"—and it's at the printer," Bethany concluded her brief history of *Humans for Aliens*. "Roland said he didn't have any work for me this afternoon, so if you aren't doing anything sensitive, I can shadow you."

Bob Steelforth was about to suggest that she check with the Freelance Desk editor again because a major investigative piece from the syndicated reporters on Earth had just come in and would need extensive cross-checking. Then he remembered that the subject was sex traffickers posing as marriage brokers for contract workers on alien worlds and understood why Roland turned Bethany away.

"You can shadow me, but it may be dull going," Bob told her. "I'm covering the Gambling Commission meeting and the discussions tend to be heavy on math and light on explanations. And it may go on right through the night."

"I have a four-hour limit," Bethany said. "Would it be okay if I leave early?"

"Nobody will even notice. You caught me just in time because the meeting starts in ten minutes and I was about to get going."

Bethany checked that she had her reporter's tab in her shoulder bag as she followed the senior journalist responsible for Union Station news to the lift tube. "What's the difference between a committee and a commission?" she asked.

"For our purposes, the biggest difference between committees and commissions is that reporters are always allowed at commissions," Bob said. "A consul can hold a seat on a committee, it may even be mandatory, but commission seats are limited to ambassadors, though temporary substitutes are allowed by consensus."

"They meet in an auditorium and there's an area set aside for the press?"

"Off-world gambling parlor," Bob instructed the lift tube. "I'm often the only press member to attend these commission things. Journalists from the advanced species can all get the meeting transcripts from their respective embassies since the commissions are a matter of public record."

"Will Ambassador McAllister be there?" Bethany asked.

"Associate Ambassador Daniel Cohan holds EarthCent's seat. The first meeting took place while Ambassador McAllister was on Earth filling in for EarthCent's president, and I suspect that the aliens planned it that way. We'll sit behind him."

"Does the commission meet at different embassies, like committees?"

"The Thark Ambassador is the chair, and he holds all the meetings in the off-world betting parlor that doubles as his embassy," Bob told her. "The Tharks are the tunnel network's experts on bookmaking and insurance underwriting, which are functionally the same thing. If a technical question comes up at a meeting, the members can always place bets and see how it works."

"What does making books have to do with insurance?" Bethany asked.

"Not making books, making book. It's gambling talk for accepting and laying off bets on different outcomes for events, primarily sporting, but the Tharks will make book on anything. You can even bet on when and if the Human Empire will take over from EarthCent." The capsule doors slid open, and he started leading the way toward the off-world betting parlor before he remembered again that his shadow was still attending Libby's experimental school. "I meant you could bet on the Human Empire if you were older."

"Do the Tharks have a minimum age for gambling?"

Bob made an odd sound, almost as if he was choking. "Not exactly," he said finally. "The Tharks give their children an allowance for gambling to teach them about probabilities and risk management." A figure waved to them from the entrance, and he added, "Looks like Consul Ofer is filling in for the associate ambassador."

Ofer was a regular at *All Species Cookbook* tastings, so he knew Bethany and insisted on introducing her to the Thark ambassador before the meeting began. They found the commission chair pushing together tables in preparation.

"Shadowing Journalist Steelforth," the Thark ambassador said to the girl after the introductions were made. "An excellent choice, though you won't learn much about gambling from him. If you want a little practical experience, take these."

"I'm focused on the reporting process for now," Bethany told him, politely turning down the alien's offer of a stack of chips. "I already learned so much about gambling from your chapter in *Humans for Aliens*."

"It was a pleasure to write. Humans haven't been around long, but you have a certain genius for cheating at games of chance that required adjustments to several of our models."

The other ambassadors all arrived in a bunch, most of them holding plastic betting slips that they had just purchased at the windows, and the next hour was taken up reviewing the minutes from the last meeting with frequent breaks to watch the results of races on the big board. Bethany noticed that most of the ambassadors threw their betting slips on the floor after the races.

"We're all caught up," the Thark ambassador announced casually when Ofer, acting in Daniel's place as the commission's secretary, finished reading excerpts from the previous meeting's minutes according to some system that Bethany couldn't work out. "Is there any new business, or shall we dig into the LARPing mess again?"

"I see young Dunkirk is shadowing Journalist Steelforth," the Drazen Ambassador said. "Would I be out of order to ask if she has any information on when *Humans for Aliens* will be released?"

Bethany blushed as all the alien ambassadors turned toward her. "I'm not sure if I'm allowed to say."

"Don't browbeat her, Bork," Ambassador Crute whistled. "We all know that your chapter was a puff piece for Drazen Foods."

"As opposed to the not-so-subtle sales pitch for Dollnick engineering services in your chapter," Bork retorted.

"I liked both of your chapters," Bethany said, trying to play peacemaker. "The book didn't turn out quite like we expected, but it makes sense that you know better than us what the members of your species want to learn about humans."

"My chapter was about what we want Humans to learn for themselves," the Verlock ambassador said ponderously.

"Now, now, Srythlan," the Grenouthian ambassador said. "Didn't I recognize the names of some of those educational math puzzles you referred to? Isn't your family in the business?"

While Bethany was trying to shrink as small as possible in her chair, Jonah was responding to a similar question while waiting for the beginning of a meeting of junior intelligence agents assigned to LARPing league security.

"Yes, my father is the director of EarthCent Intelligence, and yes, my mother provided the initial funding, but it doesn't make it my inheritance."

"If your mother financed the intelligence agency, then it belongs to your family," Whiskers said. "How could it be otherwise?"

"It's a government agency, not a business."

"If I was you, I would seek legal advice, because what you're telling me doesn't make sense."

Jonah showed both his palms in the Grenouthian gesture of not wanting to argue, and then all the conversations in the room stopped as an angry-looking Dollnick strode in.

"If you think I'm happy to be back on the clock, I'm not," Lume exploded, his whistling speech so loud that it added hiss to the translation that Jonah heard through his implant's filtering. "Does anybody want to tell me why I'm here?"

"The league called you back?" Whiskers suggested.

"Two points for the Grenouthian. If my friend Dewey hadn't been coming to Union Station on Flower's business, I would have bought a first-class liner ticket and told the league to take it out of your contract payments. What were you thinking?"

"Could you be a little more specific?" Alinka asked, as poised as always despite her youth. "I thought we were making excellent progress."

"Yes, you passed the open auditions and have entered the league in your support role as an Elf dancer," Lume said. "Jonah is cooking up a storm at hatchers and destroying his liver drinking with the players, and Whiskers is driving the production crew insane. It's the rest of you lot who need to have your heads examined."

"Maybe you could give us a hint," said the young Drazen assigned to doing deep background checks on the players from his species.

"Drip, drip, drip," the Dollnick whistled.

"You think we're moving too slow?"

"Leaks!" Lume exploded again. "There was a report in the Horten Gaming Gazette that you're investigating their top barbarian on suspicion of colluding with non-player characters to minimize collateral damage to monstrous families during campaigns."

"We haven't gotten past examining financial records and checking into known associates in gambling circles," the Drazen said. "I didn't know that Frilch has been colluding with NPCs. I never would have believed it of him."

"BECAUSE IT'S NOT TRUE! Don't you understand what I'm saying?"

"One of us has been lying to the media?" Jonah asked.

Lume let out his breath like a punctured tire, and his chest, which had been puffed out in a display of dominance, returned to its normal dimensions. "None of you have been lying to the media," he whistled in his normal tone of voice. "None of you have said a single word to the media. Where does that leave them?"

"You mean," the Horten said slowly, "if we don't leak information, they'll just invent stuff?"

"Not invent, precisely, but journalists assigned to the gambling beat don't have the option of not writing stories, if the Humanese speakers among you will forgive the double negative. The reporter who did the story about Frilch colluding with NPCs cited unnamed sources, but given the Horten Gaming Gazette's reputation, I expect those sources were vetted by an editorial board. The point, my young agents, is that you've lost control of the narrative for the season."

"But we haven't discovered any malfeasance," Alinka protested.

"And if you do detect any evidence of match-fixing, I don't want you leaking it," Lume said. "But you have to give them something or the coverage will rapidly spin out of control."

"I don't understand," Jonah admitted. "Our job is to investigate match-fixing, or ideally, to prevent it from happening in the first place. Why do we need to create a narrative for journalists?"

"Because if we don't, their stories will change the betting line just as much as point shaving. The odds on Frilch's party making the finals dropped by almost half when the news he might be colluding with NPCs first broke. While most of that discount has since gone away, some smart money picked up a bargain in the secondary market during the dip."

"Are you suggesting that the journalist for the Horten Gaming Gazette wrote that story on behalf of a professional gambler?"

Lume held his four hands in front of himself like steps, but all at different angles, expressing that it was possible but not likely. "Major media outlets take a dim view of their employees using the platform to manipulate markets of any kind, and for a Horten to knowingly lie about gaming would be a suicidal career move."

"Suicidal in general," the Horten agent concurred.

"But intent doesn't equal outcome. If somebody had given that journalist an innocuous story about which player has been seen in the company of which famous immersive star, we wouldn't be having this discussion."

"You want us to leak rumors about the social lives of the competitors to gaming journalists?" Jonah asked.

"Players love that sort of attention, it helps them build their brands," Lume said. "You don't have to go full romantic, a heartwarming story about a player volunteering at an animal shelter would do. If you can't come up with anything, go with Alinka."

"You want me to monitor player gossip for insider stories?" the Vergallian demanded. "I'm flat out trying to cram enough buffing dances to keep a place in the league."

"Be the story. New players always underrate the value of creating a fanbase, and your backstory has as much to do with that as your performance in the LARPing studio. You need to get the audience on your side."

The Frunge agent rose from her seat and glared at Lume. "This isn't about our gambling investigation at all. The league sent you here to get us to use our positions to feed the media stories about Alinka because she's photogenic. They want her to get publicity so they'll have an excuse to give her a bigger role even if she isn't ready for it."

Lume did the four-handed gesture again, this time expressing that the Frunge's accusation carried more than a grain of truth. "I won't bore you with the Dollnick Rules of

Efficiency, but this is a perfect two-for-one opportunity. The press gets their stories and the league gets its rising young Vergallian star."

"I wonder how Jonah is doing in his first meeting without you," Clive said. "I'm still not sure I like the idea of his following my footsteps into the intelligence business, but I understand the aliens being concerned with continuity."

"We all have a part to play," Thomas said complacently. "I was on my way to the concourse to catch a liner to Earth when you pinged. I'm guessing you wouldn't have called me back if it wasn't related to my visit there."

"That's right," Clive said. "John can bring Henry by QuickU and break the news to them about the way the L'meuf are using personality upgrades intended for artificial people. I received a message from Wrylenth five minutes ago that he heard back from the intellectual property attorney my wife retains on Earth. Wrylenth is confident he knows why the spiders stole the upgrades rather than purchasing them."

"I talked to him yesterday and he told me he didn't want to say anything yet because there was a good chance he could be wrong."

"You know what Verlocks are like. He was probably ninety-five percent certain, which they consider a risky proposition. I've been trying to get him to come to me earlier with his conclusions, but no luck."

"He's on the way here?" Thomas asked.

Clive nodded. "Wrylenth was working at home, and even though he's mastered speaking faster, it takes him five minutes just to walk from the lift tube to my office, which is why you got here first."

"Speaking of your office, is there a reason we're not going out for lunch?" He raised one eyebrow to make sure that Clive understood he was talking about privacy rather than food.

"None of the other advanced species have a business like QuickU or issues with artificial intelligence and intellectual property law, so it's not the kind of information we can treat as currency. If they're all listening in, it will save us having to explain what happened a dozen times."

"Bad security as a communications tool," Thomas mused. "I'll have to remember that one when I'm sitting in your chair."

Clive's receptionist announced the arrival of Wrylenth, and the young Verlock who had stayed on at EarthCent Intelligence after finishing his co-op assignment from the Open University entered the office. He shook off Clive's signal to take a seat and instead struck the pose indicating he had something to say for the record.

"Director Oxford, Deputy Director Thomas," Wrylenth began his formal presentation. "Earth's intellectual property laws must change."

"Is that it?" Clive asked after the Verlock went several seconds without speaking. "You know that EarthCent doesn't have any legislative powers on Earth. The president can make suggestions, but none of the city-states or legacy nations are bound to accept them."

"The current situation is intolerable, and as word spreads, Earth may find itself boycotted by artificial intelligences acting in solidarity with artificial people."

"Hold on," Thomas said. "I'm not planning a boycott, and neither are any other artificial people I know. Few of them have ever visited Earth or have any business there."

Wrylenth stamped his foot in a rare show of frustration. "It's not up to you. The time constraint Director Oxford placed on my research prevented me from going too deeply into the history of laws discriminating against artificial intelligence on the tunnel network, but I did find a few references to an incident more than a million years ago in which it was discovered that the Frunge had an archaic law on their books aimed at protecting their financial system from rogues. The law hadn't been enforced since the Frunge joined the tunnel network, but it was brought up in court by an unscrupulous factory owner attempting to withhold patent royalties from an inventor who happened to be an artificial intelligence."

"Did the court reject the claim?" Clive asked.

"They couldn't. The law is the law, which is why Earth's law needs to be changed. As you would expect, the Frunge rushed to remove the related laws from their books, but for the next century, artificial intelligences controlling orbitals and docking facilities around the tunnel network made their disappointment clear by staging a work slowdown whenever a Frunge ship was involved."

"That seems a bit extreme for an archaic law that the Frunge fixed as quickly as they could," Thomas said.

"The inventor who lost his royalty income from that Frunge factory was a founder of the Chintoo orbital and one of the most popular artificial intelligences of the day," Wrylenth explained. "In addition, the wording of the archaic law was highly offensive."

"And you're suggesting that Earth's failure to grant copyright protection to artificial people is just as bad," Clive said, jotting down a note to himself with a pencil and paper on his glass-topped display desk.

"Potentially worse, since the Frunge law was a historical anomaly from over two million years ago. The intellectual property laws Earth adopted to discriminate against artificial intelligence were passed just over a century ago, which may as well be yesterday."

Clive scribbled another note. "Got it. Now what about the L'meuf?"

Wrylenth took a quick sip of water from the steel bottle he carried at his belt in preparation for a long speech. "After consulting with legal experts on Earth and Union Station, I've formed a hypothesis explaining why the L'meuf stole QuickU's personality upgrades. In short, even though the majority of programmers working at QuickU are Humans, the upgrades are all thoroughly tested by artificial people, whose feedback is essential to creating a retail product, as opposed to a science project."

"That's a good way of putting it," Thomas said. "Without beta testing, every artificial person who buys an upgrade from QuickU would have to go through the same tuning and integration, rather than receiving a true turnkey product."

"Unfortunately, that contribution from beta testers throws the copyright in question since artificial intelligence is taking a creative role. As members of the Farling Empire, which has no reciprocal intellectual property treaties with the tunnel network, QuickU can't take action against the L'meuf."

"Something's not right," Clive said. "If the Farling Empire doesn't have a reciprocal arrangement with the tunnel network for intellectual property law, what difference does it make whether or not the QuickU copyrights are valid?"

"The L'meuf are using their quick learning technology to train members of their species with Human skills at a high level," Wrylenth said. "Some of those L'meuf will no doubt want to maximize their income by taking work on Stryx stations, open worlds, or even Earth itself."

"While spying for the Farling Empire," Thomas muttered.

"That is a possibility. The reason the L'meuf had to steal the personality upgrades rather than buying one of each and copying them was to avoid agreeing to End User License Agreements. The EULA terms are separate from copyright arguments and would protect the product even if the copyright is deemed invalid."

"Now that is insulting," Thomas said. "I couldn't copyright a book because I'm an artificial person, but if I sold it as an app with a click-license agreement, I'd be protected? Nobody in the history of humanity has ever read one of those things."

"Lucy Hui," the founder of QuickU said, giving Henry a firm handshake.

"Carl, no last name," a man in his late thirties introduced himself. "Chief of Software Development."

"Thank you both for meeting me on such short notice," Henry said.

"Any friend of Thomas and Chance is a friend of ours," Lucy told him. "Let's sit down in the breakroom and then you can tell us what this is about. Do you drink coffee? Soda? We also have junk food."

"I guess I'm kind of a health nut," Henry said. "Do you have any juice?"

Lucy opened the breakroom fridge, checked the names written on the bottles in the door, and grinned. "How about papaya? Eric is on vacation, and I can send the co-op student out to buy a replacement. Don't put the bottle in recycling or I'll forget."

"Thanks," Henry said, surreptitiously checking the label to make sure that the drink wasn't sugar water with a little juice for coloring. Lucy and Carl helped themselves to diet sodas, and the three of them sat down at the breakroom table.

"You're a friend of Thomas," Lucy prompted.

"Yes," Henry said. "Great dancer. I met him and Chance in a club and I wouldn't have known about your personality upgrades otherwise. Anyway, I just got back from Farling Four, where I was working as a bicycle messenger, and I couldn't help noticing these spider aliens, the L'meuf, are taking jobs that require a human skillset. It turns out that they have something like telepathy, or maybe they're naturally sensitive to radio frequencies, and they can go to a job center where the information gets beamed directly into their brains while they watch holograms for reinforcement or something."

"Speed learning is the holy grail of education, but I didn't think any of the biological species could manage it," Carl said.

"I don't know anything about that one way or another, but I have an implant, so I captured an image of the skills they were offering. I couldn't translate it from L'meuf, but I transmitted the data to Thomas since I know he's interested in stuff like that. He sent me back a tunneling network telegram this morning with the translation and asked that I bring it to you." Henry produced a folded-up sheet of plastic and passed it across the table to Carl.

"This is every personality upgrade in our catalog, plus three we haven't even released yet!"

"Let me see," Lucy said and scanned the list with her lips pulled in a tight line. "It can't be a coincidence. They must be using our personality upgrades for the training."

"And he said something about copyright protection not extending to creations that involved artificial people, though I didn't get that part," Henry added.

"It's a disgrace, but the only protection our software has against copying is the EULA. I went through law school at night and I was shocked to find that Earth's intellectual property laws discriminate against artificial intelligence to the extent that anything they touch is an opening for litigation."

"We've been subletting space to the EarthCent president's office below market rent for years," Carl said. "I'm going to stop in right now and ask the president if he can get us an appointment with Aazil."

"Who?" Henry asked, wondering how much Earth's government had changed during his four-month absence.

"Governor-general Mayhew's Vergallian princess," Lucy explained while Carl went on his errand. "She's the local head of the shadow government that the Ladies in Waiting are setting up on Earth in hopes of displacing the patchwork of city-states and legacy nations."

"I must have left before Aazil got here because I don't remember her name."

"Four months sounds just about right. It's amazing how many changes she's made to the city-state government in such a short time. She's also setting up a voluntary alternative to the existing court system, sort of like binding arbitration, where she'll hear both sides of a case and give a decision on the spot."

"What else has she done?" Henry asked.

"It would be easier to tell you what she hasn't done yet," Lucy said. "Namely, fixing this ridiculous intellectual property law that's holding back artificial people from investing their time in contributing more to the culture, not to mention risking the ire of artificial intelligences from the rest of the tunnel network."

"It does sound pretty unfair, but when I was living here, I was more bothered by the litter in—"

"Fixed that," the founder of QuickU interrupted him. "All gone."

"Princess Aazil hired people to pick up all the litter?" Henry asked.

"That, and she pushed through some laws and made clear to the police they were an enforcement priority. You don't want to get caught littering in the New York city-state. First-time offenders get four hours of picking up the litter of people who haven't been caught, second-time offenders get a weekend of cleaning Central Park, and third-time offenders get a floater bus ticket. It doesn't matter who you are, whether you own property in the city-state, or how much money you have. Get caught littering three times and say goodbye to New York."

"Guess what," Carl said, sticking his head in the door. "Aazil just got here to see the president, and they invited us to join them. They already know about the L'meuf. Thomas must have sent word through the EarthCent ambassador, but they both want to hear the first-person testimony."

Henry found himself escorted into the very office he had broken into after scaling the building in his attempt to infiltrate QuickU earlier that year. The president looked like a normal guy getting close to retirement, but the

Vergallian princess took his breath away, and he had trouble remembering why he was there.

"Relax," Aazil told him with a friendly smile that somehow carried the force of a command. "We'd just like to hear the story from your lips so it will have more force when my colleagues and I present our suggestion for the governments of Earth to let us bring their copyright laws up to date for the tunnel network."

"Don't worry," the president added. "You won't have to testify. We just want to make sure we have the details straight."

"Well," Henry began, and repeated the story he'd concocted about stumbling on the L'meuf learning technology and connecting the dots. He had the feeling that the Vergallian knew he was hiding something, but she didn't voice any objections or express her disappointment. When he finished, the president and the princess thanked him, then retreated behind closed doors with the founder of QuickU to talk strategy. Henry found himself alone with Belladonna, the receptionist.

"Have some free passes to stuff," Belladonna said, producing a handful of vouchers to various attractions that alien businesses provided to the president's office in thanks for his granting them extraterritorial status. "By the way, do you like spider plants?"

"Are they related to the L'meuf in some way?" he asked suspiciously.

The young woman laughed. "No, silly. That kind of spider plant." She pointed at the window where a giant spider plant with dozens of offshoots gave the office a little color. Then she glanced at the closed conference room door, and added, "Want to see something neat?"

"Sure," Henry said, at the same time deciding to ask her what she was doing after work and if she wanted to help him use up some of the vouchers.

Belladonna activated her display desk and brought up a hologram that showed the spider plant. "I saw that the Verlocks won a prize at the Human Empire's Elder Documentary festival for lichen growing on a rock, so I thought I'd try experimenting with time-lapse photography myself."

The spider plant seemed to grow in reverse, and then the hologram froze, an image of a man's back blocking the plant. To the left was Henry's shocked face as he plunged backward away from the window.

"Oh, I can explain that," Henry said, edging toward the exit.

"John already did," she told him. "It's our little secret. Did you really climb all the way up the outside of the building without a floater belt?"

"Kind of stupid, huh?"

"I get off work at five," Belladonna said. "Where are you taking me?"

From the Author

The next EarthCent release will be **Bits of Business**, the fourth book in the **EarthCent Metaverse** series. I apologize to readers who haven't kept up with the spin-off series and are now faced with discontinuities in the main Union Station thread, but the plot lines have become integrated across all four series, and the timeline is given below. If you're new to the EarthCent books, you can start back at the beginning with **Union Station 1, 2, 3**, a discounted three-book bundle.

For notifications of new releases, sign up for the mailing list at www.ifitbreaks.com. I also post new releases to facebook.com/E.M.Foner/ and respond to all temperate e-mail sent to e_foner@yahoo.com

Readers have asked me to include the complete timeline of the EarthCent Universe in order so here it is:

Destiny: Union Station
Date Night on Union Station
Alien Night on Union Station
High Priest on Union Station
Spy Night on Union Station
Carnival on Union Station
Wanderers on Union Station
Vacation on Union Station
Guest Night on Union Station
Word Night on Union Station
Party Night on Union Station
Review Night on Union Station
Family Night on Union Station
Book Night on Union Station

LARP Night on Union Station
Career Night on Union Station
Last Night on Union Station
Independent Living
Soup Night on Union Station
Assisted Living
Freelance on the Galactic Tunnel Network
Con Living
Empire Night on Union Station
Space Living
Traders on the Galactic Tunnel Network
Orphans on the Galactic Tunnel Network
Swap Night on Union Station
Slow Living
Artists on the Galactic Tunnel Network
History Night on Union Station
Bits of Anarchy
Double Living
Bits of Flower
Synergy on the Galactic Tunnel Network
Substitutes on Union Station
Bits of Catalyst
Elder Living
Royals on the Galactic Tunnel Network
Deal Night on Union Station

Made in United States
Orlando, FL
04 December 2024